W9-CDB-839

ALSO BY LAUREN FOX

Still Life with Husband

friends like us

friends like us

A NOVEL

LAUREN FOX

ALFRED A. KNOPF

NEW YORK

2012

THIS IS A BORZOI BOOK
PUBLISHED BY ALFRED A. KNOPF

www.aaknopf.com

Knopf, Borzoi Books, and the colophon are registered
trademarks of Random House, Inc.

LIBRARY OF CONGRESS CATALOGING-IN-PUBLICATION DATA
Fox, Lauren.
Friends like us : a novel / by Lauren Fox. — 1st ed.
p. cm.
"Borzoi book."
ISBN 978-0-307-26811-2
1. Friendship—Fiction.   2. Triangles (Interpersonal rela-
tions)—Fiction   3. Choice (Psychology)—Fiction
4. Psychological fiction.   I. Title.
PS3606.O95536F75 2012
813'.6—dc22   2011023867

Jacket photographs: (top) composite of Lori Andrews/Flickr/
Getty Images and Eva Mueller/Getty Images;
(bottom) Eva Mueller/Getty Images
Jacket design by Abby Weintraub

Manufactured in the United States of America
First Edition

For Andrew

friends like us

prologue

This is what I'm thinking about when I see her: I'm thinking about a Saturday morning, six years ago, when Jane and I decided to make omelets.

In the small kitchen of our apartment, Jane pulled a frying pan from the cupboard, and I took five eggs out of the carton. We were both still wearing our pajamas; neither of us had anywhere else to be.

"You know," I said, "my mom never let me crack eggs when I was a kid." I tapped one against the side of the bowl and plopped it in. "I used to be very clumsy!" I swept my hand to the side in a dismissive gesture—*can you believe that?*—and with that brush of my hand, knocked the remaining four eggs off the counter and onto the floor. They made a clapping sound as they hit the linoleum, four little thwacks in rapid succession, like a quick round of applause from the gods of comic timing. I clapped my own hand over my mouth as Jane stared at me in disbelief.

She looked down at the floor, yellow yolks and gooey whites oozing and spreading, then back at me. She tilted her head with a funny little smile on her face and was silent for a moment. And then she said, "I find that very hard to believe."

I'm standing in line at the bank, idly adjusting the shoulder strap on my bag, and I'm remembering how we started laughing then, and how that laughter escalated until Jane had to sit down, clutching her stomach as she gasped for breath. How just as we were regaining control, finally, just as our torrent of giggles was finally subsiding, Ben called out from the other room, "What's so funny?" and set us off again, sent us to that place you go with your best friend, to the rollicking inauguration of an inside joke that will remain hysterically funny, only to the two of you and to the annoyance of many others, for years. *I used to be very clumsy!* we would say to each other, at first when one of us had done something that was actually klutzy and then, after a while, just whenever we felt like making each other laugh—at the grocery store, on a walk, in the middle of a movie. It never failed.

This is what I'm thinking about, really, because this is how it works once in a while, when the universe cracks you over the head, when it gives you what you need, whether or not you want it. I'm standing in this long line on a Friday afternoon, and I'm remembering that careening moment of hilarity six years ago, and I'm thinking about sketching it when I get home, I'm thinking about drawing a panel where Jane, in her oversize plaid pajamas, gazes at the broken eggs on the floor and says, *I find that very hard to believe.* I'm smiling to myself, and at just that moment, I catch the eye of the baby in line ahead of me, the brown-eyed baby in the puffy snowsuit peering over his mother's left shoulder.

They're a few customers ahead of me, close to the front. The baby sees me smiling and, deciding that my smile is meant for him, returns it: hugely, wetly, toothlessly. I'm bought and sold. I wave.

"Guh-weeee!" he squeals, delighted. I waggle my eyebrows at him. "Ah doo DAH," he yells, his voice raspy with glee. The elderly woman in front of me turns around and smiles as if I'm responsible for this display of adorableness, and the goateed twenty-something dude behind me chuckles. We have morphed, suddenly and happily, from a disconnected line of distracted bank customers waiting to complete our most mundane transactions into a community of baby lovers, charmed by this dark-haired blob of sweetness.

I wave at him again. "Hello," I say. "Hi!"

And that's when the baby's mother shifts him in her arms and cranes her neck, and although she's wearing an expensive gray coat and a burgundy cashmere scarf instead of her old blue down jacket, yellow homemade scarf, and her father's Green Bay Packers cap (which together completed the fashion-forward statement: *emotionally unstable football fan*); although I haven't seen her in five years; although there are other differences, including her new human accessory, she is, unmistakably, Jane.

The baby grins again, open mouthed with pure joy.

Jane's expression I can't read at all.

Twenty minutes later, at the table by the window of our old coffee shop, I have to wrap my hands around my cup to stop them from shaking.

"So, this is Gus," Jane says, her pride obscuring whatever else is lurking underneath it. She has him propped on her lap, his snowsuit half off, as he gums a pumpkin scone. "He's nine months old," she says, her face, for the moment, as open to me as it used to be.

The industrial coffee grinder powers up with a metallic *hiss-clank*. Gus winces, and I reach across the table to touch his hand. It's wet with drool; I pull my fingers back at the slobbery shock of it and smile, trying to pretend I'm not slightly disgusted. Probably when you have a kid you get used to the general condition of moistness. "Gus," I say, drawing out the *u*. "Hi, little *Guuuu*s."

Gus chortles, then throws his head back in full-on hilarity at my joke, his fat little body quaking with laughter.

"Oh, my God," I say, enchanted, and Gus laughs harder.

Jane smiles, then casts her gaze downward at the baby's head. "He likes you," she says shyly. He reaches up for a hank of Jane's hair, which she gently works free from his fist. I feel the old bond with her, the irresistible, magnetic attraction that has always been there between us, and who cares if we're using her baby as a prop? Gus looks at me and starts giggling again.

"Is this your *life*?" I say, meaning, do you spend your days in the company of Mr. Personality, this marvelous, shining little boy? But I see immediately that she takes it the wrong way: I see by the way she hunches her shoulders and leans in protectively toward the baby, the way she seems, suddenly, diminished, as if I've consigned her to a stereotype, a supporting role, a smaller life than the one she leads. *That's not what I meant*, I want to say. *That's not what I meant!* But when you haven't seen the person who was your best friend in five years, a small misunderstanding might expose a canyon of hurt, and after all that, what can you possibly do to fix it? What point is there in even trying?

"Yes," she says, pushing her hair back. "My life. Gus, and my marriage"—her marriage; the word slices through me—"and my job, and a million other things." *Things you lost the right to know about.* She breaks off a piece of scone and chews it slowly, then rests her chin lightly on Gus's head, strokes his cheek with her hand. I look down at my latte. It's too late in the day for caffeine. I take a sip of it. I'll be up all night.

"The thing is," Jane says, and I look up at her again, startled by the gap between my expectations and reality. Jane's hair, which used to be just like mine, is smoother than it was when we lived together, shinier, the curls perfect ringlets, the color a richer shade of brown, as if she not only has the money to spend on it now, but she does; she spends it. She's wearing glasses, which she didn't back when I knew her, funky black-and-green frames, her dark eyes behind the lenses big and clear and calm. Her skin, as always, is pale and perfect. She looks beautiful.

I'm not sure how I look. Probably the same as I did five years ago: maybe slightly disheveled, because I still roll out of bed and face the world; maybe a little tired, because I frequently drink too much coffee this late in the day, and then I stay up drawing until 2:00 or 3:00 a.m.—just like I used to, only these days I actually get paid for it; maybe I look kind of okay, too, because in the wake of turning thirty I've come to appreciate certain things about myself: the angle of my cheekbones, the thickness of my hair, the fullness of my lips. Right now I just see myself reflected in Jane's face, like I always did.

Gus arches back into his mother's body, points his hunk of scone up at the ceiling, and waves it around. "Willa," Jane says, "I've thought a lot about what I would say if I ever ran into you." She pauses. My face goes hot. I nod. I think that we both do, and do not, have so much to say to each other. "Five years ago, you . . . I . . ." She makes a gesture like she's flicking a bug away. "I was shattered."

Gus begins to whimper and fuss a little, and Jane turns him around with an expertly executed lift-and-spin. He slumps right onto her shoulder, content.

Gus. I can't help but think that if I'd been in her life when he was born, I'd have had some say in name selection. I imagine, with all the brief indulgence I'll allow myself, that we're sitting here together with this baby whose name is not Gus, is Asher or Joe, Elvis, Milo, Hank; I imagine that we come here every day, that I've known him since he was born, that I still know her.

"I was destroyed," she says, her voice firmer, her back straight. She looks me in the eye. "I hated you."

"Yah!" Gus says, as if his first language is going to be German. *"Ja ja ja ja!"*

I blow on my coffee even though it's no longer hot, just for something to do. My heart is jackhammering, and my throat is thick. Of course she hated me. I'm not surprised. Still, it's on the short list of phrases you least want to hear. *You have six months to live. Turns out I have herpes. I hate you.* "I know," I say, because I said I'm sorry five years ago, and even then it rang hollow.

She flutters her hand again, waving my words away. "I've wanted to say to you . . ." She stops, sighs, starts again. "I didn't understand this back then, but I do now. I know that you thought you didn't have a choice." She nods firmly, decisively, leaving me no room to argue. "But you did. You had other options." This is what she has figured out about me. I take it. I drink it in. "You didn't know it. But you did. You had other options. You are . . . you were . . . so amazing, Willa." Gus bounces his head up and down on her shoulder. She shrugs, then exhales like she's been holding her breath for five years and pats his back. "Okay?" I'm not sure who she's talking to. She rearranges the baby and zips him up, gathers her bags, brushes crumbs from the scone into her empty cup. Her generosity stuns me. I can only watch silently as she readies herself. Gus shoves his hand into his mouth. The girl behind the counter calls out drink orders. A spoon clinks in a cup. "Okay," she says again, "I should go," and I'm thinking *Stay here, stay, please stay,* but Jane is standing, she's pushing her chair away from the table, she's wriggling herself into her coat, she's hoisting Gus onto her shoulder. She's turning, she's walking, she's gone.

chapter one

Jane sweeps a scattering of crumbs into a neat little pile. "You are quite a slob," she says as she pushes the broom across the floor with a rhythmic *swish-swish*. "And so lucky to have me to clean up your messes!"

"I know," I say, watching an ant crawl across the windowsill. "But if I weren't so messy, you wouldn't get the satisfaction of cleaning the apartment. I do it for you. For your OCD."

"Thank you, sweetie," she says. She props the broom against the wall and drops to her hands and knees, sponging up invisible spills, scrubbing our crummy kitchen linoleum into gleaming submission.

"Don't get me wrong," I continue, lifting my feet so Jane can clean under them. "I appreciate it. But it's not a favor if you can't *not* do it."

"I can stop anytime I want to!"

"You missed a spot," I say, pointing with my left big toe to a nonexistent smudge on the floor; in response, she squeezes a dribble from the wet sponge over my bare foot.

"I do appreciate your attention to detail," she says, dabbing my foot.

"Well, here's how you can repay me," I say as Jane squirts a viscous blob of liquid cleanser onto the sponge. "You can come with me tonight."

"And you know, my pretty, that there is no chance of that."

"Why not? A, you don't have to talk to anyone if you don't want to, and B, if you do, people will find you charming and interesting." Sometimes I think it's helpful to speak in outline form.

"Willa," Jane says, attacking the tabletop. "I will not go to your high school reunion. A, I'm not your boyfriend, and B, I didn't go to high school with you."

Excitement is the cousin of dread. Three weeks ago I agreed to attend my eight-year high school reunion. Eight-year reunion, yes: there it was, in my in-box, an Evite to a list of two hundred twenty-eight vaguely familiar names from one vaguely familiar name: Shelby Stigmeyer, who, the invitation explained, was supposed to get married tonight, but her fiancé called off the engagement, and Shelby couldn't get the deposit back on the room. *Aw*, I thought. *Awwww*. And in this fleeting, unfortunate moment of sympathy, I added my name to the "yes" column.

I've spent the last twenty-one days regretting it. The only thing I liked about high school was leaving it—that and my best friend, Ben Kern, nickname "Pop," but he's just another reason I should have declined that invitation. I don't want to go tonight, and I desperately don't want to go alone. Jane is, in fact, the closest thing I have to a boyfriend, and with her, what promises to be an excruciating rerun of four years of shyness could be, instead, a party. But I know her well enough to know that she's easily moved, right up until the moment she's not. "Fine," I say, defeated. I deliberately let a shower of crumbs from my granola bar fall onto the table.

She reaches around me with her sponge, unimpressed, then kisses me on the head. "It *will* be fine. It's only one night. You can leave early." She dabs at the last of the crumbs, her thin arm close to my face, her skin warm and bleachy. "Take good notes. I'll wait up."

The trip that should take twenty minutes takes me a good forty, as I deliberately navigate the side streets and drive ten miles below the speed limit, incurring the wrath of the old man in the boat-sized silver Chrysler behind me. I stop for gas, even though the tank is three-quarters full. Finally I have no choice but to pull into the restaurant parking lot and face the reunion head-on.

Inside the Hampton House's private party room, the bass-heavy thump of an eight-year-old Aerosmith power ballad bores into my skull. I squint against the swirl of Christmas lights and the confusion of faces, their features blurred, take a shallow breath through my mouth to try to minimize the smell of heavily perfumed and aftershaved bodies. Women who haven't seen each other in ages squeal with delight; men pound each other on the back like friendly apes. I'm pressed against the back wall when I think that I spot him. I crane my neck.

It's his walk that I recognize, finally, the way he moves through space like he knows in his bones that the world will never belong to him—his shoulders slightly rounded, head down, long strides meant to propel him to his destination as quickly and unobtrusively as possible. That's him. I spent four years searching the undulating sea of high school bodies for Ben's walk.

But everything else about him is a shock, electric and sweet. The man who is loping toward me, who is standing here smiling at me, is not the weird little wombat I knew years ago. He's tall—well, he's my height—and thin, angular, stretched out. His intense brown eyes are no longer planted deep in a round baby face; they stare out at me from a man's face, a man's face with cheekbones and not just a chin but an actual jaw. He's Ben Kern, for sure, but new, improved Ben, Now with Bone Structure! He looks me up and down and then grabs me in a bear hug, and that's my next surprise, the way he squeezes the air right out of me, and not just because he's stronger now.

"Hey, dingbat," he says, softly, into my hair.

"Hey, Pop," I say. He smells good, too, like licorice, another welcome addition to Ben 2.0.

"Yeah . . . no one really calls me Pop anymore," he says, still holding on.

"Well, not that many people call me dingbat, either."

He puts his hands on my shoulders and takes a half step back. "Look at you."

"Look at *you*," I reply.

"You look exactly the same," he says, and then mumbles something and glances away nervously: this is the Ben I remember, indecipherable and endearing.

"You look completely different," I say. He meets my eyes again, and we both laugh.

"Well, I've had some work done."

I squint at him, considering. "You had your lips plumped, didn't you?"

"Plus, a little Botox." He stares into the distance, his eyes wide. "See? I'm raising *and lowering* my eyebrows, but you can't tell."

I want to say that I've missed him, that I've been furious and confused and, finally, resigned to his absence from my life. But it all adds up to too much, and I can't tease out anything reasonable from the mess. "I didn't think you'd come," I say finally.

"Why not?"

The room is quickly filling up with our former classmates; I watch as each of their faces seems to register a preprogrammed sequence, from apprehension to eager recognition, uncertainty to confidence. They move around the room like amoebas, forming and re-forming into the social configurations of 1999. "Because we hated high school."

"We did," Ben agrees, following my gaze.

And that's when I realize that I came here tonight to see him, and he to see me, a sudden and visceral understanding, shocking both for its obviousness and for the fact that I didn't know it until this second. I take a deep breath, inhale the woolly, crowded warmth of the room. "Why did we . . . what happened?" I ask, but the background noise is a din of voices, and I'm not sure he hears me, because it's at this moment that Alexis Moody glides up and flings her arms around me in an unexpected hug. Alexis and I sat next to each other in homeroom. She was the kind of girl who pasted the inside of her locker with words she cut out from magazines to describe herself: *SPECIAL! OUTRAGEOUS! UNIQUE! WOW!* For two or three minutes every day for four years, she shared the juicy details of social dramas I had no part in. Her self-assurance was like a big umbrella. She could shelter anyone under it.

"Wendy?" she says. It takes me a minute to realize she's talking to me.

"Willa."

"No, it's Alexis!" she says loudly, laughing, tapping her name tag. "Poor Shelby, huh? Awww!" Then she looks at Ben with frank admiration but not a hint of recognition. "Is this your boyfriend?" She pronounces the word like it's something she's just spotted bobbing in the ocean: *buoyfriend.*

"Yes!" Ben smiles brightly at her, offering his hand.

"Oh, my gosh!" she says, her own smile twitching a bit. "Mine is over there! Actually he's my fee-*ahn*-say!" She points to a group of identical-looking men in casual wear. "Rich!" she says proudly, and I'm not sure whether she's telling us his name or describing him.

There's an awkward moment when nobody has anything to say, and, with a measure of relief, I'm plotting my escape *(Is it 8:05 already?)*, when suddenly a cluster of women in little black dresses swoops down on us, arms waving, fabric flapping—a colony of pretty bats. They emit a strong, collective odor of fruity perfumes with names, I imagine, like Delicious and Happy and Adorable. (Mine, if I were wearing any, would be called Wary or Irritable.) The bat-ladies simultaneously surround and ignore Ben and me, and I find myself moved along, Alexis's hand gripping my arm, into the larger crowd.

A woman I don't recognize holds a camera up to her face and starts snapping photos; she looks like an emergency vehicle, the camera flashing over and over. "Okay, everyone!" she shouts, and I remember who she is—Leah Reilly, former student council president and friend to everyone. "I just had a totally great idea! I'm going to take pictures of people with their former crushes!" She starts laughing maniacally. "Who did you like back in high school? Who did you *like*?"

A few people chuckle uncomfortably. All of our shoes are suddenly extremely interesting.

"Oh, *come on,* you guys!" Leah says again, her left hand on her hip, and somehow, from her, this chiding is amiable, more misguided camp counselor than plotter of evil. "We're all grown up now! High school was eight years ago! Come clean. Who did you like back then? Who did you *like*?"

Alexis turns to me and leans in close. Her lips brush against my ear. "I forgot how much I hated high school," she whispers, and I think that it is endlessly surprising, how everyone has a secret life. A short, dimple-cheeked woman giggles and points to someone on the fringes of the room, and Leah grabs her and takes off, warning the rest of us to stay put, that she'll be back.

A few of the women are murmuring to each other and flipping their hair around, clearly beginning to enjoy the opportunity to rekindle a thing or two, and I'm feeling like I actually am back in high school, complete with the attendant stomachache. I'm thinking about Ryan Cox, track star, math whiz, occasional contributor to the magazine Ben and I edited and secret hero of my fantasies *(I never knew you were so pretty behind those glasses!);* I'm thinking about how loneliness starts growing early and takes root like a weed. I'm starting to feel very sorry for myself.

And then Ben reappears and taps my shoulder. I automatically look down to find his face and then, seeing only torso, tip my chin up. "Let's make like a banana," he says, and I remember what it was like, ten years ago, to be rescued from myself. As fast as I can unhook Alexis Moody's fingers from the flesh of my upper arm, I'm following Ben out the door and into the wintry night.

chapter two

My freshman year of high school, I was constantly on the verge of a panic attack. That fall, my parents were busy lobbing grenades in their escalating marital combat zone; my brother, Seth, had morphed from beloved protector into bullying tormentor; I was suddenly three inches taller than the tallest girl in school; and overnight I had grown a pair of boobs so terrifyingly huge they threatened to rear up and smack me in the face. I felt like something out of *The Origin of Species*—a three-legged gazelle, a knock-kneed kangaroo—a certain kind of animal so clumsy and unappealing, I could only be destined for extinction. I blushed and stammered if I was called on in class. I trembled if a boy so much as looked at me—even if that boy was someone I didn't know in the lunchroom or my middle-aged math teacher with his chronic coffee breath or the janitor. If I spoke at all, I whispered. It was becoming pathological. Before I knew it, I'd be whiling away my days fingering my collection of fragile glass animals and pining over an indifferent gentleman caller.

And then I met Ben. We were paired up in our second semester honors English class and given the task of creating a literary journal.

"I do not want you to settle for average in your forays into the world of high school literary talent," Ms. Barnum advised us. Her cheeks were flushed with passion; she raised her hands to her face to cool her own ardor. "As editors," she said, "you will see that you can coax exceptional writing from students." It was her first year on the job, and she was frequently filled with this kind of exhilaration, the kind of naked optimism that perched on its hind legs and begged us to destroy it. "I want these journals to be *exceptional*," she said, bouncing on her heels. "I want you to find writing that *soars*."

"Like herpes?" Ben whispered to me. He was physically awkward and hadn't yet come to terms with the need to shower daily; he liked to share his arcane knowledge of the unusual foods of foreign cultures with anyone who'd listen *(Every country has its own version of the dumpling!)*. He had the tendency to interrupt a person by interjecting peculiar synonyms into the conversation *(Did the movie make you lachrymose? Oh, do you mean to say you bungled the science quiz?);* he frequently thought people were talking about him when they weren't; he laced his neurotic paranoia with biting wit; and he saved me.

We named our journal *The Prose Shop,* congratulating ourselves on our brilliance, and, against the odds, alone among the mediocre work of our classmates, our journal became a success. Ms. Barnum was delirious. We had submissions, subscribers, a budget. Ben did the copyediting, and I made sprightly ink drawings to fill the empty spaces and the margins. (For a short story about an average kid who wakes up one morning and discovers he's suddenly a genius, I drew a cockroach brandishing a protractor and wearing a contemplative expression; for a rhymey, earnest poem about the power of female friendship, I drew a car careening over the edge of a cliff, two clasped hands visible through the windshield.) By myself, I was a stammering nitwit. With Ben, I was confident. I was brave.

At five foot three (eight inches shorter than I was) and sporting a small, round potbelly, Ben wasn't exactly a guy, in the same way I felt I wasn't quite a girl. Together, we were a third sex, an unsexed sex, and so, like siblings, like twins, like some sort of human/lemur hybrid, nothing was weird between us. We nurtured each other with great doses of sympathy and a tiny, shimmering sparkle of mutual superiority. We made up dirty movie titles for Dickens novels—*David Cockerfield, Little Whore-it, Hard Times*—and laughed about them as if we were worldly and sophisticated instead of unkissed and clueless. We memorized passages from Shakespeare competitively, for fun. On the weekends, we devoted hours to creating a comic book called *The Overachievers,* about a band of misunderstood high school superheroes with stellar SAT scores. We wrote the story together, and I did the illustrations. We were the dorkiest of dorks. An oddball on her own is a pitiable creature, but two weirdos together are a fortress.

As close as we were in high school, for reasons unclear to me we lost touch after our first year of college. It's not that I haven't analyzed the end of our friendship, but it wasn't an obvious break; it was death by attrition, a slow dwindling, and although I still think about him often, I've never figured out why it happened. Sometimes I can practically convince myself that it didn't happen, that we're just very, very bad at keeping in touch. Other times I lie awake at night going over every detail of the final months of our friendship, replaying the last time I saw him. The one thing I know for sure is that it was Ben's doing: I called and wrote for months before I finally realized that he had stopped calling and writing back. Our distance has lived in me like the aftermath of a bad dream—I carry it around, the knowledge that we were once close, that something was lost; it's the lingering sadness of unfinished business.

. . .

The heavy restaurant doors close behind us with a *whoosh*. The parking lot is shimmering and surreal, the night sky swollen with snow. The wind has picked up since I got here an hour ago; it whips my hair across my face in hard little slaps. I feel around for nonexistent pockets in my skirt.

"This is just like that one time," Ben says, zipping his jacket.

"I know!" I glance at him, his shoulders hunched against the wind, his breath coming out in little puffs. The person who knew you best when you were seventeen will always have a claim on you, no matter how much you change. There's something seductive and magnetic about it, the feeling of being understood like that. I suppose it goes both ways.

Ben stomps his feet and blows on his hands. "Where's your coat?"

"You know me," I say, my nonchalant shrug turning into a shiver. "I live on the edge." My eyes are watering, my face slowly growing immobile. It's starting to snow, mean icy clumps hurling down like snowballs from God.

"*Willa.*" Ben says my name with a sudden, sharp irritation that reminds me of the last summer of our friendship. "Come on." He grabs my hand and pulls me to his car, and we wait in the front seat while it warms up. It feels like we were just here five minutes ago.

The wind rattles the windows. I could ask him where he's been for the past seven years, why he ended our friendship and broke my heart. Or I could tell him he's an ass and slam the car door after myself. But here he is, next to me, rearranged, and I am, too, although maybe not as noticeably. The snow is starting to stick to the asphalt and to the other cars, turning the dark parking lot into the moon.

"So," I say, when I can feel my face again. Heat blasts out of the vents, and the windows are fogging. I watch him as he fiddles with the car radio, which is not on. Like we always did in high school, we've created our own little universe without even trying. I'm catapulted back into a world of grateful love for my best friend. Still, I want to grab him by the shoulders and shake him until his bones clatter. Is there an explanation in there somewhere?

"Awesome party," Ben says, finally. He smiles without showing his teeth, moves his hands to the steering wheel, and plants them at ten o'clock and two o'clock, as if we're going somewhere.

"Who did you *like*?" I say.

The last time we saw each other was at the end of summer vacation before our sophomore year of college. Things had been strained between us for three months; I had been plagued by the constant, uncomfortable feeling that Ben was angry at me. He undercut our usual ease with inexplicable silences and frequent sighs; he snapped at me when I teased him and often tuned out of our conversations entirely. Still, through stubbornness or habit, we hung out most nights, meeting for coffee or ice cream or for beers at the High Road, the dive bar we knew that didn't card—which was especially fortunate, since Ben still looked about thirteen. That night we were marking the end of the summer. We arranged to have dinner together at the Cottage, a downtown bistro with an outdoor patio. Ben had a flight the next morning.

He met me at the door, muttering a greeting, seeming more nervous than usual. His hair was unusually neat, and he looked like he'd picked his clothes out of the closet, as opposed to grabbing whatever wrinkled T-shirt and shorts were closest to his bed when he woke up in the morning. He was fidgety, alternately tightening and loosening his watch band and tracing the design on the tablecloth with his fingertips. I remember noticing the hair on his arms—I hardly ever thought of Ben as male, and then something, a shadow across his face, a change in the tone of his voice, would remind me, just briefly. He looked like he had something on his mind, but the summer had been long and tense, and I didn't think I wanted to hear it. We were sitting outside and had just ordered our food when a guy I barely knew from school walked past our table. Without really thinking about it, I flagged him down and asked him to join us.

I could tell that Ben was annoyed with me for inviting my new friend to crash our private party, but I didn't care. I was relieved that the difficult, tiresome summer was ending; I felt as if I could finally breathe in the heat of the August night, like something important was shifting, and that Ben needed proof: if he was going to treat me shabbily, I would find someone else to be close to. So I turned my attention to Matt, laughing at his jokes, staring, rapt, as he talked, mostly about baseball. I flirted tirelessly with him, a skill I had just picked up and hadn't yet perfected. When Ben got up to leave abruptly at the end of the meal, I gave him a quick hug good-bye, and then I asked Matt if he wanted to order dessert. He did.

We could sit here all night without saying anything real. But a high school reunion, even an eight-year one, is nothing if not a reminder that time passes. "I'm glad you showed up," I try. Ben doesn't answer. "And I am pleased that you, Willa, showed up as well," I say, my voice pitched low.

He stares straight ahead, the muscles in his jaw working. He exhales loudly, as if he's been holding his breath. Without warning, he smacks his palm against his forehead. "Jesus!"

The force of this—whatever it is—takes me completely by surprise. A sudden pressure builds behind my eyes. I move toward the door, my fingers on the handle. Given the option of fight or flight,

I'll always flee. But seven years of silence and repressed feelings will make their inevitable escape. "What?" I say, pressed against the door, my voice loud and shaky. "What is it?"

"Who did I like?" I can see, even in the dim glow of the parking lot lights, that Ben's face has gone red. "Are you that stupid?"

This is not my friend. This is someone else—Ben's mean but distractingly manly cousin. "Apparently, yes, I am, thank you." And just as I'm saying it I understand, and then four years of friendship vaporize, just like that. I look down at my hands, long and alien, pinkish in the snowy light. "Oh. Shit."

"Which, in all the years I've thought about it, is not the response I'd hoped for." His voice is quieter, slightly hoarse, as if there are big Swiss-cheese holes in it where the nastiness has just been.

I scan the dashboard, trying to make sense of this revelation, but understanding only that the car has 78,997 miles on it. I tuck a strand of hair behind my ear; I can tell without looking that it's gone frizzy in the damp heat. If I had met Ben tonight, my boyfriend detector would have been clicking away; I might have positioned myself at a table near his, made some clever comment, and then turned away, waiting, faking quiet confidence. But this-Ben, new-Ben is just a superimposed image on top of the boy I used to know, my short, chubby, hygiene-challenged pal, my friend, my *best friend*.

"I just mean, you know, I had no idea," I say. "I'm sorry."

"Also not on my list," Ben says, but he sounds more like himself, like he finally remembers that beneath every statement lies the opportunity for self-mockery.

And all of a sudden I'm thinking about Jane, Jane whose friendship is a direct descendant of this one, Jane who wears sparkly eye shadow to clean a house, who never met a karaoke machine she didn't love, who dressed up last Halloween as a turkey sandwich, the *why-not* to my *no-way*. What would Jane do? I ask myself this question frequently; for her birthday last year, she bought me a WWJD bracelet. I move toward Ben, unsure of myself, but certain of the answer. He's still sitting straight in his seat, staring at the foggy, wet window as if there is an important answer encoded in the dripping blobs of slush. "Well," I say. "Like what's-her-name said, high school was a long time ago." I reach over and put my hands on either side of his face. We'll tell our grandchildren that we were friends for years before we realized we were in love, that Ben knew long before I did, that it all came together in our first kiss, in a steamy car on a freezing cold night.

His jacket makes a shushing sound as he leans toward me. He reaches his hand around the back of my head, cradling it like a baby. His mouth meets mine, and for one perfect second I'm in laser-sharp focus, I'm the culmination of Ben's drawn-out affection, I'm the fine point on it, and I close my eyes.

And then our teeth bang together. And Ben laughs, a moist, nervous exhalation right into my mouth, and I'm leaning across a gear shift kissing my old friend, which, as it turns out, is sort of like kissing my grandmother, although to be fair I've never actually felt her tongue on mine, but there's something similar about it, close and earthbound and familiar. But it's Ben! So I soldier on, praying for transformation, bracing my suddenly heavy body so that I don't collapse onto him, and I am struck by the sensation of a kiss in a way I never have been before, that it is two people trying to eat each other, one hot mouth inside the other. Then again, his lips are soft, his hand in my hair reassuring.

"Can I ask you a question?" Ben says, when we're finished.

"Please." His face is still next to mine. There is a stray eyelash on his cheek.

"Did you eat pretzels today?"

"What kind of a question is that?" I ask.

"You taste . . . pretzel-y." The rogue strand of hair has fallen in front of my eye. Ben gently places it back behind my ear.

"Is that what you ask the girl you've just kissed after pining for her for twelve years?"

"I didn't pine for you." He laughs. His breath is warm, close. "Okay, maybe I, you know, thought about you from time to time, but no, no pining."

"You pined!"

"Just tell me if you had pretzels, and we can move on." He shifts in his seat, his jacket rustling again, like wings.

"No," I say. "But I had a raw onion for lunch."

"Ah, that's it."

"And some garlic bread, and clam chowder."

"Oh, Wendy," Ben says, shaking his head and smiling. He reaches for the vent blowing on us and tips it away. Neither of us says anything for a minute, our silence punctuated by the hiss of the heater, the wind, the tinny plink of icy snow. The kiss, so clear to me just a moment ago as a misguided expression of sympathy, an intimate mistake, is beginning to transmute into a confused longing. I glance at Ben for a reading on the situation, but his brow is just slightly furrowed, his expression opaque. He pushes his hand through his hair. "So, that, uh, what we just did," he starts.

"It was . . ."

". . . weird."

"Yes!" I say. "I mean, I'm really, really glad—"

He holds up both hands in front of himself, palms out, like a crossing guard. "Can we . . . do you think we could not talk about it?"

I'm staring at his strange face, a place I used to know. "Uh-huh."

"Ever again," he adds.

My body is still awkwardly inclined toward Ben. I lean back quickly, readjust myself. "I didn't really have a raw onion and clam chowder for lunch," I say.

Ben nods. "I could go for some soup."

I imagine him at our small, round kitchen table, Ben and me and Jane, the three of us, slurping big bowls of the matzo ball soup that Jane and I sometimes pick up from Nate's Deli on Pinefield. "You should come over sometime," I say. "You could meet my roommate."

Ben smiles at me and then looks down and mumbles something else about soup, or possibly he says that the evening has been super. "I'd like that," he says. "A lot." And maybe the heat in the car has finally kicked in, but for the first time all evening, I'm warm.

chapter three

My eyes popped open at seven-thirty this morning, and I stared at the ceiling for forty-five minutes, considering everything with a mixture of relief and regret—half expecting Ben to call, the way he used to when we were in high school, early, filling me in on our plans for the day *(The Reptile Festival! The Mustard Museum!).* I know last night happened—I told Jane all about it when I got home—but maybe, in the ensuing hours, it has somehow transformed into a kind of dreamy symbolism, the closing of the book of my friendship with Ben instead of the opening of a new chapter. I wonder how long I'll let myself think about him. I'm not that kind of girl.

Jane left early for a housecleaning job. So I'm alone, sitting at the kitchen table with a half-eaten bagel and a glass of orange juice and my notebook. Before I moved back to Milwaukee, I interned for six months at Crowley, Donovan, an ad agency in Evanston run by two scruffy, displaced Irish guys who swore constantly, as if their use of the word "fucking" as verb, adverb, and adjective could disguise the fact that they worked fourteen-hour days and drove Saabs. They throw me an assignment now and then, little projects they can't be *arsed* to do, and they pay me slightly more than waitressing would, and less than almost anything else. Right now I'm brainstorming names for a new eyeliner for Vérité, a very small makeup and skin care company that is constantly on the verge of bankruptcy. "Is it you, or is it Vérité?" That's their slogan. "If it's overdue, it must be Vérité," is how Michael and Declan refer to them.

I jot a few ideas down on my growing list. This product line is targeted at *the young woman in her mid- to late-twenties . . . She's single, adrift, not yet comfortable in her own skin. She goes out to clubs and bars looking for excitement and thrills but what she really wants, what she yearns for, is a place to call home.*

We thought it'd be perfect for you, sweetheart, Declan e-mailed me last week. *Fuck off!* I wrote back, which meant *Thanks, I'll take it.*

Luminate. Luminesce, I try gamely. In the world of cosmetics, nonword variations of "luminous" are always good, as is anything vaguely European; add *-ique* to any word, and you've got a product. *Luminique?* But then there's the danger that your lipstick will sound like a porn star. Food is always a good fallback plan, since apparently women sublimate. Anything with "apricot" or "pear" will generally sell well. (But not banana; we sublimate more subtly than that.) Wordplay in limited quantities can be "fun." *Eye-dentity,* I write, but it sounds a little toothy. *Eye-dealism. Surpr-eyes! Eye-can't-believe-it's-not-butter. Eye suck!*

The doorbell buzzes, a welcome surprise. Jane is the poetic spark that ignites my brainstorming sessions; a word from her, a casual suggestion, can be enough to put an end to hours of fruitless ruminating. A few weeks ago, I was working on a tagline for Arrow, a brand of decaffeinated instant coffee favored by octogenarians, and all I could come up with were vague allusions to impending death. ("Arrow Instant. Because you haven't got a minute to waste!") Jane breezed in, glanced over my shoulder, and said, "My grandma used to drink that. She called it her morning cup of joe." And suddenly I understood that nostalgia along with references to dying would sell better than death alone. Morbidity plus sentimentality equals hope! Michael and Declan said "Arrow. Yesterday, Today, and Tomorrow" was my best fucking work yet.

Jane rings again. I pad over to the door and buzz her in. "It's a good thing you're pretty," I call out down the echoey hallway. For someone with obsessive-compulsive tendencies, my roommate forgets her keys a lot.

"Thanks!" A voice that is decidedly not Jane's reverberates back, and it's Ben who ambles toward me down the long corridor, a white paper bag in one hand, a big, goofy smile on his face.

My breath catches in a gasp; for a second the whole inhale/exhale system that has always worked so well balks at the sight of him. My day crashes open, bright and unexpected. "Ben!" I yelp.

"Willa!" He stops at the door, gives me a little poke. "You look nice," he says, still grinning.

I glance down at myself and realize I'm still in my monkey pajamas, which are now dusted with bagel crumbs and, I notice, newly spotted with orange juice. "See?" I say. "That's what phones are for."

"For removing orange juice stains from monkey pajamas?"

"For calling first so people can look presentable when their friends come over."

Ben shrugs, then hands me the bag, which is full of baked goods—muffins, doughnuts, scones. I pull one out, a long, sugar-dusted cookie. "Remember?" he says, and I do, a long-ago morning at Baywood Bakery involving a man who didn't speak English, and the word "ladyfingers," repeated over and over in increasing volume, accompanied by much useless hand waggling and, at one point, the grabbing of an actual, unsuspecting lady's fingers, until Ben and I, in line behind the man, were doubled over; and then, when it was our turn at the counter, Ben, with an innocent gaze and an improvised Russian accent, ordering bear claws. This is like finding twenty dollars in the pocket of my winter coat on the first cold day of the year, like discovering my favorite, long-lost necklace behind the dresser. This is the shorthand, finally, of a long friendship. I bite into the ladyfinger and recognize its sugary density, along with a slight cardboardy staleness that I choose to ignore, because I know a peace offering when I taste one.

When my parents finally split up, toward the end of high school, mostly I was relieved. Their divorce was a quiet détente after three long years of volcanic arguing and festering ill will. But what made sense during the day grew leaden and confusing as the sun went down, and for months I lay awake every night, counting my own shallow breaths, trying to soothe myself to sleep by conjuring up situations in which it would be impossible for my parents not to admit that they still loved each other. (Most of these dramas involved me, weak and pale on my deathbed, rasping judgment as my weeping mother and father finally came together in their shared regret. *Too late . . . too late!*) In the end it was Ben—not my parents, definitely not Seth—who saw through the flimsy shell I built around myself, only Ben who didn't flinch when I broke down crying over Hallmark commercials, who didn't freak out when I abruptly turned from myself into a snapping turtle. It was Ben who brought the Rocky Road when he came over to study, Ben who stayed on the phone with me until I fell asleep, Ben who drove me to the DMV three times until I passed my driver's test. If this was all motivated in part by a crush he was secretly nursing, it doesn't change our history.

I offer him half of the ladyfinger, and we stand in the doorway for a while, chewing, before I remember to invite him in.

"So," he says, settling himself on the sofa and looking around the neat, spare living room. "How'd you do on that math test?"

"Huh?" I'm standing at the kitchen counter, pulling plates and napkins down from the cupboard. The coffeemaker gurgles. I turn to Ben, confused, a crackle of irritation sparking through me. He's as twitchy and inscrutable as ever. Math test? "What?"

"Well, I thought we'd pick up where we left off." He glances down at the doughnut in his hand as if it has just appeared there, as if it's some kind of strange, tiny puppy that has just hopped into his palm. He considered how to handle this moment, I realize. He tried out different versions of what to say to me, here in my apartment, how to appear casual and unstudied and charming and easy, and now that his joke has fallen flat and the air between us has gone still, and without the last decade as ballast, we're losing heft, starting to drift.

I walk over and plop down next to him, reach for his doughnut. "I skipped that test and got high in the parking lot," I say, and I take a huge bite of the doughnut, lick my fingers. "Do you have a job?" I ask. "An apartment? A girlfriend?" I ask the last question out of courtesy; something tells me the answer is no.

"Did I not mention that I've been married and divorced three times?"

"You did not," I say.

"Yes! And I have, um, twins. Four-year-old twin, uh . . . boys."

"Really!"

"Yes, and from different mothers!"

"Interesting. What are their names."

Ben grins, looks quickly around the room. "The twins. Their names." His gaze settles on the bookshelf. "Um . . . Biff." He shrugs again, a habit he seems to have picked up over the last seven years, the slouchy, unassuming gesture of someone who doesn't understand the high-voltage power of his good looks. He's still smiling. "Biff and, you know . . . Happy. We call him Hap."

I stand up and walk back into the kitchen, which is really part of the living room, which is more or less the same thing as the dining room. I hold up a mug; Ben nods. "Biff and Hap! Hmmm, I bet they're a handful," I say as I pour Ben a cup of coffee and bring it to him. "I bet they require a lot of *attention*."

"Attention must be paid," he says, and winks, an exaggerated facial contortion, a sort of this-is-not-a-wink wink. So much of our friendship in high school involved plucking out memorable lines from the literature of our AP English class and quoting them back to each other as punch lines, the inside jokes of the supremely nerdy. I'm surprised by how much this game still comforts me, how easily I can slip back into our script.

"I'm going to get dressed. I look forward to hearing more about your three ex-wives." With his free hand, Ben salutes me.

I wonder how long we'll be able to keep this up, this skimming, gliding dance we're doing. In my room, I rummage in the closet for my best jeans and find them on the floor, pull them on with the blue sweater that Jane admired the other day.

I rub ChapStick on my lips and drag my fingers through my hair in a futile attempt to create a flowing mane out of a Brillo Pad. I try to catch a glimpse of my reflection in the window next to my bed, but all I can see are the bare arms of a silver maple brushing against the side of the building. Two squirrels dash madly along the branches in hot pursuit of one another. Squirrels are at the top of the list of things that scare me, even before bats with rabies. It's the way they live among us. You never know if they're going to change their minds. I sketch them sometimes and imagine their secret lives, the way they probably plot against us but then get distracted by acorns.

I look up, past the tree, at the only square of sky visible from anywhere in this apartment, and there's the moon, too, even though it's the middle of the day, a blurry smudge in the bright blue sky, faint but unmistakable. Maybe I'll walk back out into the living room and tell Ben, gently, to go home; maybe this is the part where I explain to him that unrequited love is one thing, but to leave a friendship comatose for seven years is to give it up for dead.

When I emerge, Ben is staring into his mug of coffee, his face serious.

"Ben?"

"You know I am not a fan of sincerity," he says. There's a small rip just below the left knee of his jeans, and he worries it, plays at the fraying denim. "So I'm going to say this quickly."

I think about the way those squirrels chased each other, switching places at what looked like a predetermined moment, so that the chaser suddenly became the chasee. We are the squirrels!

"You don't have to say anything," I say. My voice is, unexpectedly, squeaky.

"No, but, of course I do."

"Is it about the twins? Is there a problem with the twins? Are they *Siamese*?" Just two minutes ago, all I wanted was something real between us, something quiet and true, and now I can't shut up about the twins. I twist my hair nervously.

He sighs. "Yes, they are Siamese twins. Now please let me talk. I shouldn't have cut you out of my life. You know me . . . or, you knew me, and you know that I didn't really have a handle on . . . well, I wasn't sure how to . . . be an adult . . ."

"But we weren't." I want to sit down, but suddenly every available chair seems wrong. The armchair? Too close. A kitchen chair? Too far away. I grip my hands behind my back and list a little bit, like a sailboat.

"Willa, I'm sorry. Can you forgive me?"

"Yes," I say, with a big bright smile, but it's all just too much— Ben, here, full of regret, the two of us, trying to salvage what we've lost. Seven years is too long; we'll try and we'll fail. And worse, I know with the tense clarity of a patient on the receiving end of a needle that *this will hurt.* "Yes!" I say again, my hands still tightly clasped behind my back.

And then there's a jingling sound that takes us both by surprise, a key in the lock and the *whoosh* of the door, and Jane. She's turned toward the coatrack, so she doesn't notice us at first; she shrugs off her winter jacket, revealing a tight purple T-shirt underneath and gray sweatpants, her hair up in a loose bun, tendrils curling around her face: an angel of grime. She drops her bucket of cleaning supplies onto the floor, kicks off her shoes, and sighs and says, "Fuck," the sound of her exhaustion intimate.

And I am frozen in place, standing in the middle of the living room between Ben, sitting, and Jane at the door, and who do I think I am? But I'm holding my breath, and I'm suddenly certain, like a magician or a mental patient, that I'm the one who'll turn it all around.

With a quick glance to the side, she sees Ben and me.

"Honey, you're home," I say.

She straightens and smiles, wipes her forehead with the back of her hand and says, again, "The fuck?" only this time it comes out throaty and cheerful.

"Not in front of the company," I stage-whisper.

Ben stands up and we both walk over to her; he holds out his hand to Jane, who takes it and looks at me.

"Ben! Jane!" I shout their names like I'm directing movers: *This chair here, next to the piano.* I recognize the volume of my voice but can't seem to control it.

"I'm sorry," Jane says. "I don't usually meet people this way."

"What way?" Ben asks.

"Um, sweaty from a cleaning job and reeking of Pledge?"

"I thought I smelled something lemony fresh."

Yellow rubber gloves poke out of the pocket of her sweatpants. "Willa has told me a lot about you," she says.

I cringe at the way that innocuous expression exposes my secrets, cracks my attempts at a cool exterior. *No, I haven't thought about you much over the years.* . . . Ben looks down, embarrassed or pleased.

"Well, mostly just about last night," Jane says after a beat, and we stand there, the three of us, in silence, until Ben snorts, a rhinoceros laugh, and then Jane giggles, and I grab one yellow latex glove from her pocket and swat her with it; she snatches it back.

There are moments—maybe everyone has them—when I'm outside of myself, peering sideways at my own life, telling myself to pay attention. I'm not saying, Willa, enjoy these moments, for they are fleeting and precious, or even Willa, stop eating all that cake. Just: look. See how the front of that car is dotted with dead bugs like an abstract painting? Or, watch that little kid, he's wiping his nose on his mother's shirt and she doesn't notice; or, listen to the neighbor's dog, how if you close your eyes he sounds like a wolf. This is one of these moments: the look on Jane's face changing from weary guardedness to expectant joy, Ben leaning toward her, bouncing on the balls of his feet a little bit and not even knowing he's doing it, the pull between them, and I'm right here, a part of it.

Jane lets her yellow gloves fall into her cleaning bucket. It looks like a bottle of Windex has suddenly grown hands, is waving to us. "Jane gets her best material from cleaning houses," I say to Ben, eager to offer him a glimpse of Jane's quirky brilliance.

"Well. . . ." Jane nods. I remember too late that she can be sensitive about how she makes her money, sometimes defensive about its honest, intrinsic value, other times insistent that every swipe of the mop is in the service of her poetry. Also, she really does smell quite bad, and I silently will her not to raise her arms. "You know, people's lives, and the things they leave out, the things they forget to hide, and, I mean . . ." She does this sometimes when she's nervous, drifts off, skidding down a slippery slope of unfinished sentences and disconnected thoughts.

"Your best material! Ha! Remember when you stole that dildo?"

Jane eyeballs me, and I know I've gone too far. *We were having a ball,* I'll explain to her later. *I thought we were becoming a unit. I didn't mean to be cocky.*

"It was . . ." Jane allows herself a half smile. "I didn't steal it. I liberated it. I was cleaning the house of the owner of Mr. Hump's Sex Emporium."

Ben is newly enthralled by the mention of this famous local sex-toy shop, the way guys are.

"The dildo was huge. I mean, epic." She raises her hands and measures the air, then, dramatically, moves her hands apart six more inches.

"And orange!" I say, wanting in on the action.

"Bright orange," Jane agrees. "Wide, circular base. I'd never seen anything like it. Not that I'd seen so many. They had an eight-month-old baby," she adds. "Mr. Hump and his wife."

"Mrs. Hump," Ben says.

"And I thought, *No, you cannot leave a fourteen-inch-long bright orange dildo out here in the middle of the living room when you have a baby! It's just wrong!*" Jane reaches out and touches Ben's arm. "I thought I was performing a service."

"So to speak," I say, and she looks at me and rolls her eyes. I breathe in and lean toward Jane a little bit. I want her to reach over and touch me with her other hand, but she doesn't.

"So to speak. I buried it at the bottom of my bucket of cleaning supplies. Underneath the bleach."

"But it wasn't a dildo!" I pipe up, glancing back and forth from Jane to Ben.

"It was a baby toy," Jane says. "One of those . . . where you stack the rings on top of each other?"

"A stacking toy!" I clap my hands gleefully and then immediately feel like an idiot.

"Which Willa helpfully pointed out to me later."

"Sometimes a stacking toy is just a stacking toy," Ben says.

"Exactly!" Jane, I notice, has not let go of Ben's arm this whole time. He doesn't seem to mind.

"So Baby Hump," I say, "is still wondering where his favorite baby toy has gone."

"And, not surprisingly, I have never been called back to clean that house."

"The home of Mr. and Mrs. Hump," Ben says.

"And poor Baby Hump."

"But she wrote an excellent poem about it," I say.

"An okay poem," Jane agrees. She does reach over now and picks a stray bit of lint from my sleeve.

"About toys," I say.

"About perspective," she says.

Ben nods slowly, his eyes on Jane, the smitten grin on his face the replica, I realize, of how he used to look at me, and with the slightest twinge I think, *This is it, this is right.* He's like a check I have signed over. *Pay to the Order of Jane Weston.*

"I'm going to shower," Jane says. "And then I think we should all go bowling."

And because we have nowhere to be, because there is not a single obligation among us beyond the imperative to move steadily forward through a day that is suddenly and completely ours, bowling is both a fabulous idea and as good as anything else. And it is exactly what we do.

chapter four

Baxter's Basement Lanes smells of Doritos and communal footwear, beer, and the light sweat that comes from very minimal physical exertion. I breathe it in. This dark, underground room is one of my all-time favorite places. When I was growing up, it was an old-fashioned Milwaukee bowling alley, smoky and dank and serious, All League Nights and *Wednesdays! Ladies Drink Free!* Our dad used to take us here once in a while on a Saturday afternoon when our mom needed a break, and Seth had his tenth birthday party here. Over the past decade, it's gradually been colonized by the college-aged residents of its east side neighborhood, but never completely, so that these days team tournaments and trophy dinners coexist with ironic hipster dudes in black leather jackets throwing noncommittal spares and girls in short skirts giggling over gutter balls or huddled together on the plastic bucket seats, sipping beer made by blind Belgian monks.

"This is my favorite sport!" I say, taking another deep, nostalgic breath as Jane tests out bowling balls of various weights, settling on a speckled green eleven-pounder.

"You've always been a very athletic bowler," Ben agrees. He tightens the lace on one of his scuffed, red-and-blue shoes.

I nod. "It's all about endurance."

"And an extreme level of fitness, of course."

Jane holds up her foot. "I don't really understand why we have to wear these shoes that so many others have worn before. What would be so bad about letting us bowl in our socks?" There's a sign above the entrance: YOU MUST WEAR BOWLING SHOES AT ALL TIMES. Someone has scrawled DISEM in front of the word BOWLING in purple marker.

"It levels the playing field," Ben says. "For example, some people might be able to afford fancy bowling socks, which would give them an unfair advantage."

"This way," I say, "we are all equal in the eyes of God."

"There's no such thing as fancy bowling socks," Jane says, gazing from me to Ben and then back to me. "Is there?"

"Will," Ben says, "do you remember our senior year phys ed class?"

"Golf is not for the faint of heart!" I announce.

"No freakin' crumpets at this tee time!" Ben adds. Ben and I had tried to sign up for bowling, the popular physical education elective for the sweat averse, and, failing to get in, we registered for golf instead, believing that it would be the next easiest, somewhere in the vicinity of archery but not as exacting. But Mr. Karlinsky, the golf coach, was a task master and a sadist. Strength training and three-mile runs were a regular part of the class. It was the hardest twelve weeks of my life.

"Remember how we tried to earn extra credit by writing that report on the golf courses of Scotland?" I say, "and Mr. Karlinsky told us to give it to the Loch Ness Monster?" Ben covers his face with his hands. I reach over and pretend to try to pry them off. "How is it that we were so phenomenally dorky back then, a mere few years ago, and yet we are so cool today?" Ben shakes his head, his hands still hiding his face. I hold up my bowling ball. "I mean! Nerds in high school, awesome bowling phenomenons today!"

Two lanes over, a white-haired senior bowler in a lime-green team shirt rolls her ball down the alley; I watch, mesmerized, as it slowly, slowly makes its way toward the pins. It seems, momentarily, to defy the laws of motion. It almost stops, possibly even rolls backward for an inch or two, and then, miraculously, it continues its wobbly journey to the end of the lane and knocks down every last pin. I look over at Jane to see if she's noticed. She's perched on the edge of one of the low plastic chairs, leaning forward slightly, and she's drawn a vague and pleasant screen over her features, her lips pulled into an unreadable little smile, her eyes focused somewhere in the distance behind Ben and me. Ben, unaware, tugs on the lace of his other shoe and grins at me, falling back under the spell of our old friendship. I rub my eyes against the haze of cigarette smoke that hovers around us; the rumble of falling pins is a sudden, thunderous cacophony.

There's a threesome in the lane next to ours, two girls and a guy, all in their twenties, our age, maybe a couple years younger. One of the girls has very white teeth and a long, sharp nose like a pretty rodent. The other, holes in her tights, auburn hair down to her waist, laughs like Woody Woodpecker, an annoying/charming rapid-fire machine gun. The guy, skinny and pale, is trying to teach the girl with the long hair to bowl, although he himself doesn't know what he's doing. They clink plastic cups, cheer each other on.

What separates us from them? We all think we're snowflakes, but we're Tinker Toys, held together by our interchangeable parts.

I can see myself ten years from now. This day is a fuzzy memory, a flash: Ben and Jane are two people I once knew, and time has won out over history and love. But what if this concoction we're brewing right now will be our magical potion? Someone a few lanes away bowls a strike, and a smattering of applause erupts. *Good one, Betty!* "Hey," I say. I take a half step away from Ben and turn toward the bar, gesture in its direction. "Should I get us something to drink? Do you two want something to drink?"

Without waiting for an answer I sprint to the grimy little counter where a bored-looking guy pours soda and beer, a toothpick dangling from the corner of his mouth, his eyes glued to a little TV next to the cash register. I linger over the menu, a collection of Gothic typos: *Died Coke, Rot Beer, Spite;* when I come back with our beverages a few minutes later, Ben and Jane are sitting together at the lighted scoring table, and Ben is telling Jane how to add up a spare. He draws a slash through one of the little boxes, then demonstrates how you calculate the numbers in the next frame. "I'm embarrassed that I know this," he says, and Jane laughs and says, "I don't understand scoring in tennis, either," and Ben says, "How about Ping-Pong?" and Jane laughs again. The dirty light from under the glass casts a faint glow on their faces. I'm holding a cardboard tray of watery Cokes in my hands, watching them.

Later I'll recall how after every gutter ball Jane threw that afternoon, Ben would say, "Try to get it just a *little* closer to the edge"; how once, after she managed to knock down four pins, he hugged her. I'll remember how Jane nervously smoothed her purple shirt every time she got up to bowl, how she licked her lips after she took sips of her Coke. I'll think about the way Ben stared at her, how Jane pretended not to notice. I won't recall what was said, but I'll remember how I sat there, subdued and watchful, happy to let them talk to each other, warmed by the glow of their ambient heat.

chapter five

Seth is elbow deep in an almost-empty bag of barbecue-flavored potato chips. A breeze blows in through the open window. On the sidewalk below our apartment, a woman yells something in Russian. I can't tell if she's angry or happy.

"It's like everything finally fits," I say to my brother. "It's like I'm home!" Across the kitchen table from me, Seth nods vaguely, then crams too many chips into his mouth and crunches loudly. "I thought Ben was gone from me forever," I tell him. "And I mourned, you know, the loss of my best friend. And then I met Jane, and she filled that hole. Even though of course I would always be sad about Ben." The chip bag crackles, indicating Seth's interest, although not necessarily in what I'm saying.

Ben has come to our apartment every day since the bowling adventure, self-conscious and shiny and bearing small, neutral gifts for both Jane and me. He handed us two bars of fancy chocolate the first time he stopped by. *Just thought I'd see what you two are up to!* he said, with a hearty nonchalance so obviously rehearsed I had to cough to stop myself from laughing. Yesterday, just as the cold twilight was sharpening into an icy, dark evening, he buzzed our apartment and yelled through the intercom, *Hey, I brought soup!* And we sat together, the three of us crowded around our little table, just like in my fantasy, only the soup was chicken noodle.

I want to describe it to Seth, to explain how it feels to be an ingredient in this happy, new friendship pie. "But all of a sudden he's back in my life, and the three of us are hanging out together, and, Seth, it's *perfect!*" Heat rises to my face as soon as the words are out of my mouth. Seth leans back in his chair and gazes past me. It's a good thing that he is not, it turns out, even remotely listening to me, because along with barbecue potato chips, my brother eats sincere emotions for lunch.

"I don't blame Fran and Stan, you know," he says, tipping the last of the chips into his mouth. That's what we call our parents—Fran and Stan—although our father's name is actually Roger.

"Huh?" I say, baffled by his sudden change of gears. Powdery orange crumbs fall like nuclear snow around his mouth. Later, Jane will spot the flecks on the floor, and she'll make them disappear. I blow on my fingernails, which I've just painted a bright and glittery red, from Vérité's disastrously named I'd Nail That line of polishes. Jane is dragging me to a party tonight. I don't like parties, but I do enjoy the occasional opportunity to shine myself up. I shaved my legs earlier, and I'm even contemplating wearing lipstick.

"I don't blame them for how things turned out."

"Seth, you came home from Madison after your first semester freshman year and you waved your Intro to Psych textbook in front of Mom and yelled, 'You and Dad screwed me up! I have *proof!*'"

"Well, I don't blame them anymore."

"Really, you don't blame Stan for the time he stormed out of the house and didn't come back for two days? For those months before the divorce when he just stomped around and didn't talk to any of us? For moving in with Lesley six months after he left?"

"Do you have any more chips?" Seth asks. I shake my head. "Or, um . . . Pop-Tarts? That's what I want. Did I see blueberry Pop-Tarts in your pantry?"

"You don't blame Mom for the constant stream of bitter poison that didn't dry up until the day she married Jerry in Arizona, without us, *and called from Tucson to tell us?*"

"No," Seth says, licking his fingers. When we were growing up, my brother refused to submit to my mother's requirement for good table manners; his stubbornness backfired, and now he's incapable of not being disgusting. "But *you* still do!"

"Well, whatever," I say. "You're the one whose girlfriend just kicked him out." I pull my favorite pink sweater from the back of a kitchen chair, where it's been hanging since last week, and slip it over my head.

"And that's my point," Seth continues. He's up and rooting through the cupboards. Five nights ago, Nina tossed him out of the apartment they shared on the east side. I loved Seth and Nina's place, the big living room with its sea-blue walls, deep, welcoming couches, and antique lamps glowing yellow in every room. And I loved Nina, the way she teased Seth, softened him. She's a herpetologist who specializes in mutations. I wanted them to get married, to share in the care and feeding of Nina's three-legged frogs and then, eventually, of Seth and Nina's hopefully two-legged human babies; I wanted them to redeem our fractured adolescence with a happy, functioning family. They were supposed to be the template.

Seth won't tell me why their relationship imploded, but I have my suspicions. His last relationship, with a coworker named Shelly, ended in a spectacular display of fireworks when he cheated on her with her half sister, Kelly; he broke it off with his college girlfriend, Libby, by sleeping with his high school girlfriend, Nora, whose heart he had broken, years earlier, by making out with Merry, a sad-faced girl he'd met at math camp. I don't have Seth's degree in statistics, but it's not that hard to figure this one out. He's been sleeping on his friend Pete's sofa but spending his days here, plowing through all of my food and spouting self-help clichés whenever his mouth isn't full. "You have to own your problems. You can't play the blame game!"

I cut my eyes at my brother. This is the boy who caught me practicing French-kissing the mirror one day when I was fourteen, and, for a full year, whenever the mood struck him, he would make slurping, licking sounds, frequently accompanied by a passionate make-out session with his own hand. In front of my friends. At school. Worse, after he graduated from high school, the brutal mockery morphed into hard indifference. He ignored me completely, disowned us all, neglecting to come home for holidays, never phoning or returning my calls. We had adored each other growing up. The shock of losing him to the nastiness that had colonized his soul was unbearable. So I pushed him out of my mind, cultivated my own cool detachment. For a time after college, even my closest friends were surprised to learn that I had a brother.

And then, three years ago he met Nina, and she convinced him I was worth knowing. Within weeks he had invited me back into his life, and I RSVP'd with an emphatic yes. I happily resumed my role as little sister, repressing the hard feelings that had simmered for over a decade, banishing any pesky, residual resentment. I showed up at their apartment empty-handed and allowed myself to be fed. I watched movies on their couch on cold nights, toasty in Nina's slippers and snuggled under, *yes, thank you,* their cashmere blanket, met them for Sunday brunch and took home all the leftovers. I claimed what was mine.

But how much of Seth is mine without Nina? In the absence of her domesticating goodness, will he hop away, gone? The truth is, I'll happily keep him swimming in trans fats if that's all it takes to make him stay.

"Finding anything good in there?" I ask. He's still foraging in the cabinets, rustling bags and examining jars.

He holds a silver foil-wrapped package up to me, triumphant. He's managed to locate a box of very old Pop-Tarts in the back of the cupboard. They may have been here when Jane and I moved in. He tears it open and starts gnawing at the petrified edges of the thing as if he has just emerged from the forest. A low growl of pleasure escapes from him as he chews.

"I'm fixing you a salad, Kaspar Hauser," I say, and I resolve to call Nina tomorrow. *Your voice sounds scratchy,* I'll tell her. *Frog in your throat?* And she'll laugh, she'll say, *Gee, Willa, I've never heard that one before,* and at my gentle prodding her anger at Seth will loosen, her chest will expand to take in oxygen, and she'll realize that she can't live without us.

"Hey, um, maybe you should come to this party tonight," I say halfheartedly, and Seth rolls his eyes at me in response.

"That sounds *awesome,*" he says, which means *Hell, no.*

"Or you could stay here and throw some things down the garbage disposal," I say, pointing at him for emphasis.

"Nah," he says. "I'm outta here. All you guys have left in this place is cottage cheese, yogurt, and sunflower seeds. And, I mean, Christ, I'm not *desperate!*" We both laugh, then, and I have the disorienting feeling, for a second, of nostalgia for something we've never really had: an adult friendship, a bond separate from our heavy family baggage. He grabs his jacket and pats me on the head as he leaves, which is about as close as Seth and I have ever gotten to an expression of love.

Al's apartment is hot and crowded. The party was in full swing when we arrived, and Jane and I found refuge on the love seat, where we're scrunched next to each other. "Sometimes I worry..."

She pauses, holds up one finger, and takes a very long guzzle of a drink that looks like coolant. "Vile!" she says, delighted, and offers it to me. It tastes like liquid cough drops. My face immediately feels warm. I take another swig and hand it back to her. Al's small apartment is filled with friends from Jane's creative writing classes—a master's degree most people refer to obliquely as "the program," like it's rehab for people addicted to clever symbolism. Jane calls it the Road to Nowhere.

In the corner, two poets Jane has introduced me to, Bridget McCarragher and Penelope Tan, are arguing passionately. I presume they're debating the finer points of the sestina or the questionable merits of Ezra Pound, until I overhear Penelope, her high-pitched voice rising above the din: "Kylie shouldn't have been sent home before G-Lance! His tango was a fucking travesty!" Bridget McCarragher shakes her head vigorously and smacks her forehead in distress over the latest elimination on *Celebrity Dance-Off*.

We haven't moved from this spot since we arrived an hour ago. The strum and thump of loud flamenco music fills the air, making everybody look somewhat sexier to me than they are.

"You guys," someone yells. "I'm transferring to the Business School! I just found out that poetry's dead!"

Jane and I met during our senior year of college, in Madison. I was majoring in drawing and painting, working on a graphic novel about two star-crossed bird-watchers, called *We'll Always Have Parrots*. I thought that a creative writing class might broaden my skill base: this way, after graduation I could work in a restaurant *or* a bar. Most of us in the Art Department accepted our fates with weary resolve, undercut by constant neurotic fretting. We drank a lot of beer and cultivated superior attitudes about having to work retail jobs at the mall to pay the rent on our crappy off-campus apartments. There was also a plasma center off State Street that paid thirty dollars per donation and gave out cookies, and which sometimes looked like one of the wine and cheese receptions they held for fine arts students on Friday afternoons.

By the time senior year rolled around I was pretty sure I was just about finished with all of that. But I had no idea where I would go next. In addition to my book about bird-watchers, I had also devoted an enormous amount of time to a series of drawings of imaginary animal crossbreeds (hippophant, skunkey, flamenguin). I felt like I was pursuing my dream and wasting my time simultaneously. There weren't that many jobs for people who could draw a really majestic polar beagle. I didn't know what I was supposed to do with my life. And I had the vague sense that I ought to have already figured it out.

I was in the middle of drawing the snout on a dolphig when Jane walked in on the first day of class, silver rings and earrings sparkling, her curly hair bursting out of its ponytail holder like loose springs. Twelve of us sat at a big square table—an arrangement, I would soon learn, well suited to the process of ritually immolating one another's work. Jane came in late and slid into the last available chair.

We started with Owen Schiff, straight spined and shiny eyed and wearing all camouflage, including, I noticed, his socks. He told us that he was writing a series of Shakespearean sonnets devoted to his passionate love of military history. He recited his poem, "Iraq: My Brains," and seemed happy to interpret the stunned silence that followed as approval. Then Jane read hers, "The Universe Is a Vacuum Cleaner." Her voice was clear and deep and unaffected, and when she was done, when her tongue had loosed the final, debauched *k* in "suck," she looked across the table and smiled at me, a great beaming grin. I stared back at her, startled, smitten. It was love at first sight, and also sort of like looking in the mirror on a really, really good day. I saw that Jane was just like me but better, an observation she would later, with a laugh, firmly deny.

Jane had managed to sidestep the unearned cynicism the rest of us were afflicted with. Her poems were about the search for meaning in a sparkling kitchen sink, the persistence of mildew, dust bunnies, and stubborn love; she cleaned big suburban houses to pay her rent. She wasn't afraid of latex gloves or of rhyming "dust" and "lust," "clog of hair" and "fog of despair." She seemed to have found the intersection between her life and her art. She had a purposeful glow about her, a clarity—or at least bravado—that I was drawn to, along with the lingering scent of lemon. Plus she was pretty, and tall like me. We went out for coffee after class. From that moment, like eager lovers, we were inseparable.

In the dim light of Al's living room, Jane looks at me, blinking. She gives her hair a self-conscious flick. "Sometimes I worry," she says again, "that men find us intimidating." My dangly turquoise earrings swing from her ears. "Because we're always together. Like we're a package deal or something?"

"Maybe so," I say, glancing around at the other partygoers, couples locked in conversation, a few women dancing, groups of friends laughing and gesturing to one another, every interaction made extra hilarious by Al's high-octane fruit punch.

"I'm not thinking about anyone in particular," she says, and giggles. "Really, Willa, no one in particular!"

Nearby, Rafael, one of the new poets, is standing close to Amy, a thirty-year-old blond fiction writer perennially looking for love, whose short stories are always about twenty-nine-year-old blond fiction writers looking for love. Amy, Jane has told me, has dated every grad student in their department, each relationship lasting precisely long enough for her to suggest that she'd be open to not using birth control. But Rafael doesn't know any of this. He's leaning against the wall, talking to her intently, and she is staring up at him, her eyes huge with need that could easily be mistaken for adoration. I can see, even from here, that this and the spiked punch would be a heady mix for an attention-craving artist.

"Remember Ed?" I say. A burst of laughter erupts from Al's kitchen.

"Ed." Jane snorts. He went out with her for three weeks, and then, after it fizzled, he and I met for drinks a few times, followed by beery kisses on his porch among the fireflies.

"Ed," I say again, "who wrote the poem about us."

"'Tall Girls'!"

"Before he got kicked out of your department." Out of the corner of my eye, I see Rafael, still talking, leaning nearer to Amy, whose eyes, I notice, are closed.

"'Tall girls, Amazon hearts,'" Jane announces dramatically.

"'Warriors,'" I say, clenching my fists in front of me.

"'On the tender battlefield of love'!"

This is not the first time Jane and I have recited Ed's ode to us; with each rendition we add more sweeping gestures and exaggerated emotion, and each time, by the end, we're screaming with laughter—although lately I've begun to feel, despite the hilarity, that this particular joke has a specific shelf life, that it will die— not now, not yet, but eventually, like a sputtering car running out of gas.

Jane takes a deep breath and another sip of her noxious drink. I reach my hand up to smooth my hair. A man and a woman I don't recognize seat themselves on the very sunken, 1970s plaid sofa across the room, and then seem to disappear into the dip in the cushions.

"I think guys see us," she says, "they see our friendship, and they know they don't have a chance."

"Remember Josh?" I absently run my palm along the worn nub of the love seat's arm. Last year, Josh the city planner broke up with Jane because he said he felt like he was the third wheel. Josh's area of expertise was bus and bicycle lanes. He used a lot of vehicle metaphors.

"I did not prefer him," Jane says. "He was needy."

"I know. He was a third wheel!" One time we went to a movie with Josh, and it wasn't until after the closing credits that Jane and I realized that, while he'd been in the bathroom, we'd changed our minds and gone to a different film.

Al walks out of the kitchen carrying a huge, steaming vat of chili. Behind Jane, Rafael bends awkwardly toward Amy. She strains on her tiptoes, her blond head tipped back. He looks like he's in imminent danger of toppling onto her. They kiss, finally, and Jane, noticing that my gaze has drifted, cranes her neck to see what I'm looking at. She laughs. The music has grown louder; the guitar comes to a throbbing crescendo, an ache that reaches inside me, takes me by surprise.

"Well," Jane says softly, below the din, "those two probably won't last the week, but in fifty years, when we're in the home, we'll still have each other."

"You'll have to pluck my chin hairs," I say.

"I will," she says. "I promise." She squints at me, stage-whispers, "You have one now."

The song ends abruptly. The apartment is warm and smells like beans. "Come and get it," Al calls cheerfully from the dining room table, where he is beginning to scoop the chili into deep blue bowls.

Jane leans her head back onto the edge of the love seat. Her long neck is birdlike, suddenly vulnerable, and I have the urge to pet it. "Let's go," she says, but neither of us gets up. Rafael and Amy unclench and quickly separate. Dozens of party guests begin to move en masse toward the food. They drift past us, and it seems for one dreamy moment as if they are under water, or I am.

chapter six

In May of my sophomore year of college, my dad drove up to Madison for a visit. It was his fiftieth birthday, so I baked him a cake. I used a Duncan Hines mix and slathered the finished product with frosting from a can, but for me it was a Herculean effort. It was my first year living off campus, and it had taken me a long time to get the hang of things: it was the year my roommates and I didn't realize our oven was broken until one day in early April when our landlords were being stingy with the heat, and we tried to turn it on to warm the apartment. Even though I put the frosting on when the cake was still too hot and most of the top layer crumbled up into the thick, gloppy icing, and one side of the cake ended up about two inches higher than the other, it still looked and smelled remarkably edible.

We met at A Tale of Two Zitis, the bookstore/Italian restaurant on State Street frequented by students and their visiting parents. At every other table there was a version of us. Dad had brought his girlfriend, a pleasant, petite, leather-skinned woman Seth and I called Tan Lesley. Lesley's presence neither delighted nor disappointed me. She'd been a part of the scenery since a few months after our parents divorced, and Stan and Lesley had recently gotten engaged. Lesley didn't speak much. At any given moment you could tell if she agreed or disagreed with my father by whether she placed her tan hand on his upper arm, or rolled her eyes and clucked her tongue at him. Whenever she talked to me, she announced my name first. *Willa! It's lovely to see you. Willa! How are your classes this term?*

"Willa! Do you know where the little girls' room is?" I pointed her in the right direction, and she tottered off on her very high heels.

"Stan!" I said. "Will you guys come back to the apartment after dinner?" I wanted to surprise him with my cake.

My dad nodded happily and took another bite of his fettuccine alfredo. When Lesley came back from the bathroom, he jammed another forkful in, and Lesley said, "This place reminds me of that cute little café in Florence we went to a few years ago. The one with the chairs." She touched my dad's shoulder and smiled, then popped a cherry tomato into her mouth.

But my dad returned her sunny gaze with a look of distress. His mouth was still full of pasta, his eyes bugged with alarm. It took me all of five seconds to catch on: Lesley. Florence. She was referring to a trip our family had been planning when I was fourteen, about two years before my parents split up. We had been talking about it for ages. Fran and Stan had always wanted to take us to Europe—when we would be old enough to appreciate it, they said, but before Seth went away to college, before we were too grown up to enjoy a family vacation. This was going to be the big one, the big splurge: Austria, where Stan's grandparents had come from; France; Italy. We had already gotten our passports. I'd spent my babysitting money on travel guides and sketch pads and a leather-bound European trip diary. But one night, a few weeks before we would have left, Stan and Fran called us into the living room and told us that the vacation was off. Just like that. Stan clasped his hands behind his back and told us that an important business trip had come up for him during the exact same two-week period, that he had to go to Albany and couldn't get out of it, that he was terribly, terribly sorry to disappoint us. Fran sat on the edge of the ottoman looking ashen.

"Willa," she said. "Seth. We'll reschedule the trip. I promise we will." She covered her face with her hands, and we knew not to ask any questions.

In the restaurant, a waiter rushed past our table; glasses and silverware clinked. "Dad," I said. I pushed my plate away. My appetite had died, had been crowded out by the tidal wave of disappointment and disgust that was washing over me. "God, Dad."

Lesley looked at me, her pretty, lined face a relief map of confusion. "What's wrong, honey?"

I shook my head. Nothing was her fault. Still, I wanted to stab her with my fork.

"Will," my father said, and I turned to him. I thought about how this could go; I thought about how if he apologized, after all this time, I might never talk to him again: I would look back in thirty years and say, *That was the day I stopped talking to my father.* He kept his small brown eyes fixed on me as he reached for Lesley's hand. "You know that things have turned out for the best for all of us. I think you do know that." He leaned over to Lesley and kissed her on the cheek, and she turned her face to him, surprised and pleased. "Well, it's not always easy to do the right thing," he said. "We take so many wrong turns."

Lesley, still smiling to herself, still a bit bemused, turned her attention back to her garden salad.

"Love can be ruthless," he said. He ran his hand through his hair, which was full and curly and only just starting to go gray. "But we do what we have to do. We make our choices."

"I have to go," I said.

"Willa."

I got up from the table and thanked them for dinner and said I had to get back to study. The restaurant went blurry for a second, and I gripped the edge of my chair.

Stan stood up and walked around the table and put his arm over my shoulders like a man who would not, in fact, apologize for his own happiness, not even to his daughter. And what could I do about that? How could I argue with it? I leaned into his embrace, but only for a second. "Okay," I said. "See you."

When I got home I took one look at the birthday cake I had baked, and I wanted to stuff it down the drain, but I also wanted to call Stan and tell him to come over after all. I stared at that lopsided chocolate cake for a full five minutes, and then I carved myself a huge, crumbly slice of it. I called out for my roommates, who were studying; I called out, "Guys, cake break!" and they came, and slice by slice, we ate the whole thing.

But what seems jagged and wrong at nineteen can change, over the years, and seven years is a long time to think about a thing, to turn it over and over in your mind. My dad and Lesley are happy. My mom and Jerry are happy. Seven years is long enough to turn an excuse for the worst kind of behavior into a flawed nugget of wisdom. Take it or leave it. It had always been up to me.

chapter seven

"You have to acknowledge your inner truths," Seth says to me. It's been a week since he was here last, and he's slumped at my kitchen table again; he's unshaven and wearing the same frayed blue T-shirt and sweatpants he wore last week. For a moment it seems possible that he has never left. Right now he's methodically dipping his index finger into a container of powdered hot cocoa mix and then licking it.

"My inner truth is that that jar of Nesquik is yours," I say. "You can take it home with you." I regret instantly my use of the word "home," because Seth still doesn't have one. He's still camped out on his friend Pete's sofa.

"That's your outer truth."

"Okay," I say lightly, "but I'm not interested in your cooties becoming a part of my inner truth."

"Oh, my cooties?" Seth glares at me, his voice suddenly serrated, his features twitchy with disdain; immediately I curl up inside myself like a roly-poly bug. This is the thing about Seth, how when I'm with him, time will sometimes whirl backward in a dizzying spin, and without warning I'm the scorned fourteen-year-old little sister, the embarrassed blob of developing flesh, the trash bin for his misplaced anger. I finish drying a mug and, still stunned, carefully place it right back in the dish rack. When I notice what I've done, I leave it there, too proud to move it to the cupboard, to let Seth see he's rattled me.

I hang the dish towel on the oven door and glare back at my brother, who of course is no longer looking at me. But the fact is, I am just as much Willa-then as Willa-now, just as much fourteen-year-old kid as twenty-six-year-old adult, and although Seth may have the power to flatten me, it helps to remember that I'm not the one who got himself kicked out of his own apartment, I'm not the one spouting self-help platitudes while nursing an endless, insatiable sugar jones, currently licking powered cocoa mix from one wet, wrinkly finger. I'm not the one who, I am just noticing for the first time, has a brand-new silver dollar-sized bald spot on the top of his head.

"So how's it going at Pete's?" I say, restraining the urge to plant my hands on my hips. "How's that couch treating you?" *Baldy.*

Seth pauses, considering. "Lumpy," he says. "And lonely. It's the perfect combination."

"Right," I say, loosening. "How psychically unbalanced would it be if you were sleeping in someone's well-appointed guest room, on six-hundred-thread-count Egyptian cotton sheets?"

Seth nods. We're back to normal. If there's one thing I've learned from my brother—and there may be only one thing I've learned from my brother—it's that opportunities for forgiveness are unlimited. "I know!" he says. "One of the great things about getting dumped by Nina is that all of my friends are pathetic losers like me."

Seth's best friend is Pete Moss, a chubby computer genius who sometimes confuses his online avatar—star soccer player for an Italian club—with his real-world self.

"Pete Moss," I say. I just like to say it.

"Pete Moss," Seth agrees. "Hey, where's *your* loser roommate?"

He looks around the apartment in an exaggerated way, craning his neck as if he's just noticing that Jane isn't here, which obviously is not the case, because he's had a crush on Jane since he met her. But that's an uncomfortable fact we don't acknowledge, given both Seth's former relationship with Nina, and also Jane's startling resemblance to me.

"She's out."

"Out?"

"Jane is out for dinner with Ben. On a date." I straighten the dish towel, which is suddenly in dire need of my attention. The corners are really uneven. ESCAPE TO WISCONSIN! is emblazoned in bright red on the white cloth. Depending on how you fold it, you can also make it say ESCAPE WISCONSIN! or SPEW SIN! I pluck at one side, then the other. "They're on their first date, technically, although the three of us have hung out. But this is just the two of them."

Seth is silent, except for an unpleasant wet suction slurp. Other than that, he's quiet for a long time. I crumple the dish towel and look around for something to wipe off, tension inexplicably balling up in my chest. As usual, except for whatever damage I've just inflicted on it, the entire kitchen is spotless, sparkling.

"Huh," Seth says finally.

"Huh?"

"She's out with Kern?"

"Yes!" I say, slapping my hand on the ancient yellow Formica countertop. *It's from the Plasticine Era,* Jane says. "What is the big deal?"

"Nothing! Just . . . dude always had a thing for you."

"You knew?"

"You didn't?"

"Noooo," I say, contemplating whether to tell my brother everything. "Why didn't you tell me?"

"What, back in high school?" Another fact we barely acknowledge: the entire history of our strained relationship. Seth wouldn't
have let me in on his observation about Ben in high school; he was
too busy smoking pot, running track, and conducting his lengthy
campaign to bulldoze my self-esteem.

"Actually," I say, "I arranged it. Their date." It was predictably
simple, the time-honored technique of eighth graders everywhere.
I told Ben; I pretended Jane had no idea I was spilling the beans:
a little tug on his arm, *She likes you.* And Ben, with the easy confidence of a customer whose new toaster comes with a money-back
guarantee, asked Jane out.

"Wow," Seth says. And then he doesn't say anything else. Outside, a siren screams past our building.

"I think it's great," I say. "I think they might make a really good
couple." A thick, savory smell wafts through the apartment: our
neighbors' Friday night dinner. We have never actually met Mr.
and Mrs. J. Smith of apartment 7, but we know a lot about them.
Garlic, Italian opera, dramatic arguments. It's too obvious, the
generic name, the old-world odors and sounds: witness protection
program. "What?" I say finally. I sit down across from Seth and,
in spite of myself, reach for the cocoa powder and dip my finger
into it.

"Nothing," he says, smirking.

"Did you know that you're starting to lose your hair?"

"Oh, little sister," Seth says, and his smirk, poised between
gently mocking and ugly, twists up in the direction of his narrowed eyes. "How can you not know how this is going to play out?"

I sigh. The evening ahead with my brother suddenly seems
interminable. "Enlighten me."

"One," he says, holding up the index finger of his right hand.
"Jane and the Kern dog will break up, and you'll be caught in the
middle. Two," he continues to hold up just one finger, "and less

likely, they'll actually stay together, and you'll be . . ." and he rakes that finger across his neck.

"Can I ask you a question?" I say. Seth nods. "Why do you always assume the worst?"

He looks at me, and for a second I see a glimmer of something sad and true, before his lip curls again. "Were you not raised by my parents?"

"Okay." I push away from the table, my chair shrieking across the linoleum. "We'll see, I guess. We'll just see how it goes." My voice is louder than I mean it to be, and I am filled with rage, with the sudden, trembling urge to run from my apartment, to leave Seth behind, once and for all, this slouched, beaten-down amalgam of base instincts and poor choices, this boy-man who shares my DNA but not my heart. *Yeah, well, you cheated on Nina!* I won't let him slither under my skin. I turn away from my brother, move toward the television, and, so that he won't be able to see that my hands are shaking just a little bit, start fumbling through the collection of DVDs he's brought over. "I think things will turn out just fine," I say, meaning it.

chapter eight

In college, my friends and I used to play a game we called Special Family. It was a competition, and sometimes a drinking game, in which, one by one, we compared the sordid details of our messed-up families. There were eight of us, and we played it over and over; we never ran out of material. There was only one rule—never embellish—and a clear winner always emerged. Sometimes it was the person whose parents were the most narcissistic and oblivious, like my friend Violet, who overheard her mom, mid-divorce, say to a friend, "Hell, if I hadn't had kids with Tom, I would have had them with someone else." On another night the victor might be the one whose parents had caused the most spectacular damage, had burned the broadest swath through their son or daughter's childhood, like Ari, whose parents woke him up one night when he was six, stood together in the dark at the edge of his bed and said, "Choose!" I had my share of victories: the way my parents told Seth and me they were splitting up during Christmas Eve mu shu at our favorite Chinese restaurant; how I overheard them screaming at each other in their bedroom one night and then suddenly grow eerily silent, and when, finally, overcome with concern, I went to investigate, I found them rolling around on their bed, pale globes of flesh in the dim light. I got a special tinfoil medal for that one.

One lonely winter weekend my junior year I even drew a comic of it, twelve pages of Special Family Commemorative Moments: Evan's mom with a glass of wine in her hand, weepily telling her eleven-year-old son that he looked just like his father but that she loved him anyway; Katie's dad removing all of the light fixtures from their house when he moved out, insisting they belonged to him. I thought they would be funny, my black-and-white drawings, a joke to share with my friends at our next pot-and-poker night. But it turned out they were just depressing.

All of this is why, when Jane invites me to come home with her for the weekend, I assume that it will be a piece of cake, that the trickiest thing I'll have to navigate will be Jane's mother's overuse of the phrase "That's *real different*!" Every happy family, I figure.

"They're not Ozzie and June, you know," Jane says as we pull into her parents' driveway, a smack of gravel against the car as it slows, then stops, the engine ticking to silence.

"Ward and Harriet, you mean, and look! Over the front door! A banner that says WELCOME HOME, JINXY!" There's no banner, but Jane did admit to me as we were leaving Milwaukee three hours ago that her dad used to call her Jinxy, and I've been taking advantage of that information ever since. "Come, Jinxy," I say, unbuckling my seat belt and patting my thigh. "Come!"

"Hang on," Jane says, reaching across me to rifle through the glove compartment; she pulls out a bright yellow scrunchie and tucks her hair into a ponytail.

"Your glove compartment is a time machine to 1994!"

"My mom says she likes it when she can see my face," she says, unembarrassed. She glances in the rearview mirror and then slides out of the car. I watch as she walks around the front of the car to my side, her long loping strides, her head bent slightly against the wind, and not for the first time today, I see my friend as the object of someone's affection. Will Ben notice the way she rests her hands on her stomach when she's thinking? How her hair is slightly curlier on the left side than it is on the right? Jane and I spent the first hour of our journey analyzing every detail of last night's date. He was nervous; he spilled a glass of water. They told each other stories about past loves. *Not me, I hope, ha ha.* They kissed. "Every first kiss doesn't have to change your life," she said, matter-of-fact, and then, "I like him," before I could respond, which I would have, but then I didn't. Her eyes were fixed on the road. I imagined their faces. It was the start of something. Any idiot could see that.

"Come on," she says, opening my car door. "Your list of ways to make fun of me is about to grow significantly longer."

Sure enough, Jane's mother greets us at the door with a plate of cookies. "Hi, girls!" she says, cookies aloft, and I'm thinking, *Give me a fucking break,* and also, *Maybe they'll let me move into Jane's old room,* when her mother slaps Jane's hand away. "Not for you!" she says, with surprising force. Mrs. Weston is wearing a zigzag-striped sweater, a horrible, mesmerizing thing in pinks and browns that, I feel, could be used for nefarious purposes. *You're a duck! Quack like a duck!* She's at least six inches shorter than Jane and I, her brown wavy hair cut to just above her shoulders. She reminds me of a doll I had when I was little whose appearance you could change by snapping different hairstyles onto its head.

"Hello, dear." She places one hand on my upper arm and squeezes; she seems like a person who understands the nuances of a good arm squeeze. "You must be Willa. We are *so pleased* that you're here." *Squeeze.* She juts her chin toward the plate of cookies.

"I was just going to run this over to the Tylers'. Dougie's getting divorced!"

"So you baked them cookies," Jane says. She reaches for the plate again and takes two, offers me one. Oatmeal raisin, the Miss Congeniality of cookies.

"He's over there now," Jane's mother says, her voice a sudden, conspiratorial whisper. She nudges Jane. "Go on, you take them over."

"Oy vey, Mom," Jane says, raising her palms dramatically. Mrs. Weston purses her lips a little and tilts her head as if she is hearing distant, complicated music. "Dougie and I grew up together," Jane says to me. "My mom and his mom have been trying to get us together for . . . twenty-five years?" Her mother nods. "Since preschool. Dougie is a salesman for a sporting goods company. He still gets drunk every Saturday night with his college frat brothers. Still calls them his brothers. Last time I saw him he bragged to me that the only reading he does is the sports page while he's in the bathroom. Except he didn't say 'in the bathroom.' We're perfect for each other!" Jane glances at me above her mother's head, raises her eyebrows; clearly, you don't tell a woman like this about the promising first date you had last night with a boy who works part-time at the library and plans to become a social worker.

"Scoot them on over, Janey," Mrs. Weston says, doing a convincing impression of someone who hasn't heard a word her daughter just said. She passes the plate to Jane and then, her hand still gripping my upper arm, leads me inside.

The door opens into the warmth of a small entryway with just enough room for two people to stand too close to each other and a living room with a shock of fluffy, salmon-colored carpeting and everything else in shades of white: cream-colored sofa, puffy beige armchair, off-white throw pillows scattered about. I have the disquieting feeling of being inside someone's mouth. Mrs. Weston glances around, looking pleased.

"You have a *lovely* home," I say, which is stupid, because I haven't seen any of it beyond this humid corner, and also so unlike me that I think Mrs. Weston's arm squeeze may have been some kind of alien personality meld. I resolve not to say anything else until Jane reappears.

"Do I hear our *city slickers*?" A voice booms from a nearby room, then a clank of pots and pans. "Oops! It's okay! I'm fine!"

Mrs. Weston clears her throat, then guides me through the living room into the bright, cluttered kitchen, where Mr. Weston is standing over a steaming kettle of something. He's wearing an apron, in the style of men who believe that they cook frequently. He raises the lid of the large pot and inhales deeply. "It's water!" he yells, in what I fear is his normal decibel level. "I'm boiling water!"

Mr. Weston is tall. He's more than tall. He's stretched out, elongated, every limb like pulled taffy, gangly and loose, and he looks elaborately ill at ease bent over the stove.

"Charlie," Mrs. Weston says.

"I'm making supper for our *gals about town*, if they're not too sophisticated for Charlie Weston's old-fashioned spaghetti and meatballs!" I look down at the kitchen floor, feeling awkward and bony, like a twelve-year-old girl who really loves horses.

"Hand over the wooden spoon, Charlie," Mrs. Weston says, finally letting go of my arm and moving toward her husband in quick steps, heels clacking. She snatches the spoon from him and puts her hand on her husband's upper back—she has to stand on her tiptoes to do it—and pushes him away. "Scoot," she says, for the second time in the past minute and a half. "This is a man who does not belong in the kitchen," she says cheerfully, her body to the stove as she dumps a package of spaghetti into the water. Mr.

Weston, serene, defeated—*Who, me?*—folds himself into a kitchen chair.

I'm trying to figure out what's unsettling about this scene, and it dawns on me that it's the lack of rancor, the routine good nature between them. She didn't mutter a cruel remark as she grabbed the spoon from him; he's quiet, but clearly not freezing her out. They're just doing their thing.

And I'm midrealization when Mr. Weston notices that I'm here, standing in the kitchen doorway, unsure where to look. I smile weakly, even more abashed in the face of their relentless normalcy. My hands are clasped in front of me so tightly that when I try to loosen them, they feel like hinges. My mind cartwheels, searches for something to say. *Hello! You have a lovely home!*

"What rhymes with 'spaghetti'?" Mr. Weston asks suddenly. Sitting, Jane's father is almost as tall as I am.

I stare at him, a mute game-show contestant in the spotlight. "'Uncle Freddy'?" I say finally. He studies me for a long few seconds, then winks.

Mrs. Weston turns, an expression of horror on her face. "Oh, Willa!" she says. "My goodness, I'm so sorry! But if you'd seen some of Mr. Weston's more spectacular kitchen disasters, you'd forgive my rudeness."

She lowers the heat and steps toward me again, and I'm bracing myself for another arm squeeze when Jane charges into the kitchen and drops our bags on the floor. If I squint, she's fourteen, tossing her school backpack at her feet. Her mother wheels around.

"Did you see Dougie?" Mrs. Weston asks, as Mr. Weston stands and swoops Jane up into a hug.

"Mmmph," Jane says.

"Little Janey Jane has a walnut for a brain!" Mr. Weston

announces, letting her slide an inch away from him, but apparently only so that he can squish her again with the force of his embrace. "And almonds on her toes, and a peanut for a nose!"

"Cashew!" Jane says, muffled inside her father's bear hug, and Mr. Weston says, "Gesundheit," and frees her.

"Dougie?" Mrs. Weston repeats.

"Yeahyeahyeah," Jane says. "I gave him the cookies. He says thanks." But then, when her mother has turned back to attend to the stove and her father has carried our bags away, Jane leans in and whispers to me, "I lost my virginity to Dougie when we were sixteen!"

"I find that very hard to believe," I say under my breath. Jane chuckles, low and lascivious. And only later, much later, will I realize that this feeling, vague and inchoate, is the shock of illumination. I thought I understood my best friend inside and out, but the truth is I knew just enough about her to think I knew everything.

Dinner is early at the Westons', and it is, conspicuously, not spaghetti—as if the spaghetti incident never happened, which makes me think that maybe it didn't. Dinner is not actually anything I recognize, having been raised on the fractured-marriage menu of frozen pizzas, Lean Cuisine, and canned soup, but Jane has prepared me for this: it's Bonnie Weston's specialty, tuna casserole, with green beans and Jell-O salad on the side. The tuna casserole is sprinkled with cornflakes. Is it dinner? Is it breakfast? It doesn't know! Mandarin orange slices float in the red Jell-O like prehistoric fish. My eyes flicker around the table, trying to find someplace neutral to land. Jane won't meet my gaze; she's too busy playing some kind of poking game with her father. The serving dishes are decorated with geese flying around their edges. The tablecloth is flecked with clouds, a linen wild blue yonder. Steam from the casserole wafts up, dissipates.

"This is real midwestern cuisine!" Mrs. Weston says to me as she surveys the table and spreads her napkin on her lap, as if this is some kind of exotic locale to me—*Real Tibetan delicacies here on the mountaintop, Willa!*—as if I hadn't been born and raised in Milwaukee.

"Real midwestern cuisine!" Mr. Weston echoes. Jane laughs and jabs her father. Jane's parents live in Marcy, Wisconsin, founded by a Christian dairy farmer with, legend goes, either poor penmanship or a very heavy German accent. *Lord have marcy,* they say around here, an inside joke among the 4,102 residents. *Marcy me.*

"I like the geese," I say. A curl falls in front of my eye; I swat it away from my face.

"Aren't you lovely?" Mrs. Weston says. "These two don't care for my motif, do you?"

Jane reaches for the tuna casserole and helps herself. "Makes it easy to buy you birthday presents, though," she says through a mouthful of food. Her father beams at her as if she has just uttered her first complete sentence.

Mrs. Weston reaches across her daughter and passes the dish to me. "Manners, Janey," she says, but mildly, and it strikes me that although on her deathbed she will probably remind Jane to tuck in her shirt, she's also someone who gives the people she loves the benefit of the doubt. I feel swamped, suddenly, in self-pity, trapped in a Jell-O salad of melancholy. I glance over at Jane, her elbows propped on either side of her, her body loose and hunched over her plate, confident, entitled. A person could be anything if she were raised in a family like this. What could possibly stop her?

"Hon?" Mrs. Weston says to her husband, and he piles first my plate, then hers, with green beans. The beans look otherworldly for a blurry second, like alien pods, like mermaid hair. Then back to beans.

I smooth my napkin over my thighs, feel my own reassuring flesh beneath the layers of cloth.

"Yum, Mom," Jane says, her mouth still full, but no one cares, and she really seems to mean it.

Mr. Weston pops up. "Oh, water!" He walks around the table to the sink, fills a glass pitcher, returns with it.

Mrs. Weston upends a slab of casserole onto her plate and looks at me carefully. "You and Janey really do resemble each other," she says. "Even I can see it."

My thoughts careen past each other like eleven-year-old boys on ice skates, skidding, flailing. Family outings that turned into screaming matches between my parents. Days when they would only talk to each other through Seth and me. The time Fran sat down at the table in front of the lasagna she'd made, clearly pleased with herself, and Stan looked at the dinner, rolled his eyes at me and Seth, then turned to my mother with a grin on his face and said, "Oh, my favorite! Cold, congealed, salty lasagna! How did you know?" He was an expert at taking her down, a master of the surprise attack.

I look down and notice suddenly that I've been picking the cornflakes off the surface of my tuna casserole. Quickly, I shuffle them back to their home. "We could eat the leftovers for breakfast tomorrow!" For one fleeting, hopeful breath I believe that maybe I've just thought this and not said it out loud. But then Mrs. Weston, Mr. Weston, and Jane all stop eating at the same time and look at me. The refrigerator motor hums. Mrs. Weston's geese lift off from the plates, flutter their wings, and circle around my head. *So long, everyone! Thanks for the Jell-O!*

After a few seconds, Jane laughs, a snort of sisterly derision, reaches across the table and pats my hand. "Sure we could, sweetie."

"We're so glad Jane found such a nice roommate." Mrs. Weston is still looking at me, kindly.

Mr. Weston nods. On the long journey from his plate to his mouth, a bean falls off his fork.

"So, girls, I thought we might go to the mall tomorrow. Have you finished your Christmas shopping yet?" Mrs. Weston picks up her glass and looks at me with an expectant smile, and I see that this is her hand reaching into the ocean and gently plucking me out.

"Not really," I say.

"Mom, Willard is Jewish." Jane rolls her eyes. She wants distance from her parents' convivial small-town presumptions, and what better way than with a Jewish roommate?

I shrug, the words *I'm really not that Jewish* already forming on my lips. I'm ready to convert, to sell my soul, whatever it takes; I want in.

"You are!" Mrs. Weston says to me. "I had forgotten. That's interesting!"

"Did you know that the Jewish people only have nine commandments?" Mr. Weston says, and before I even fully register my shock, before I can open my mouth to correct him, I recognize an evil glint in his eyes.

"True," I say. I catch a glimpse of Jane's twitching smile before she covers her mouth with her napkin.

Mrs. Weston gazes at each of us, one after the other, her eyes narrowed skeptically. "Oh, you all are pulling my leg, and I know it!"

"Mrs. Weston," I say, placing my fork carefully next to my plate. "It's not that commonly known, but it is true. We don't have the one about adultery."

"Mom, Mom, Mom!" Jane says, her fourteen-year-old personality fully at the fore. "I didn't believe it at first, either. But it's totally true." Mr. Weston just nods peacefully, as a wide and receptive chamber of my heart pumps to life.

"Plus instead of 'Thou shall not kill,' we have, 'Thou shall not kill, except bugs and rodents,'" I say.

Mrs. Weston shakes her head and slaps her hands on her lap.

"Ah, Willa, too far," Mr. Weston says.

Jane throws up her hands. "Willa, we had her!"

"You three are awful!" Mrs. Weston says. She points an accusing finger at each of us in turn. "And it's too bad, because I made tiramisu for dessert, and now none of you will be having any."

"Sorry, Mom!"

"Sorry, Mrs. Weston."

"Oh, Bonnie, forgive us," Mr. Weston says, his voice pitched low and insincere, a newscaster's baritone.

Jane's mother pushes her chair back from the table and moves over to the refrigerator, pulls out a large glass bowl, and shows us its custardy contents, then hugs it dramatically to her chest, as if she alone will consume the entire dessert. She shakes her head again, then reaches for the serving spoon, unable to commit to the role of vengeful mother. I'm right here, at this table, with the Westons: I'm a part of this oddity, this entity, this group of people who love one another. I soak it in. I let it fill me up completely. Mrs. Weston begins scooping big blobs of tiramisu into dessert bowls while Jane laughs at something her father says. I know it's not real. This is not my family. But for one brief, passing moment the idea that it could be fills me with indescribable sweetness.

chapter nine

Ben leans back against the brick wall of our apartment building. He holds two fingers up to his mouth and puffs on an imaginary cigarette; a cloud of his breath wisps away. "I don't understand," he says.

Jane and I got back from Marcy last night, and now the three of us are sprawled out on a blanket in the grimy courtyard behind our building.

"What don't you understand?" I ask, pulling my long gray sweater out like a tent and tucking my knees under it. We're bent on enjoying this midwinter thaw, but it is still January in Wisconsin.

"For starters, why does a tea bag need to be inspirational?" He runs his palm over a small patch of weedy grass, untouched by snow or rain. Our little communal space back here manages somehow to be both overgrown and half dead at the same time. Adjacent to a row of garbage cans, one thin, moldy mattress leans against the wall; four discarded tires are arranged in a row next to it. It looks like someone was assembling parts for a garbage-powered mattress-car. All in all, this is not a place that invites outdoor lounging, and yet we spend quite a bit of time out here.

"Because," Jane says with a shiver. "People who drink tea are not drinking coffee." She takes a sip of her strawberry margarita, her gloved hands cradling the glass. Actually, it's much too cold to be out here.

"Yep," I say. "And that makes them sad."

"And wistful." Jane is on her second margarita. "Or wishful. Are those both words?" She giggles.

"I drank only tea when I was a nanny in England," Ben says, and I look over at him to see whether he's kidding, whether this is one of Ben's weird jokes that you end up laughing at only because of the gap between how funny he finds it and how incomprehensible it is.

"Was this before or after your year on the space station, orbiting Jupiter?" I ask, and then my brain closes the distance, and I remember that there are seven dead years in the history of this resurrected friendship, that Ben could have spent a year as a nanny in London or three years driving a taxi in Dubai for all I know. He might have wandered around England or Iceland or Auckland, he may have pursued the brief but strangely obsessive interest in Ecuador he cultivated for a few weeks senior year . . . and I wouldn't have been privy to any of it, obviously. Those rambling, homesick letters on airmail paper, the overly descriptive, hyper-self-conscious e-mails from Internet cafés in foreign cities, would have been sent to some other friend, a college roommate at a desk job in New York, a pretty ex-girlfriend named Becca who teaches fourth grade in Minneapolis.

"After," he says, raising an eyebrow at me, and Jane, who is leaning against him, turns her face and looks straight at him and shakes her hair behind her and smiles, smiles like she's thinking, *Oh! Another interesting thing for me to learn about my shiny new boyfriend, another layer of this bright package that I will unwrap in time.* Flustered, I turn to my notebook and rifle through it, even though my notes are right here, right in front of me.

"Um," I say, my pages whiffling in the chilly breeze. "Declan told me he wants 'witty, encouraging phrases for the urban tea drinker.' Nothing condescending or cute, he says, but complicated enough that it might take a moment to register with the consumer. And each one has to be under ten words." Declan also told me that this would be the last assignment he'd have for me for a while, and that's a fact that I don't share right now.

A few years ago, I had interviewed for an internship in the fledgling art department at Declan's ad agency. Two days later, he called and told me they couldn't afford an art department after all. He offered me a job writing copy for him instead. He was cute, and I didn't really have any other leads, so I said yes.

We flirted for a few months. He drew me a picture of a smiling tree with curly hair for branches and wrote *Willa tree* underneath it. He left a small, tinfoil-covered chocolate turkey on my desk for Thanksgiving. He wooed me with his accent, his poor posture, the way he pushed his fingers through his messy hair when he was concentrating and left it sticking up in odd places, how he walked around the office in mismatched socks. He was like a little boy who needed a mother to straighten his sock drawer and lick down his cowlick. But I didn't want to take care of him. The more time we spent together, the more I wanted to be like him, a person who lived inside his body and his brain at the same time, a person who could forget to eat for a whole day and then delightedly inhale an entire quart of cashew chicken with peapods. He was appealingly strange. He would spend hours in his office plugged into his iPod, occasionally yelling, "I really need to be left alone in here!" when no one had bothered him.

Whenever I came up with a good slogan, or even a promising turn of phrase, Declan would grab my shoulder or hug me or give me a peck on the cheek. We worked late some nights, just the two of us; Michael had a family to get home to. All I had to do was turn my head, and Declan's playful kiss on the cheek turned into something better. It was that easy.

We made out in my cubicle a few times, as furtive and frantic as teenagers. Each time he stopped it, once with his fingers poised on the hook of my bra, once as his own shirt was halfway off. His torso was long and pale and surprisingly dense. I was willing. "But I'm your boss," he said, breathing hard, or, "We can't. I'm too old for you."

I didn't believe his dramatic protestations. And I felt my affection for him growing. My heart beat uncomfortably in his presence, like something trying hard to escape. During the day, he wandered around the office in his socks, sipping tea from the thermos he brought from home even though the office had a kitchen and a kettle and a bottomless supply of Irish tea. I would think about his mouth against mine, and I'd feel slightly displaced, as if my center of gravity had been lowered. Declan acted exactly the same as he always did, which I took as a good sign, since he was slightly odd to begin with.

One night after everyone else had gone home, we met in the hallway near my desk. He was carrying his bike helmet in one hand, and his right pant leg was rubber banded at the ankle, as if his shin were a loaf of Wonder Bread. The fluorescent light above us flickered. Declan smiled, and I reached out to touch his face.

He caught my hand before it made contact with his cheek, held it for a second, kissed it, then pushed it gently back toward me. He said, "You're killin' me, Willa." I was tingly and hot with embarrassment. I leaned against the wall of my cubicle, the mauve nubbly carpeting of it always a surprise to me. Why was it that cubicle walls were covered in carpeting? It was insulting, as if a person could be fooled by a poly-wool blend into forgetting the flimsy, impersonal nature of her surroundings. Declan and I were still standing close enough that I could feel his breath on my face. It smelled of strong tea and spearmint gum, or maybe just spearmint tea.

"Um, okay," I said. "I don't want to kill you."

"I really like you, you know," he said, taking my hand in his again and squeezing it. "But . . . the thing is, Willa. The thing is that I've been seeing someone else for a couple of weeks."

I narrowed my eyes and stared at his face, at the dark stubble just starting to appear, his handsome gray eyes, his straight nose. He had remarkably even features. It took me a second to feel the cut, the slice was so clean. He had a girlfriend.

"She's not my girlfriend," he said. "It's nothing serious. Only . . . I'm starting to think I might like it if it were."

"Okay," I said quickly. "I understand." I did—he was choosing someone else over me. I contemplated taking the sting of humiliation and turning it into an invigorating hatred. It would have been easy. Those gray eyes were too small, I decided, like a rat's. Oh, look, it was already happening! But then I saw something in the way he was looking at me through those rat eyes, something raw and real and honest. He didn't want to hurt me. I felt like I could see inside his heart, and it was a clean, spare place, a room filled entirely with inexpensive Scandinavian furniture. I mustered up a smile, the one I'd practiced for just these sorts of occasions. "Well, I'll see you tomorrow!" Declan exhaled, obviously relieved. *You're a great girl, Willa.* That was one of his expressions.

I had three more months of my internship left in that office, so I stayed, faking it, mostly, and acting nonchalant while underneath I felt like a human tuning fork, like my entire body was vibrating at such a high and terrible frequency that I would soon attract the neighborhood dogs. Over time, though, I was relieved to feel all that nerve-jangling hurt slowly draining out of me. My fake carefree smile eventually became authentic, exactly itself.

The winter sunlight in the courtyard is thin and weak and almost completely defeated by the shadows cast by our apartment building. The air is getting colder by the minute. Jane holds up one finger. "The path to enlightenment is steep," she announces.

"Nice," I say, jotting it down.

Ben nudges my foot with his. "Oh, you tease," he says. I look at him, confused; he's staring back at me with a half smile that makes me nervous before I understand. Oh, you teas.

"*Very* nice," I say, scribbling.

"Oolong! Farewell!" Jane says, waving, then shakes her head. "No. Sorry."

Nobody says anything for a few moments. The neck of a broken bottle glints on a patch of sandy soil beside us. I doodle a picture of a tea bag with a face and wearing swim trunks, sunbathing on a beach towel. *Tannin is good for you,* I write underneath it, then slowly ink over the whole thing. I jot down some tea-related words. *Drink. Hot. Spills. Dregs. Leaves.*

Ben adjusts his sunglasses and looks up at the darkening blue sky. "Why is it that none of us has a real job?"

I pretend to write the question down. "Wait, that's not inspirational."

"I have a real job." Jane bounces her shoulder against Ben's.

"I'll get paid for this," I say. *Willa,* Declan wrote, *This will be it for a while, I'm afraid. Revenue's down, budget cuts and all that. It's the feckin' economy. You know I'll give you a great reference.* Too bad great references don't pay the rent.

"You know what I mean," Ben says. He drapes his arm around

Jane, and she hunkers in. Ben took a few night courses in public health almost a year ago and has been studying for the GRE ever since. In the meantime, he slogs through his part-time library job and fantasizes about joining the Peace Corps. Together, we probably earn one decent salary. Our collective underemployment makes me anxious.

"Well, if we had real jobs, we wouldn't be sitting here at three-forty-five on a Thursday afternoon," Jane says.

"Brooding," I say. "*Brew*-ding."

Ben rolls his eyes. Jane offers him a sip of her margarita, and he lowers his mouth to the glass. Their intimacy is light and new but not exactly tentative; they look like a couple who has been together for a long time. The energy between them is surprising, not the electric buzz I've felt with every guy I've been with, the giddy question with one inevitable (frequently wrong, but inevitable) answer; between Jane and Ben it's gentle, expansive, roomy.

I imagine us years from now, sitting on a real deck behind a small white house somewhere, and the configuration is almost the same, although in my mind there are four of us, Ben and Jane and someone for me, someone hazy, unformed . . . faceless (but attractively faceless!). He sits next to me in a cushioned lawn chair, close but not too close, his long legs extended. And there are a few kids running around in the yard, cheerful little children who don't demand much attention. But mostly in my imagination it's this feeling, adjusted for practical considerations: the happy ease of the family you've created, the one that doesn't fall short, the one that doesn't disappoint.

"I can't think anymore," Ben says. "I'm too cold. My ass is too cold."

"You know," I say, "that I am contractually obligated to make a joke about where your brain is."

Jane pats Ben's shoulder and nods. "She is."

He ignores us, starts packing up the supplies of our little Arctic picnic. "How about, 'When your friends force you to sit outside on a blanket in the middle of winter and your extremities freeze, hot tea will at least raise your body temperature to the point where you might not die immediately.'"

"Good," I tell him. "But more than ten words." I'll need to find a real job soon, that's for sure.

Jane laughs and hoists herself up; she wobbles a little, steadies herself against Ben. "Because you can't drink R or S," she says, and he looks at her, confused.

I'm sitting on this blue wool blanket, craning my neck at the afternoon sky and at my friends who are suddenly towering, shadowless, above me. Ben and Jane each extend an arm for me, two cold hands to pull me up, and Ben mutters, "Shit, I'm freezing," and for a passing second I wish we could actually freeze, the three of us, just like this.

chapter ten

Early in my friendship with Jane, when our favorite thing to do was to compare notes, to establish and reestablish the specific degree of our astounding similarities, Jane asked me about my parents' marriage. "How was it between them?" She scooped a handful of our favorite nuts *(Pistachios? Me, too!)* and passed the bowl to me across the table. "What was your parents' marriage *like*?"

And I thought: Like? There was no like, as far as I could tell, only dislike, and that was on a good day; on a bad day, it was much worse. Fran and Roger Jacobs were two people who had probably once thought they were alike but discovered—oops, too late, they'd heedlessly created two hapless, helpless children—that they were deeply *un*alike and did not like each other at all, not one bit.

I didn't say this to Jane. Instead I told her about the time when I was ten years old, alone in our basement playroom. I was moving a family of tiny, colorful, wooden dolls around a dollhouse that I was much too old for, but it gave me a comfort I couldn't explain. It eased me sometimes just to be down there, to take refuge in the faux-wood-paneled room whose shelves were still stacked with Candy Land and Chutes and Ladders, floor cluttered with train sets missing tracks, chunky foam balls and bright yellow nets, games and toys that implied, if not exactly recalled, happier family times.

Kristina, the blond-haired little girl doll, was performing a Christmas ballet for her doll family. My fantasies always involved Christmas and little girls named Kristina or sometimes Heidi and once in a while Heidi-Kristina. The mother, father, and brother dolls (nameless) were arranged in a row, watching, rapt and supportive. I heard my dad come downstairs and begin to rummage through the pantry in the laundry room where we kept extra cans of soup, rolls of paper towels and toilet paper, boxes of cereal and macaroni and cheese.

"Where is the oatmeal?" he muttered. He was on a sort-of health kick back then, as much as someone with an insatiable appetite could be, and he liked to have a huge bowl of oatmeal for a snack, drizzled with honey and sprinkled with wheat germ and raisins and sometimes chocolate chips or M&M's if he thought no one was paying attention. My mom bought boxes of Quaker Instant in bulk for him at the Food Warehouse. "Fran, where's the oatmeal?" he called. He still hadn't seen me. I was in the corner of the playroom, crouched behind the dollhouse.

My mother's voice came from the kitchen at the top of the stairs. "There's some up here!" Her tone was neutral, pleasant.

But then my dad ramped it up, the way one of them always did, the way one of my parents would without fail glance around and say, *Hmm, yes, the low road is the better option here.* "There is no oatmeal upstairs, Francine! If there were any goddamn oatmeal upstairs, I wouldn't be down here looking for it!" I could see from my perch my father's face pinking up, like a baby's, the color spreading from his neck to his cheeks to his forehead, until his entire face was a flushed red orb, like the bike lights he made me and Seth use even though he forbade us from riding at night.

"There is no goddamn oatmeal in this house!" His voice was suddenly a carnival of meanness, a rip-roaring circus of blame.

"I am holding in my hands a fucking box of oatmeal!" my mother screamed. They had long ago given up many things; appropriate language in the home was among the first to go.

"Oh, for God's sake," my father muttered, still angry but also, all of a sudden, deflated and pouty.

That's what it was like, I told Jane. Anything—a phone call, a birthday party, oatmeal—could turn into hatred between them and then, without warning, into defeat so palpable it made your heart stop. Until they finally ended it, their marriage was another planet, a harsh, extraterrestrial climate—scalding mornings followed by blue-black evenings so frigid no life could possibly be sustained there.

Jane crunched on another handful of pistachios. "Huh," she said. Sometimes, in those early days, we didn't know what to say when one of our experiences so obviously didn't match the other's. Later, with relief, we would figure out that it was okay to say nothing. "That's a bummer," she said; through her mouthful of nuts it sounded like *There's my thumb, or . . .* "My parents are not like that," she added, stating the obvious, because although I hadn't met them yet, I knew that the Westons were, if nothing else, still together. "They're boring." She looked at me as if for permission to go on with her story of lesser angst. "They're boring and utterly predictable except that they never mastered the art of parental alignment. So whenever I wanted something, some toy or sugary treat or something, and one of them said no, I could go to the other and that one would probably say yes." Her eyes widened at the *insanity* of it.

"So then what?" I asked. I was holding a pistachio shell. I tucked it into my curls, like a barrette.

"Then what what?"

"If one of them said yes, did you always get what you wanted?" I imagined Jane a spoiled princess in a pink-carpeted room, ruler of the kingdom of whatever-the-hell-she-wanted.

She looked at the blue bowl of nuts, mostly empty, and at the second bowl into which we had been depositing the shells. With a little shudder, she pushed both of them away. "No!" she said, indignant. She thought for a moment, then shrugged. "But actually, pretty often."

I pointed to the pistachio shell in my hair, secured there by the spirally strands, and then I fluffed my hair showily, like a movie star, a slightly mentally ill movie star.

"Very gorgeous," Jane said, and she plucked a shell from the bowl and wriggled it into her own curls, and then we were the same again, two girls with pistachio-shell barrettes suspended in our curly hair.

chapter eleven

Even in your closest friendships, you're alone. Maybe it's your best friend who, in fact, reminds you, just by making it her business to try to know your heart, that no one can—that our fate is to suffer in isolation and then die. But it's our collective fate! So I guess I'm an optimist.

There are plenty of things I don't tell Jane, bits of information I edit out, stories I don't share—so that the picture she has of me is incomplete, a self-portrait I present to her, and if she sees light where there should be shadow, well, she can choose to be dazzled, or she can fill in the darkness herself.

When Seth was a senior in high school, Stan decided that we would take a family road trip to Philadelphia. Seth had just been accepted to the University of Pennsylvania, along with a slew of other top-tier colleges my parents couldn't afford. "The Ivy League," my dad kept saying, the week Seth got the fat envelope from Penn and then, after that, the one from Dartmouth. "I'll be damned." He would say that and scowl and rub his fingers hard across his eyebrows, as if trying to pay for an expensive private college really would consign my father to hell.

This was months after he had canceled our trip to Europe, and we were suspicious and raw. Fran took to referring to our impend-

ing journey with a vaguely Italian accent: *Pheeladelphia,* she would
say; *I cannot wait to see the sights of Pheeladelphia, to enjoy its fine cuisine,* just subtle enough so that Stan might or might not notice. I
noticed.

On the first day of spring break, we piled into the car and
headed east. The night before, Fran had made egg salad sandwiches
for us—dozens of egg salad sandwiches. Every time we stopped for
gas or coffee, whenever someone had to use the bathroom or my
dad needed to get out and stretch his legs, she would offer up the
sandwiches, like a sacrifice to the gods of family harmony. After an
hour, the car smelled like swamp gas and candy; our mother had
also come prepared with an endless supply of red licorice, which
was one thing we all agreed on.

I took my cues from my brother and pretended to be deeply
unattached to the fact that we were trekking across the country
on a mission of familial unity and support. *Whatever,* I said to my
parents when one of them asked me a question: *Would you like a
Sprite? Whatever. Did you and Ben finish the issue of* Prose Shop *you
were working on last weekend? Yeah, I don't know. Whatever.* Secretly I
was thrilled, thrilled that we were all together, my grumpy, muttering father; my mood-swinging mother; my brooding, gimlet-
eyed brother; and me. I propped my bare feet against the back of
the seat and read the Brontës for hours. *(What are you reading, Willa
Gorilla? Nothing. Whatever.)* Seth spent the entire trip plugged in
to his portable CD player, staring out the window or at the calculus textbook open on his lap. My parents argued. But they had
been arguing for so long that it seemed almost pleasant, an off-
key tune, the jangling notes playing so frequently you don't even
realize they have caused you to rearrange your entire definition of
"music."

"Fran, did you write down the mileage at that rest stop?"

"Oh. No."

"I asked you to write down the mileage."

"Well, I'm sorry, but I forgot."

"How could you forget? What else are you thinking about that you could forget something as simple as writing down the mileage?"

"Oh, Roger, back off. Here, have a damn sandwich."

"I don't want a damn sandwich."

I'll have a ham sandwich, I wanted to say. But I kept quiet and stared out the window.

We made it to Cleveland by early evening and pulled into the E-Zzzz Rest Inn, a cut-rate motel off the highway where my father had, absurdly, made a reservation. "We're the Jacobses, and we have reserved two rooms for tonight," my dad announced, and the girl behind the desk pulled a wad of gum out of her mouth and laughed.

"I'm going to go swimming," Seth said to me, pointing to a small, steamy pool behind a wall of glass, and I nodded. It wasn't an invitation, but it was as close as I would get.

"All righty," Fran said, lugging her big suitcase, dragging it awkwardly behind her. "Let's go find our rooms." My father came up behind her with his smaller, lighter duffel bag slung easily over his shoulder. "Oh, that's all right," Fran said, huffing. "I've got it," although Stan hadn't offered.

We headed down the chlorine-scented hallway, and when we got to rooms 16 and 17, Fran and Stan inserted their separate key cards into separate doors. Seth glanced at me and dropped his backpack on the floor. "Wait, no." He shook his head, horrified. "Dad, *no.*"

Stan tilted his big head toward Seth. "You're bunking with me, son."

Seth crossed his arms over his chest. "Dad, no," he said again. "I can't!" Our father's snoring was legendary. His rumbling shook the rafters. There were several states in which he was not welcome. I looked down at the cabbage-rose-strewn, industrial carpeting and tried not to smile. Seth wanted to share a room with me. Yes, he was trying to avoid sleeping next to Mount St. Stan. And, no, it wasn't as if he wanted the two of us to eat M&M's at midnight and giggle at bad romantic comedies together. Still. I was used to taking what I could get from my brother, and I would take this.

"Mom," I said, fingering the sleeve of my worn jean jacket, "can't you sleep with Dad?" My face flushed hard. "I mean, can't you guys, like, sleep in the same room?"

Our parents looked at each other. My mother sighed, my father shrugged, and everyone seemed to soften; even the cabbage roses looked hazy and pretty for a moment. "Well . . ."

"You're with me, Seth," Stan said abruptly.

My mom bristled. "Come on, sweetie," she said to me. Fran and her big suitcase disappeared into our room; I caught the door just as it was about to close.

I changed into my swimsuit while my mom showered. The rush of water against the plastic tub sounded like thunderous applause: *Congratulations, Jacobs family, on remaining intact for another day!* As I was adjusting the straps of my old Speedo and tugging it out of various cracks, Fran stepped out of the bathroom, naked and dripping, a towel twisted into a turban around her head. I saw my future in her large, sagging breasts, her bulgy middle, the fleshy tops of her thighs, and I felt a hot, tender shame for both of us.

"Oh, don't look at me," she said, laughing, as she stepped back into the underwear she had been wearing.

"Ugh, Mom, gross," I said. I grabbed a towel, tucked it around my waist, and went to get Seth. Their door was ajar. My dad was already conked out on one of the beds. Seth was sitting on the edge of the other one, staring at the TV. There was a pillow over my dad's face like a scene from *One Flew Over the Cuckoo's Nest,* but

I could hear his snoring—had heard it from the hallway—so I knew there had been no mercy suffocation. "Hey, come on," I said to Seth. "Let's go."

He looked at me, then turned quickly back to the television—he was watching a European soccer game, but on mute, so it looked surreal, the enormous stadium packed with silent fans in bright shirts, people on their feet, arms waving, mouths open. Seth turned to me again and sneered. "I'm not going swimming with you," he said. *Not with you.* My brother could break my heart a thousand times a day. He could tear me in two. He could burn a hole in me with his eyes. He was a superhero of scorn.

"Okay," I said, my eyes stinging. I thought about my mother in the next room, bent over naked, stomach pocked, breasts swaying, pulling her light pink underwear up over her legs. Little blue veins decorated her calves, her thighs. She was one of the slimmer, more-well-kept moms, among the middle-aged mothers I knew. Still, she was ravaged. "Fine," I said to Seth. "Whatever." I wished I had wrapped another thin motel towel around my shoulders. I braced myself for what he would say next. It might have been anything.

He leaned forward and rested his elbows on his knees, his chin in his hands. "Maybe later," he said to the TV. "Maybe I'll go swimming with you later."

In the car, on our way back home, after our walking tour of Philadelphia, after our visit to the campus and my parents' meeting with the financial aid officer, my father would tell Seth not to get his hopes up. "Lower your expectations," he would say, and Seth, headphones still clamped to his head, would act like he hadn't heard.

We could have rescued one another—the four of us, together, or any combination. But we didn't. We left each other alone, and for a long time after we stayed that way.

chapter twelve

I spend my days watching Ben and Jane become a couple, and I will myself to happiness. I make myself a scientist of them, an expert in my narrow field, a Ben-and-Jane-ologist. How close can I get without compromising my subject? *Move closer, a little closer.*

One Saturday in the middle of March, we go bed shopping. We try out the extra-firm mattresses at the Box Springs Eternal Bed and Furniture Warehouse, roll around like little kids in a bouncy castle on the double-plush pillow top, lie shoulder to shoulder to shoulder on the king-size Super Sleep Superluxe. The three of us.

"Hon," Ben says, from his prone perch on the Superluxe. He reaches across my chest to rest his hand on Jane's elbow. "If you bought this one, I bet we'd never fall off again, like we did the other night."

So that was the crash I heard. I clear my throat and move Ben's arm. Okay, maybe this is a little strange.

"Benjamin!"

Lately Jane has taken to calling Ben by his full name, claim staking and maternal, and every time she does, a small, evil creature that lurks inside my brain crawls along the edges of my skull, hissing.

"This bed would not fit in our apartment, much less my bed-room," she says.

I flex my calves. I can extend my legs completely on the Super-luxe, and my toes still don't dangle off the edge—a rare luxury for a tall girl. "Remember in college, how you would sleep on a twin bed all night with your boyfriend, and you didn't care?" My lying-down voice sounds funny to me, as if someone else is talking.

"I didn't have that many boyfriends in college," Ben says, and Jane laughs.

There are days when I feel like every step I take outside my apart-ment is an opportunity, every trip to the grocery store, every walk to the corner mailbox, are chances to reinvent myself, to embrace the possibility that I might meet someone, see something, catch someone's eye, that in a split second, everything could change. Then there are the days when I feel like everything I've done has brought me here, to where I am and will always be: right here, lying trapped between my two best friends on a bed that hundreds of other couples have lain on in search of the best place to have hot sex and then sleep comfortably for the next eight hours. I turn from Ben to Jane and back again. The problem is, some days I can't tell the difference.

A young couple on the bed five feet from ours has been whis-pering urgently for a few minutes, and their voices are gaining vol-ume. I prop myself up on my elbow and look over.

"But when you yelled at him this morning, you *shamed* him," the woman says. She has huge blinking blue eyes and long blond hair fanned out on the pillow behind her head.

"Well, he took my book and ripped it. Maybe a little shame is a good thing." The man is her photographic negative, dark and scruffy. They're attractive, almost disturbingly good-looking. They look like a magazine ad, but a weird, unhappy one, maybe an ad for couples therapy or rained-out vacations.

"Jesus, Jeffrey, what's *wrong with you?*"

"Nothing. Natalie." He says her name as if it's a small insult, a suggestion of things gone to seed. "I just don't want him disrespecting my things, my personal things. It starts with a book. Where does it end?"

"I don't know where it ends. Maybe with you in therapy dealing with the legacy of your abusive father?"

I'm starting to feel very sorry for their child, the little miscreant. Given the genetic windfall, though, he's probably beautiful enough to overcome his dueling parents.

I elbow Ben, whose eyes are closed. "They remind me of Fran and Stan," I whisper, "but prettier."

Jane sits up, too. She twists a long curl of her hair around her finger. "Let's go look at another bed," she says sternly, as if Jeffrey and Natalie will overhear her mildly scolding tone and promptly change their ways.

"I think we should just *sign him up!*" Jeffrey says. They're not even attempting to whisper any longer. Natalie snorts her derision. Jeffrey bangs his hand down onto the mattress. "You didn't even know what I was going to say!" he growls.

Ben rolls over and stares at them; we're watching this spectacle unfold. I want to tell them that they haven't actually bought this mattress yet, haven't shipped it to their house and set it up in their bedroom. *We can hear you.*

"You want to take him to obedience school!" Natalie starts to cry, and then Ben laughs so loudly, such an explosive exhalation, a true guffaw, that we all roll off the bed in a tangle and hurry over to another section of the store.

Jane grabs my hand and pulls me along. "Oh, my God," she says.

"Oh, my dog," Ben says, catching up to us in the children's furniture department, a bright enclave of red and blue bunk beds, superheroes, fussy canopies, and pink princess comforters.

"Hey!" Jane hoists herself up a ladder to the top of a race-car bunk bed, her legs flailing behind her as she disappears behind a tower of pillows. "Maybe I'll just get myself one of these!" Ben flicks a Spider-Man lamp on; it plays the theme music from the cartoon, and Ben starts singing along. I know he won't stop singing until he's gotten through the entire tune, because he knows all the words and is compelled to display his knowledge, and suddenly I just have to get away from them.

The truth about two people who don't like each other much is that their fights can be small, gnawing things. I know something about this. I know that this is how people destroy each other, in ugly increments, slivers of their lives falling away until, all at once, they topple. I imagine Jeffrey and Natalie as furry, sharp-toothed beavers. I want to go find them, wherever they are in this vast furniture warehouse, maybe chewing on a table leg somewhere, and tell them: *Handsome rodents! Stop nibbling away at your own happiness!*

In flight from Ben and Jane, I wander into the recliners section of the store, rows and rows of big empty armchairs in a sad rainbow of earth tones, a shipwreck of abandoned Barcaloungers. I run my hand along the top of a dark green suede behemoth with what looks like a sidecar attached to it. Upon closer examination, it turns out to be a cooler.

"This would look good in your living room," Ben says, from behind me. He pats my shoulder, and I turn to face him.

"I would be willing to get rid of all of our other furniture," I say, "and just have one of these in every room."

"The kitchen?" Ben says.

"Yes."

"The bathroom?"

"Obviously."

He points to the cooler. "For storing toilet tissue."

"'Tissue' is one of my favorite words," I say. "It makes every-thing sound fancier." I plop myself into one of the chairs, a dark, mannish thing that immediately flings my body backward, hoist-ing my legs up higher than my head; I feel like a beetle, a strangely comfortable beetle.

Ben places his hands on an armrest to steady himself and hov-ers over me. "Are you okay?"

I look up at him, his face squinched with concern. "Ach," I say, with a wave of my hand. "Natalie and Jeffrey!"

"And Spot!"

"Poor Spot."

Ben just keeps staring, leaning over me, and I can't help it, I think about him and Jane, about what it must be like to lie beneath him, his body close, features gathered in concentration. I remem-ber the bumbling kiss in Ben's humid car, the sound of our teeth clacking against each other like tiny tap dancers. I see that his lips are a little bit chapped, and I turn my face away and pretend sud-den fascination with the dark maroon leather of the cushion.

He touches my forehead gently. I force myself to stay still. "For someone who's in her twenties and hardly ever even talks to her parents," he says, "don't you think it's about time to get over their divorce?"

He's right, of course. But nobody likes her blindingly obvious failings pointed out to her by her best friend when she's belly-up on a Barcalounger.

"I talk to them!" I say.

In fact, just last week Fran called me from her car, driving down a Tucson highway, on her way to meet Jerry for an early din-ner. *Seth can't maintain a relationship,* she said, *and you never seem to have them. Did your father and I do this to you? Is this your father's fault?*

I held the phone at some distance from my ear; if it came too close, I thought, it might burn a hole in my brain. *Are you on your cell? I yelled. I can barely hear you! I'll call you again soon!*

"We talk all the time!" I insist.

"Which is not exactly my point." Ben leans down closer, so close that for a second I think he really is going to kiss me, and my stomach squeezes with the thought of Jane. It's so easy in the moment to know what you're going to do, as if life were a pointillist painting of moments. "Look over there," he whispers, tilting his head toward Sofas and Sectionals. Natalie and Jeffrey are wandering around, heads together, holding hands.

". . . perfect for the living room," Natalie is saying, and Jeffrey murmurs something about getting rid of his grandmother, who is old and loves beets.

"Your grandma's old love seat can go in the basement," Natalie says.

"That's not them," I whisper, even though it is.

Ben looks at me funny, and then, clearly making the decision to humor me, he wiggles his fingers above his head, devil horns.

"*There* you two are." Jane is winding her way through the rows of recliners, like a giraffe among the underbrush. She stops short and plants herself in front of us, and I look up to see my friend, her face flushed, taking in the tableau of Ben and me. Her eyebrows furrow, her mouth just barely moves, and then she composes her features as I crank myself up, the chair's footrest lowering with an incriminating *clunk*. Ben wraps his arm around Jane's waist and kisses her cheek.

"I was up in that top bunk," she says, "talking to you guys. I had an entire conversation before I realized nobody was there!"

"What were you talking about?" I grip the squishy arms of the chair. Warp speed!

"The time I fell out of a bunk bed when I was ten."

"Aww," Ben says, kissing her cheek again.

"Poor Jinxy."

Jane rolls her eyes at me and relaxes into Ben's hug, forgiving us for whatever it is she thought she knew. "I was talking to myself," she says. "Up there. Like an idiot." She laughs then, a loud *haw*, and nobody says anything for a while; the *haw* just hangs there in the air above the recliners, until Jane looks around and notices for the first time where we are. "Willapede! I would like one of these for the apartment!" With balletic grace she twists her body around and slides into the recliner next to mine, pulling Ben down with her; they land together and the chair squeaks in protest.

They're squished, Ben and Jane, in the overstuffed armchair, laughing as Ben tries to wriggle his left leg out from under Jane's right, and suddenly I am wide open with longing. I want to be between them again, I want to be one of them, Ben or Jane, just to be next to someone, leaning against the solid mass of someone else's muscles and bones, a rising chest, a beating heart. Jane has finally reconfigured herself so that she is draped over Ben's lap, their four long legs entwined, a denim sea creature of limbs, her body turned sideways in the chair. Ben glances over at me and I think with surprise that he is reading my mind as he lifts one shoulder, a fleeting acknowledgment of something we both know will never happen, or maybe just another small attempt to make himself comfortable against the soft crush of Jane's body.

chapter thirteen

This morning, Jane and I stood together in the bathroom in our apartment, getting ready for Amy and Rafael's wedding. Jane was wrapped in a fluffy yellow towel. There was a tiny red dot of blood on her shin where she'd nicked herself shaving. "I wish I had your collarbone," she said, spreading cocoa butter lotion onto her shoulders and neck. She smelled like a cookie.

"I need mine." I worked some useless gel into my coarse hair. "What's wrong with yours?"

"Yours is elegant. Mine just sits there!"

"Oh, my God," I said. "I wish I had your elbows. Mine are so pointy!"

"Eeek!" She waved her hands around. "I hate my wrists!" She stood close to me and we rifled through my container of Vérité freebies, samples they sometimes send me from failed product lines. My favorite is the ill-fated On the Town collection, a series of nonsensically labeled lip glosses whose names bear no relation to actual colors. We held up Embarrassing Night at the Karaoke Bar and examined it, then Jane dabbed a bit of Get Your Hands Off My Boyfriend, Bitch! on her little finger and smoothed it onto her lips, and I smeared some Whoops! I'm Soooo Tipsy! on mine.

Ben appeared in the doorway, munching on a banana. "You

look pretty," he said, and Jane and I both said "Thanks," simultaneously. And then there was a confusing half beat when no one said anything, and I felt my face grow warm. I studied my reflection, pressing my shiny pink lips together.

Jane tilted her head. "We do look pretty," she said, glancing at Ben in the mirror.

It's June, humid June, six months since the day they met, one hundred eighty-three days since the moment I stood between them in our apartment and waved my magic wand, the good witch of setups, the problem-solving guru of complicated friendships.

Well, sure, there have been instances. Occasions. Would I relive the time I overheard them having sex, startled awake at 1:00 a.m. by a moan that I thought, at first, had come from my own throat; a loud thump against my wall, then another, and another; how—too late!—I folded my pillow over my ears to try to drown out the sound of their bodies slapping against each other, the unmistakable thwack of skin on skin? No, I would not. (Would I relive the next time I overheard them, or the time after that? Well, I suppose I've sort of gotten used to it.) Or the night we made lasagna, how Jane lit candles and we sat together at our little round kitchen table drinking wine, Ben turning from Jane to me to Jane, his lips a grapy purple, a grin creasing his face like he couldn't believe his good luck. And then, after dinner, how we cleaned up together, me gathering plates at the table, Jane and Ben in the kitchen washing dishes, and when I went in with my stack of plates, midsentence, ". . . that's when I realized I had accidentally hit REPLY TO ALL!" there they were in a clutch at the kitchen sink, lips locked, Ben's hand cradling Jane's head, yes, like a baby's, the faucet on full blast, water pouring down the drain, and me, awash in the sudden awful knowledge of where, exactly, I stood.

No, I probably wouldn't revisit that one, either.

Yes, there have been moments. But more than that, there have been days and weeks of happy ease: long mornings at Rock River, the coffee shop near our apartment, where we play a complicated drawing/guessing game that I invented and always win; late-night games of Scrabble that I always lose; muddy, early spring tromps through the woods and chilly hikes along the shore of Lake Michigan; Sunday brunches cooked by Ben; movies. I look back with very little perspective and feel like I have been dating my two best friends. What could be better than that?

Jane and I find seats in the middle row of folding chairs set up in Latvian Hall, meeting room 2, a no-frills, bare-floored space with overly good acoustics that probably usually hosts motivational speakers and rained-out church picnics but today is decorated with fresh flowers and origami birds and strings of white lights for Amy and Rafael's very low-budget wedding. *Shabby chic,* Amy wrote in her e-mailed invitation, *or possibly just shabby!* But it all looks perfect to me, the flowers and the paper birds and the party lights, fresh and hopeful and earnest in a good way, although I probably won't admit that to anyone.

"Oh, my God, this is *weird*," I whisper to Jane as murmurings start at the back of the room, and the wedding guests go quiet. Jane shushes me so loudly that the elderly lady in front of us turns and shakes her head at us with a ghoulish wobble of loose skin. I poke my elbow into Jane's rib cage. "That was your fault," I whisper again. "Offer her a peppermint!"

Jane elbows me back and scowls a reproach, but then, Jane-like, she relents and throws her arm around my shoulder; Willa-like, I wriggle it off.

To the opening notes of "I Got You, Babe," which is either an excellent preemptive strike or the strangest shotgun-wedding song choice of all time, we crane our necks toward the door. "Oh!

Here comes the bride," Jane says, *Oah! Here comes the br-eye-id,* her Wisconsin accent thick, the way it is when she gets emotional, as our friend appears, beaming. With a little shrug, Amy starts walking, unaccompanied, down the makeshift aisle, to Cher's warbling alto; she's wearing a bright yellow sleeveless dress, her hands wrapped around a small bouquet of white daisies and resting on her bulging belly as if that's what it's there for, a little shelf, a portable hand rest. Rafael stands at the front in black pants and a blue linen shirt, his face very pale. He looks like the flag of a tiny, neutral, Alpine country.

Jane and I chipped in on a set of pretty salad bowls that Amy and Rafael had registered for, but I can't help but think that they'll be spearing baby spinach and cherry tomatoes from those burnt orange glazed pottery bowls long after they've forgotten Jane and me. Which doesn't distract from my enjoyment of the day, not at all; in fact, my irrelevance fixes me right here, solidly in the moment, as if I'm watching a play, or maybe *in* a play, but with no lines—other than "Offer her a peppermint," I guess.

"I never thought I'd find myself here," Rafael says, his hands gripping Amy's, his voice shaky, "with you." Jane sighs. The party lights cast an ethereal glow around the windowless room, like stars in a planetarium. A box fan rattles in the corner. "Amy," Rafael says, "since you came into my life, everything has changed."

"Except diapers," I whisper to Jane. "Diapers will be changed next." At the Yom Kippur services of my childhood, Seth and I used to try to make each other laugh with jokes about the ladies in fancy outfits *(She's atoning for the murder of all those minks)* and the jowly-cheeked cantor *(He's storing nuts for winter),* but now I see that Jane is wiping a tear from her eye, and the feeling of being a spectator shifts and settles in me, a dense and strange amalgam of yearning and embarrassment and full-on surprise.

"I can't believe how lucky I am," Amy is saying, looking up

at Rafael, "to have found you." Her blond hair is swept up in a complicated twist, pretty tendrils framing her face. Rafael nods in agreement, and then Amy sneezes, and everyone in the room laughs.

"Why was that funny?" I ask Jane. This is the first wedding I've ever been to. I guess it's obvious that this is the final destination for two people in love. And soon enough it will cease to shock me—those fat envelopes addressed to Ms. Willa Jacobs and Guest; budgeting tea kettles and place settings and linen napkin sets into my monthly expenses. But right here, as the ceremony continues, I feel bewildered by it, as stunned as if I'd stepped out of my apartment building to find that I was in another country, smack dab in the middle of a busy jumble of bodies where everybody knows the language but me. Where was I when the instructions were given to pair off, to slice away from friends and re-form as a couple? What boat have I missed? "Why was that funny?" I ask again, although maybe that's not the right question.

Jane is digging around in her bag. "I'm starving," she whispers, and when the old lady in front of us turns, inevitably, to glare at us again, Jane leans forward and offers her a candy. To my surprise, she accepts.

chapter fourteen

For a time after Amy and Rafael's wedding, I floated through my days—sleeping, drinking coffee, drawing, hanging out with Jane and Ben, who did have jobs: generally existing as if I had a trust fund. In the end maybe it was a good thing that my bank balance dipped to $74.92, because how long could I have kept it up, my princessy, jobless drift, the days piling up like pretty snow, a formless heap of pleasant hours? Probably for quite a while.

It was on one of those long, lazy afternoons that Ben brought home a job quiz from the library, a page torn from a career counseling workbook someone had left behind. *What are your goals?* the quiz asked. *Would you rather plan a wedding or build a road? Style hair or predict severe weather?* And after I filled in my answers (style the hair of people who have survived severe weather), I put down my number 2 pencil and admitted to myself that all I wanted to do, all I've ever wanted to do, was draw. It turned out that I didn't have goals, only a dream: compelling, impractical, and useless as a hair stylist in a hurricane. Which left me feeling both despondent and, strangely, free.

So I went out for a walk in my bustling little neighborhood, and I gazed at the world of industrious, productive humans. A man in a brown uniform lugged a huge package from his double-parked truck while two blond women carried trays outside the Blue Roses Café, and a priest, in full regalia, hurried down the sidewalk. It was a bright children's book out here, a scene from Busytown—the mailman, the grocer, the baker; Leo, the friendly, chain-smoking gay man who owned Spexxxy Time, the weird store that sold upscale eyeglasses and, in the back room, sex toys. Okay, Leo might have been exiled from Busytown, but still, here he was, in the real city, making his living. Did none of these people have rich inner lives, dreams of their own? Of course they did. I was waking up to it all, it seemed, for the first time.

I was also calculating the maximum number of days through which I could stretch $74.92. I got to twenty-two if I was willing to consume a lot of canned tuna when the HELP WANTED, PART-TIME sign in the window of Molly's Blooms caught my eye—like a message from God: *Willa, you hate tuna!* I pushed the door open, little bells like angel's wings tinkling after me.

The store was empty, damp, and cavernous. Buckets of flowers stood neatly along the walls, two or three deep, the colors of the petals splashy and chaotic, a shade or two brighter than what you see in nature—like genetically engineered combinations of flowers and neon signs. The glass door of one of the coolers was ajar, and I gently tapped it shut.

A woman emerged from behind the counter. She had flowing red hair and bright green eyes. Her neck was long. She looked like she was made to work with flowers, like she herself was part flower. She looked like the kind of person who might start dancing spontaneously to no music. "May I help you?" she asked.

"I'd like to apply for the job," I said, gesturing toward the help wanted sign.

She asked me if I had any floral experience, and I pictured my grandmother's old sofa. I tried to think: *Do I have any floral experience that I have forgotten about?* I shook my head.

"My last part-time employee called in sick on Mother's Day." She tilted her head and fixed her gaze on me. She was sizing me up.

"I would never do that," I said. "I have an excellent immune system." I was suddenly self-conscious under her gaze. She was surprisingly steely for a redheaded flower sprite. I liked her.

"You're hired," she said, and she reached out and shook my hand.

It's cool in the shop today, a relief from the June heat wave, the fog of wet lethargy that has been sitting on the city for the past two weeks. I've only been here for ten minutes, only just flipped the OPEN sign around in the window; the sweat from the short walk over is still drying above my lip. I'm pinning my name tag onto my apron when the bells ring. "Be right with you," I say, as I fasten the pin. Every day I make myself a new name tag. Yesterday I was Xena. Today, Saffron.

"Well, isn't this just grand," a familiar voice says. *Grand.* "Her ladyship can't be bothered to help a customer."

It's Declan, tall and lanky. The prototype for the word "rakish." Pushing one hand through his hair, which is unkempt, convincingly bed-headish. In his other hand he holds a paper coffee cup, lifts it to me. I haven't seen him in three years. He flashes me a huge grin. His left incisor is slightly crooked. I had forgotten that.

My hands drift down, from my name tag to my sides. I'm wearing my pretty purple sleeveless dress, the one with the swingy skirt and the neckline that sits just below my collarbone. *Good thinking, forty-five-minutes-ago self!* For a second, for the one that matters, the thump of my heart that I'll remember later, I feel like my entire body is levitating. Just for a second. I feel as if I'm an elevator—not that I'm in one, but that I am one. I'm off the ground, and then I'm back. It's Declan of the mismatched socks, Declan of the dirty jokes. Declan of the I-choose-someone-else-over-you. I extend my arms like I've just sung the last note of something loud. "Well."

"Never you mind. I'll just take my business elsewhere." He's wearing a loose gray T-shirt and black biking shorts, and his skin is, as always, winter pale; he looks like he's just cycled out of a cave.

I tuck my chin, look up at him, flutter my eyelashes. We know a thing or two about each other.

He lopes over to the counter, four long strides, and leans across it to kiss me hello, once on each cheek. And I'm right here in it, feeling his smooth cheek on mine, breathing in the vaguely familiar, menthol smell of his skin . . . until I remember, with a sudden bolt, all the strange, wrong moments in our brief relationship: the misunderstandings, the long waits. The forgotten birthday. The Valentine's Day card that said, *To a terrific pal!*

"Hey," I say, more sharply than I intend, as Declan retreats. "What are you doing here?"

He looks down at the counter, embarrassed or pretending, I'm not sure—we're two actors in a bad high school play, all exaggerated gestures and slightly off-key emotions. Then Declan's gaze settles on my name tag, and he grins. "Well, Saff, I'm here to see you, of course." He pushes his coffee cup to me across the counter. "There are five packets of sugar in here," he says. "And about a liter of half-and-half. I know you like your coffee to taste like melted ice cream."

I take a sip; it's disgusting, and just the way I like it. I lick the foam from my lips. "Yummy!"

He takes the cup back from me and drinks from it, winces.

"Willa. You poor thing. Were you not allowed sweets when you were small?"

"My mom tried to convince us that prunes were candy," I say. "Oh, and also? Seriously. What are you doing here?"

"Ah, luv." Declan has heard too many times that his Irish accent is sexy. It's no longer even an act; he just pours it on and splatters everyone within earshot. And who can blame him? It is sexy. He runs his hand through his hair again. "I really am here to see you." I roll my eyes. "All right. I'm here to have lunch with a client." He raises one eyebrow. "And dessert with you?"

I nod slowly, recognizing this for what it is, matching his suggestive look with a half smile of my own. "Maybe. But probably not." The air conditioner's fan kicks into high gear, blowing a cool breeze through the vent above us, and Declan meets my eyes with what looks, finally, something like honesty. "I'll get coffee with you, though," I say. "More coffee, that is. I'm off at two. You can meet me at my apartment."

I drum my fingers on the smudged top of the counter, glance at the door. People don't buy as many flowers when it's hot outside. I've recovered from the initial surprise of seeing Declan, the first sizzle of recognition, and I feel dulled, suddenly, and cautious. I remember the way I had opened up to him, three years ago, and the unexpected heartbreak.

But then all the longing of the past six months, all the mixed up pleasure and regret of watching my two best friends fall in love in front of me, next to me, near me, practically on top of me; every *Good night, good night* at the doors of our respective bedrooms, every *Bye, babe*, every thigh pressed against thigh on the couch two feet from where I sat, it all just floods over me, and I decide on a leap of faith. "Two o'clock," I say again. "Thirty-two seventeen North Bradford." And I take another sip of the oversweet coffee he's brought for me and then rest my fingers lightly on the warm paper lid, thinking that this might be an answer, although of course everything depends on the question.

I'll say now that I know you can't change a person. I know that you can't mold him to be who you want him to be. But maybe you can hone in on certain glimmers, you can recognize certain buried elements or unrealized traits, and you can hope—when you want something.

When I come home from work, I'm bursting to tell Jane about Declan, to unwrap the glittering details of our reunion and examine them with her, to see if, after six hours, they still shine. But when I walk in the door, the apartment is quiet, save for the whirring of the window air conditioner, and dark, even for our usually dimly lit rooms; the shades are down, and I wonder with a shudder if I'm walking in on something. Did they think they had the apartment to themselves for the afternoon? Oh, God. "Hello!" I shout, even though the place is so small there is never any real need to shout. I drop my bag with a thump, kick my shoes off with extra vigor. "Hello?"

The living room lamp flicks on, and there is Jane, hunkered down in a chair, covered in a sheet, her right hand on the switch, her left shielding her eyes. She turns the light off again. I half expect to find a bunny simmering in a pot on the stove. "Janey?"

"Hey," she says, and I feel my way over to the couch, plunk myself down across from her, wait for my eyes to adjust to the darkness. Has Ben broken up with her? It's all I can imagine.

"What's going on?"

There's a long silence, and then, finally: "My dad . . . just . . . left."

What was Charlie Weston doing in our apartment? I swipe

my hand across my perspiring forehead, my hot cheeks. My palm smells like roses. "He left? Where did he go?"

She turns the light on again. The room is aglow; all the smudged details—the edges of the brown coffee table, the frayed blue-and-green rug—are sharp in the sudden glare. The hand that was shading Jane's eyes covers her whole face. "That was my first question, too," she mumbles, through splayed fingers. "'Where did he go?' Actually, though, it turns out he left my mom."

I swallow. "Oh, Janey."

"Well," she says, "apparently it's *temporary*." She hangs air quotes around the word.

"What happened?"

"I don't really know the details," she says. "He made some bad investments, I guess, without telling my mom, and they tanked. He lost a lot of their money. Like, a lot. They might lose their house." Jane blushes and the unexpected intimacy of it all, how the failings of our parents still, at twenty-six, embarrass us. "Do you want to know how they told me?" She doesn't wait for me to answer. "My mom sent me an e-mail. She got herself a new computer last month, and she's so proud of herself, of how well she's adapted, you know, she'd be a technological wiz if this were 2002. Anyway, she sent me an e-mail. 'The e-mail,' she calls it. 'I'm going to check *the e-mail*.' She wrote, *They're opening a Walmart in New Hamburg. Also, Dad left.*"

I cross my legs, then uncross them. My skin sticks to itself like cling wrap. "She didn't."

"She did! She asked him to go. So he packed a bag and left this morning. He's in a hotel for a few days until they can both cool off." Her voice cracks, and she starts breathing heavily, sighing slowly, repeatedly, through her nose, the sound underneath her exhalations a high, whistling wheeze, like a tea kettle. I would like to tell her that: *You sound like you're about to boil.* But I don't.

She looks up at me, her eyes bloodshot. "Gack." She tries to laugh. "This is ridiculous. What am I, twelve?"

And memories of my childhood do not pour over me, images of my parents' divorce do not come flooding back. A deluge of sadness does not rain down upon me. I don't even think about my parents, or Seth and Nina, or Ben. Every relationship is weak and shoddy, every bond always, always, just one light tap away from shattering. Why do more people not know this? I reach across the coffee table, fumble for Jane's hand, find her fingers, which are limp and cold despite the heat, her palm clammy. I squeeze, suppressing an urge to let go of it—the bony, dying starfish; I squeeze, and Jane holds on, even after it becomes a little bit uncomfortable, after the gesture is complete.

"So . . . are you going to go home to Marcy?" I ask. "Are you going to go see them? Do you want me to come?"

Jane kicks the striped sheet off her legs and finally slips her hand out of mine, reaches up and swats at her hair, which is frizzy and matted on one side of her head from resting against something for a long time, a pillow or a phone. "Do you ever lie in bed and worry that you won't be able to fall asleep ever again?" She's wearing a red tank top of mine and a pair of Ben's boxers, as if she woke up this morning and assembled herself out of parts. "Like, you're tired, but nope, it's not going to happen anymore—sleep is a thing of the past?"

I tilt my head. "Um . . . ?"

"Because that's how I feel," she says, with an embarrassed smile. "Like I'm going to be awake forever."

"You could get a lot done if you were awake forever," I say. "You could get one of those make-ninety-five-thousand-dollars-a-year-working-at-home jobs they advertise on the Internet."

"I've always wondered about those jobs," she says. "Is it stuffing envelopes? Like, just a ton of envelopes?"

"I thought it was webcam porn."

"And that's what you were suggesting to me?"

"Well, I wouldn't care. I'd be sleeping."

"I should call Ben," she says. "But I don't really want to." I raise an eyebrow at her. "He'll be so kind and sympathetic." She shakes her head and looks down at her lap, and I'm staring at the crooked part in her hair, the thin line of naked scalp. Jane's childhood is a rubber band that has just snapped back hard.

And then we are both jolted by the sound of the doorbell ringing and a simultaneous knocking on the door, a jaunty little song, a charmingly impatient announcement. The voice on the other side of the door says, "*Jaysus*, it's hotter than balls outside," and Jane raises her head and looks at me, puzzled, and then she snorts a laugh and says, "You've gone all blotchy!" And I think, not for the first time, that if all of my dating stories, horror and otherwise, grease the wheels of my friendship with Jane, if they do nothing more than serve *this*, then it's worth it, all of it. I stand and bow, kick a little shuffle-ball-change to the door, *Thank you, ladies and gentlemen.*

"And, ah, by the way, Willa," Declan says, before I've even fully opened the door, as if we were in the middle of a conversation, as if I've just clicked back from call waiting, "Molly's Blooms? *Molly's Blooms?* It's an offense to my people." Declan has always held a proprietary grip on Irish culture. "How would you like it if I worked in a handkerchief shop in Dublin called A-Jew's?"

I laugh, as much at his audacity as at the wretchedness of the pun. We're standing toe to toe in the doorway, an echo of Ben's first visit to the apartment on that cold winter morning six months ago. "It's my boss's name," I say. "Molly Blumenfeld!"

"Also, I was going to bring you flowers, but then I thought that would be like bringing a leg of lamb to a butcher." He holds a brightly colored slip of paper in his hand, offers it to me. "So I've

brought you a lottery ticket. If you win, you can split it with me."
He exhales with relief, and grins.

I look down at the lottery ticket. There's a cartoon drawing of
a friendly looking badger on it, along with nine boxes, each decorated with a neon-orange hunk of cheddar cheese that you scratch
off. Do badgers eat cheese? It makes absolutely no sense.

"A handkerchief shop called A-Jew's?"

"D'you like that one? I've been working on it all day."

Jane, still sitting in the living room, clears her throat loudly.
She's leaning forward, her elbows resting on her knees, looking,
for the first time since I got home, delighted. If she had antennae,
they'd be quivering. "Declan," I say, loving the feel of his name on
my tongue. I throw open the door. "My roommate and best friend,
Jane."

I hold my breath as they take each other in, but all I see on
Declan's face is pleasant, vague curiosity, polite distance. Something loosens in me, a knot I didn't even know had been pulled
tight. "I remember hearing about you a few years ago," she says.

He walks over, shakes Jane's hand. "Listen," he says to her.
"We're not splitting our winnings three ways, and there'll be no
discussion about it, so you'll just have to hope your roommate and
best friend Willa is generous, right?"

"She'll take care of me," Jane says.

Declan digs around in his pocket and hands me a dime. He
smells of coppery sweat and of the spicy deodorant I remember.
Something about the heat wave, the fleshy closeness of it, the
thick hot air that is only slightly undercut by our valiantly clunk-
ing window unit, something about it makes me feel as if Jane and
Declan and I are in the midst of something bigger than we are. "I
think we're going to win!" I say, scraping silver and orange paint
from the little scratch-off boxes. Declan stands close; I can feel his
breath on my neck. Jane is still peering at us from her perch on

the chair, too intent. I recognize that look, the laser-sharp focus of the magical thinker, the quiet attention of a girl making a quick bargain with the universe.

I hold up the ruined ticket, shavings of shiny metallic paint falling from it, pass my hand underneath it like a game show hostess. "Ahh! So close!"

Jane's concentration breaks, and she rises. "Oh, well!" Her voice is unnaturally loud. "Nice meeting you," she says, as she abruptly heads to her room, the striped sheet balled up in her arms like a tabby cat.

Declan is standing in the middle of the living room with his hands stuffed into the back pockets of his khaki shorts. I idly straighten the spines of a few cocked books on the shelf. "Can we postpone our . . ." I won't say *date*.

"You need to take care of her." He tilts slightly, like the books, toward Jane's room, and I nod. "I'll be back next week," he says. "We've a new client in town. And anyway, even if we didn't." Years ago, Declan told me that no Irishman looks good in shorts. It's true. On him, they look strangely both too long and too short, baggy, yet also somehow taut. He shifts his weight. "Why are you looking at me like that?" And instead of answering—*Because nobody said anything, but you know Jane needs me; because your legs look like white fence posts poking out of your shorts; because you were sort of my boyfriend for about ten minutes, three years ago*—I move closer to him and lean in, press my warm cheek to his: a suggestion of a possibility, a very likely *maybe*.

chapter fifteen

Ben comes over to our apartment late. From my bedroom, I hear them argue.

"Because!" Jane says. "Because I would rather do this alone. Well, it's as good as being alone when I'm with Will. It's just easier with her."

Ben's low murmur is harder to make out: . . . *want to support you.*

"It's not supportive to insist on coming with me when I don't want you to!"

. . . *as if you don't trust me.*

"You're not hearing me!"

They don't fight often; they're not very good at it. I lie in my bed and squeeze my eyes shut, listening hard. Long silences are punctuated by confusing outbursts. *Whatever you want! It'd be nice if you meant that!* Eventually, very late, Jane's door clicks shut. I hear the soft thump of footsteps, a pause outside my door. And then the front door closes with a thud.

It's still dark when Jane wakes me. I squint at my clock, which glows with numbers that should only exist if they're followed by P.M. I look up at Jane, her round face like a full moon looming over me. My eyes are bleary with sleep. "Really?" I croak.

"Sorry, Willard," she whispers. "Come on. I'll drive, and I won't say a word. You can just keep sleeping." She pulls the sheet from my shoulders. "You won't have to do a thing, baby. Just lie back and think of England!"

I hoist myself out of bed and throw on a shirt and jeans, trudge behind her, zombielike, out the door, down the stairs, and across the street to the lot where she parks her car.

But, as we drive away from Milwaukee, as we pick up speed and barrel down the vast and empty County Trunk Highway CCC toward her hometown, Jane's calm exterior begins to crumble. The closer we get to Marcy, the more anxious she becomes. As the wheat fields blow past, she white-knuckles the steering wheel and starts talking.

"How could he have done this?" she asks, and doesn't wait for an answer. "Do you know, my dad had a special arrangement with our local grocery store when I was a kid, to buy their recently expired yogurt and overripe produce for cheap?" She purses her lips, remembering. "I had no idea until very recently that bananas were supposed to be yellow. I honestly can't recall him ever buying himself new clothes or a watch or anything. He wears the same slippers he's had since I was a kid. Blue fleecy things. Imagine how gross they are!" She smacks the edge of the steering wheel. "Like dead animals! His glasses frames are from 1985. They're so out of style I think they might be back in. When I left for college he gave me a suitcase he bought on clearance at Macy's, monogrammed with the name JAN." She launches into a passing imitation of him, her voice low and jolly. "He said, 'That *e* would have cost another two hundred dollars!' So this is the guy who blows his life savings in a pyramid scheme? I mean, who *is* he?" She slurps from a cup of rest-stop coffee then and rattles off a list of her options for dealing with her father: mature sympathy, quiet reserve, lawyerly interrogation. "Petulance," she says finally, with a little chuckle. "I think I'm going to go with petulance."

An hour later, we arrive at the Marcy Motel and House of Pancakes, where Mr. Weston has been staying. In the sunny lobby, he hugs Jane and ushers us right back out to the parking lot. "We can't eat pancakes here!" he says cheerfully, and Jane nods, as if, *No, of course we can't eat pancakes at the House of Pancakes,* as if this is the most obvious statement in the world.

In addition to the possible typographic error that is its name, Marcy, Wisconsin, is famous for its pancakes. On the town's seven-block main street, sandwiched between a Walmart and a massive Home Depot, you can enjoy breakfast at Pancakes-n-More (which serves only pancakes), the Flapjack Flappery, the Marcy Motel and House of Pancakes, and, according to its sign out front, the world's only drive-through pancake restaurant, Millie McMaple's Griddle Hut. The Flappery, Mr. Weston and Jane agree, has the fluffiest cakes.

I pull my chair up to the table and reach across Jane for the syrup, examine my options (orange infused? apple-cinnamon?) and then remember that I don't like syrup. I pour some on my pancakes anyway.

Charlie Weston, in a canary yellow T-shirt, his thin hair sticking up in spots like a sparsely seeded lawn, is in a talking mood.

"You know, and I mean no offense to your mother by what I am about to say, Janey." He lets loose a flood of syrup onto his tall stack with a dramatic flourish. "Because I love your mother. But Bonnie has always been extremely rigid about breakfast foods. Not to be eaten for lunch or dinner!" He replaces the container in the syrup caddy and passes the whole thing across the table with his freakishly long arm. "Ms. Jacobs?"

Jane presses her fork into the soupy pulp on her plate and glares at her father. "Fabulous," she mutters. I guess she wasn't kidding when she said she had settled on petulance. "Can you even afford this meal?" She points her empty fork at her father and holds it there for a second, then sets it down next to her plate and rests her forehead in her hands.

"Oh, honey," he says. His gaze slips from hers, drifts around the room. "Did you know," he says to no one in particular. "Did you know that I was Chuck before I met Bonnie?" Jane shudders but doesn't look up. A swath of curls falls across her forehead. "But she didn't like Chuck. She said it made me sound like beef. Like meat. And I said, Well, meat! That could be good!" I look up at the ceiling. *Do not tell us about your sex life. Do not tell us about your sex life.* "But she didn't like it, so she started calling me Charlie. And before I knew it, everyone was calling me Charlie. And now it's who I am. Amazing, the ways we change each other."

Pam, the bottle-blond waitress from central casting, swoops in and refills our coffee cups. "You folks still working here?" she asks, and for a second I'm confused. Has Mr. Weston taken a job here? Things are even worse than I thought.

"Not quite finished," Mr. Weston says. He watches as Pam sashays away. "Jane." She sighs audibly, her head still in her hands. "Look at me!" he commands, too loudly; a toddler in the next booth obeys and then starts to cry.

Jane scowls at her father, death rays shooting from her eyes. "I'm *looking*," she says. She must not have gone through a teenage rebellion. I haven't felt this disgusted with my parents in years.

"Well, this is me." He shrugs, then flicks a crumb off the edge of the table. "I screwed up."

Jane exhales. She glances at me for moral support; craven, I stare down at my lap. I wish I were home, in bed. Not for the first time today, the thought of Declan crosses my mind. "I guess I just don't understand how a fifty-three-year-old husband and father manages to *lose everything*." She scrapes her chair away from the table and then, changing her mind, pulls it back in.

One morning toward the end of my junior year of high school,

I woke up, stumbled downstairs, and banged my shin on a stack of cardboard boxes piled at the base of the stairs. My parents were sitting together at the kitchen table, drinking coffee, talking in low voices. They saw me at the same time, turned tired faces toward me in unison. I closed my eyes, rubbed them, tried to remember what I'd been thinking about just seconds ago at the top of the staircase. *Tengo, tienes, tiene, tenemos, tienen.* When I opened my eyes, my parents were still staring at me, and the boxes hadn't disappeared. For a full minute, nobody said a word. Then my mother got up from the table, shuffled over to the sink, and poured her coffee down the drain. "Well, it's not as if you didn't see this coming," she said, and sighed. She handed me a brown bag. "I found a pudding cup in the fridge," she said. "It might be from last summer, but those things never expire. I put it in your lunch."

"Remember when you and I used to make pancakes on Sunday mornings?" Mr. Weston says.

Somewhere in the back of the restaurant, a chorus of voices launches into "Happy Birthday." Jane takes a sip of my water. She looks at her father blankly.

"We did," her father says. "Don't you remember? We used to let your mom sleep, and we'd rustle up a batch of pancakes together every Sunday. Almost every Sunday."

Happy birthday to yoooooou.

"You slept late on Sunday mornings. I went to church with Mom."

Mr. Weston opens his mouth, then closes it. He looks a little bit flustered, his confident shell cracking. "Well, maybe it was Saturdays, then."

Jane sits up straight, her shoulders pulled back. "Sorry, Dad. I don't ever remember making pancakes with you." She tilts her head at him. "Maybe it was your other family."

Later Jane will tell me, "Of course we cooked breakfast together, we made banana pancakes every Sunday all through my child-hood." And I will think, *But we're adults. We're not supposed to let our parents' mistakes turn us into children.* But they do. That's what they do.

A waitress, not ours, careens past our table, plates balanced on her arms. Mr. Weston pours more syrup onto his pancakes, then looks at his food with regret. For a while, no one speaks. I tap the table. "Hey! Did Jane tell you about her poem?" One of Jane's poems was recently accepted for publication in a very small liter-ary magazine. In fact, that's what it's called: *Very Small Literary Magazine.* I know that Jane hasn't mentioned it to her parents; she told me so just the other night.

Jane waves her hand in front of her face. "No. I'm done with that," she says, before Mr. Weston can respond. "There's no money in that! I'm done writing poems."

"Honey!"

"No," she says again, and I'm reminded of Princess Jane, ruler of her pink childhood kingdom. *Off with his head!*

An old lady in plaid pants gets up from the table across from ours; a crumpled brown paper napkin slides from her lap like a large dead moth. Mr. Weston looks around the restaurant. Jane blinks hard and downs her water in three fast gulps, and I squeeze her knee under the table. Soon we'll head to her parents' house for round two. But as far as I'm concerned, we could get in the car and drive back to Milwaukee now, because she's learned everything she needs to know. Your parents will fail you. Lovers will fail you. In the end it's this: your best friend in a pancake house, witness to your despair. I want to tell her it's okay. *This is what it is, and it's okay.*

In the six minutes since we walked in the door, Jane's mother has offered us five different snacks. "Aren't you girls even a little bit hungry? Why don't I whip up some popovers?" Her suggestions grow increasingly bizarre. *Grapes? French onion soup? Corn casserole? Leftover Swedish meatballs?* An exorcism of the marital kitchen, or the menu of the unhinged. "It's early still," she says, bustling about. She pulls out a whisk. "Maybe you need something more breakfasty."

"We've had breakfast, Mom," Jane says, fiddling with her hair.

Mrs. Weston shakes her head vigorously and flaps the hand that is not holding the whisk. She's just gearing up. "Breakfast," she says, a hint of suspicion tightening her voice. "*Did* you? On the way here? On the road?"

"Downtown. With . . . um . . . we met Dad." Jane tugs a curl straight and makes a mustache out of it.

"Don't play with your hair." Mrs. Weston is standing with her back to her daughter, but somehow it doesn't surprise me that she knows what Jane is doing behind her. She replaces the whisk in the drawer, stands on her tiptoes, reaches into a cabinet, and pulls out, for no apparent reason, a salad spinner. "Well." She turns the knob on the empty spinner; it sounds like an engine revving.

Jane shifts her weight from one foot to the other. I can see the straps of the same shirt she wore yesterday—my red tank top—underneath her pink T-shirt. I feel my customary urge to break the tension by sacrificing myself on the altar of weirdness. "I am not a big fan of pancakes!" I say, as the whir of the salad spinner dies down. "I mean, syrup! Who needs it?" Jane and her mother both turn and look at me as if I ought to be gently guided back to my room. I shrug. Mission accomplished.

"I think I'd like to take you shopping," Mrs. Weston says, clapping her hands once. This seems like a strange offer, given their new financial circumstances, but Jane's mother is insistent. She surveys us, her eyes narrowed with maternal discernment; her gaze settles first on Jane's feet, in their green flip-flops, and then on mine, in pink high-tops. "Shoe shopping!" She claps her hands again; I half expect the kitchen lights to turn on and off.

Jane shakes her head in horror. "But you can't . . . we can't," and I nudge her.

"Of course," I say. "Thank you, Mrs. Weston." I think this is her mother's way of reassuring her, and it feels like a kindness to accept it. Plus, new shoes!

The doorbell rings, and Jane tears out of the kitchen to answer it. With her daughter out of earshot, Mrs. Weston quickly moves over to me, stopping an inch too close, and I stiffen in surprise. If only we'd accepted her offer of popovers. Melba toast. Chicken fingers. Anything!

"It's not her business," she says to me, leaning in and looking up. "As an only child, Janey was frequently privy to more adult conversations than she ought to have heard." Her words come fast and clipped; her breath smells strange, pungent-sweet, like sardines and cinnamon, a recipe of wrong ingredients. I nod, breathe through my mouth, force myself not to turn away. "This is between Charlie and me." She reaches up, presumably to squeeze my shoulder, but since she is so much shorter than I am, a squatty shrub to the tree that is me, she misses, and her small, warm hand lands squarely above my left breast. "Mr. Weston and I will be fine. I mean, financially, we'll be fine. Well, to be honest, I don't know. And there you have it." Mrs. Weston turns away from me purposefully, back toward the kitchen sink, grabs a sponge and starts attacking the green backsplash tiles with Jane-like fervor. There I have it? *There I have what?* Oh, Marcy. Marcy me.

"Oh-em-gee," Jane says. "That was Dougie." She lopes back into the kitchen, flushed and smiling, her flip-flops smacking the floor. "Good old Dougie! He noticed my car in the driveway and wanted to stop over and say hi. So nice! He wants to meet up tonight. I said we would. Let's go shopping!" She looks at me and then at her mother. She presses her lips together and plants her hands on her hips, her pointy elbows forming a rhombus of defensiveness. I won't say a thing. I'm relieved, grateful for this distraction, and definitely not worried about the look on my friend's face, about how excited she seems, suddenly, to see good old Dougie, or about how she hasn't mentioned Ben once today.

Jane's mother tosses the sponge into the sink and dries her hands, then grabs her keys from the kitchen table and jingles them at us. "The mall awaits!" I raise my eyebrows at Jane and grin, happy to play along.

The shopping trip is an all-afternoon marathon under fluorescent lights, an exhausting forced march from store to store in search of the existentially impossible. But it's also kind of fun. By the time we get home and get ready to go out and meet Dougie, I feel like a pleasantly numb facsimile of myself, a person who shops all day and goes out at night, the kind of girl who is ready for anything.

Polka music blasts into us as we walk through the doors of the Deutschland Beer Haus, the accordion providing both melody and jolly, relentless backbeat. Dougie Tyler, zapped by a bolt of recognition, hops off his bar stool. He grabs Jane in a rough hug, lets go of her, then looks at me, does a comic double take. "Whoa! For a second there, I thought I was hugging the wrong girl!"

Jane wraps her arm around my waist and leans in. Not far from where we're standing, an older lady with a silvery helmet of hair dances by herself to the music, hopping from one foot to the other like an impatient toddler. "It's true," Jane says. "We have been told on occasion that we resemble each other!"

This afternoon, a grandmotherly saleswoman at one of the shoe stores clucked about how lovely it was to see a mother and her two daughters doing a little shopping together; the pretzel girl glanced at Jane and asked me if I was going to get anything for my sister. "We look alike?" I say to Dougie. "No, I've never heard that."

Hanging in Jane's bedroom in our apartment, above her desk, is a sketch I made a few weeks ago, a drawing of the two of us, our faces nearly identical. When I gave it to her, she knew right away. She pointed to the face on the right. "That's me! My hair's slightly shorter than yours," she said, "and my eyes are just a little bit lighter. And my mouth is totally different." She studied it for a moment. "You're really good, Willa. You're really talented." The truth is I stared in the mirror as I drew the picture. I used myself as the model for both of us. I'll think about this drawing, months from now, and wonder why I did that.

Jane giggles now, tosses her head, flicks her hair behind her. "I know! Weird!" she says. She laughs again, a trill of notes, a high-pitched twitter. I wouldn't be surprised if a flock of excited male birds flew toward the sound and knocked themselves out cold against the windows of this restaurant. "This is Willa!" Jane is shouting now, above the din. She squeezes my waist and plants a moist kiss on my cheek. Dougie tilts his large head, smiles at me, takes in what must be the very peculiar image of his high school girlfriend exuberantly smooching her look-alike.

Jane is using me to flirt with Dougie, although amid the confusion of the crowded bar, I can't wrap my mind around exactly how it's happening. She kisses my cheek again and grabs my hand. Maybe I'm her stand-in, her stunt double. Maybe I'm like one of those mannequins we learned CPR on in seventh grade. Place your open mouth on the doll's lips, press your hands onto her still chest, and bring her mechanical heart back to life. *Willa, Willa, are you okay?*

"I need a beer," Jane says.

Dougie leans across the bar and flags down the bartender, holds up three fingers. The refreshment choices here are regular and lite, but it's okay: the crowd and the noise and the feathery skim of Jane's hair against my shoulder are starting to get to me, to stir up the sediment inside me. "Dougie's cute," I whisper-shout to Jane as he's paying the bartender. "Oddly."

We stand for a while, the three of us sipping self-consciously, smiling, smiling, then make our way to a booth in the back, where there are fewer people and it's slightly quieter. A middle-aged waitress in a red-and-white dirndl stands over us and asks if we're interested in the special.

"Sorry, I missed that," Dougie says, wiping foam from his lip.

The waitress bends toward us. "Schnitzel," she says, her voice low and tired, her right thigh braced against our table. "Tonight's special is schnitzel!" The pronouncement sends Jane into a sudden convulsion of laughter.

Dougie shakes his head at the waitress, and she turns and walks away. With nothing but a few bites of pancake, this afternoon's pretzel, and half of a beer in her, Jane is loose—her arms and legs a little wobbly, gestures imprecise, her conversation unfiltered. "Oh, God, I don't know why that was so funny," she says. "Schnitzel." She wipes tears from her face with the back of her hand, and Dougie looks at her, concern furrowing his low-hanging eyebrows.

"So, Willa," he says quickly. "I got divorced recently." His face immediately goes pink. "I don't know if you knew that."

I cringe. I recognize this galumphing attempt to redirect the conversation, but that doesn't make it any more graceful. I know the feeling of trying to play the piano with a sledgehammer. "That must have been rough," I say, and he raises his beer stein to me.

"Divorce! Betrayal!" Jane guzzles her beer and plonks the glass down on the table. "Love's in disrepair!" she sings.

"Are you still in touch with your ex?" I ask.

"Erin. Her name's Erin. And, nah." And then Dougie Tyler, former frat boy who is indeed wearing an Alpha Sigma Sigma sweatshirt, baseball cap sticking out of his back pocket, holes in his jeans, divorced Dougie Tyler who sells sports equipment and lives in his parents' basement and lifts weights for fun and says *I know, hey* when he agrees with someone, Dougie Tyler laughs: at himself, at the mundane misfortune of being a divorced twenty-six-year-old man who's still pining for his ex-wife, at the incongruity of sitting at a booth in a small-town bar with his crumbling mess of a former girlfriend and her best friend.

Her intriguing best friend? Something passes between us, and I revel in it, in the surprising, off-beat thud-*thud* of my heart. *Hello.* "Erin," I say. "What a bitch."

"I know, hey." Dougie nods.

Jane fiddles with the edge of a paper coaster. "Did I ever meet her?"

"You did, you met her at Fisk's graduation party. She wore a back brace in high school?"

"Oo, sexy!" Jane says, and Dougie laughs again.

"Yeah, but it was good for a while. It worked." He looks at me and finishes the last of his beer.

"You know, you should come visit us in Milwaukee sometime," Jane says dreamily. "You should!"

"I'll go get us another round," I say, a little wobbly now myself.

I stop in the bathroom first, then make my way to the bar, where I wait for a while, sandwiched between bodies, brushed by the occasional, accidental sweep of fabric or skin. It feels good to be in the thick of things, even if it's hard to breathe in here, even if polka music makes me nervous—*Enjoy it! Or there will be consequences!*—even if the small flame inside me has been ignited by the unlikeliest of sparks.

The bartender slides three mugs to me, and I arrange them carefully. Right now I'm here to take care of Jane; she needs me. And Dougie sees me. Although he may see me as a new yet familiar country, although I may just be, to Dougie, Canada, still, he sees me. I'm walking back to our table, three cold glasses of beer balanced in my hands, and I'm thinking about upping my game, about letting him know that the interest is mutual. This is how it all comes together. I get it; I'm late to the party, but I get it. I may be semiemployed and single and directionless, but I can be good at this. I feel the vibration of this place, the low and pleasant thrum of hope, fleeting and fine.

And then I see them. Jane's long, white arms draped around Dougie's neck, his big, blond head tipped down toward her dark one, the two of them, their faces pressed together; I can actually see the wet pink flick of someone's tongue, Dougie and Jane locked in a sloppy kiss, *Oh, of course,* and me, nine feet tall and thick as a tree, lowering three glasses onto the table with a slosh of beer.

They part, faces flushed with what may or may not be guilt. I stare as Dougie removes his hand from inside the front of Jane's shirt. His hair is sticking up on one side. They must have gotten right to it, as soon as I left. Slowly, and without looking at me, Jane rebuttons the three top buttons of her shirt and adjusts her bra strap. Dougie looks down and tugs at his sweatshirt.

The inside of my mouth is suddenly pasty and dry. "Hey, you two. Hey, now." I slide into my seat across from them. Dougie slings his arm over Jane's shoulder. Jane runs her tongue over her teeth and blinks slowly, like a lizard. I grab one of the beers. "So, what were you two talking about?"

Jane laughs a little and then turns her focus to the skin underneath her right thumbnail. "I could go for some potato salad," she says, licking her lips. "Is what I could go for."

Dougie, recovered, leaps up from the booth. They dish out sides of German potato salad and sauerkraut here, pale little dumplings, and an array of tiny sausages in rolls—greasy little men in sleeping bags—straight from the bar. He scurries off to fulfill Jane's request.

I watch my friend tending to her cuticles. "Seriously? Did I really just see what I think I saw?"

She turns to me slowly, eyes narrowed, thumb resting on the ledge of her lower lip. "I don't know. Yes. I thought . . ." With her teeth, she rips off a shred of skin from the side of her nail; a bright red flower of blood blossoms there. "You were flirting with him. With Dougie! I got . . . I felt . . . proprietary."

My heart thumps hard and then takes off at a sprint. I fill my mouth with beer and swallow it in a huge, bitter gulp. I look at my friend's face, and in this charged, tipsy moment I see her as she must once have been, a smooth, pink, fuzzy-headed baby with round eyes and wet, red lips, and as she will be, cheeks like deflated balloons, wrinkles creasing down from the sides of her nose to the edges of her mouth, the cartilaginous tip of her straight nose sagging. What is the weight of conflict with my best friend? How do I balance these scales? She and Dougie kissed—made out, pawed each other, in a bar, cleared at least a couple of bases—and she's blaming me for it. She has a boyfriend. Ben! Ben is her boyfriend! She could have given this one to me, if it was hers to give. But is it worth leveling an angry accusation at her when she's vulnerable? My heart pounds faster, my engine floods; I'm stalled out.

Before I can figure out the answer to my own question, Jane extends her hand, bleeding thumb and all, across the dark wood of the table. "Oh, Willa, oh, shit, I fucked up." At the table behind us, someone laughs, low and bleating, like a goat. I shake my head to try to clear it, a gesture that probably looks to Jane like I'm dis-agreeing with her.

Dougie, stocky and bowlegged—I hadn't noticed it before, his cowboy swagger—returns to the table and displays his treasure: a plate of things, unidentifiable objects, red, pickled slices of vegetables, dollops of cream, meats, and a low, gelatinous mountain of potato salad. He smiles at Jane proudly and deposits the dish on the table. I swallow the urge to slap the grin off his wide face.

Jane unfolds herself from the booth. "I'm so sorry, Dougie. We have to go." I stand up quickly and slide away from the table, smiling, nodding. "We have to go," Jane says again, tucking her hair behind her ears, "because Willa's not feeling well." On cue, I squeeze my smile into a grimace of pain, clutch my stomach and moan softly. We're back in cahoots, where we belong. She waves her hand toward the plate of food. "Can I give you some money for that?" She asks the question like a person who probably doesn't have five dollars in her wallet, who maybe doesn't have a wallet at all, who knows she doesn't need one.

Dougie, crestfallen, shakes his head. He slides his hands into the pockets of his jeans and tilts toward Jane as, with an elegant arch, she backs quickly away.

In the car on the way home to Milwaukee the next day, I drive and Jane is quiet. An hour in, we stop for gas. It's drizzling, a light mist that keeps promising to swell into something more but then doesn't, the kind of rain that evaporates before it hits the pavement, too weak and unsure of itself to cool the humid air.

I'm filling the tank as Jane walks toward me from the convenience store, waving two packages of Twinkies. "It's not a road trip without junk food," she says happily.

"It's ten a.m.," I say, shaking my head in disgust. "Way too early for Twinkies. You should have gotten Ding Dongs."

She leans against the car, eases one foot out of its flip-flop, and scratches her calf with her toe. "Willa, I need to say . . . I want to ask you . . ." She taps the plastic Twinkies package against her bare leg. "Please promise me that you won't tell Ben what happened last night? With Dougie? Please?" She inches away from the car and rolls her shoulders, straightens her back, revealing the flesh above the low waistband of her shorts. She meets my gaze. For a second Jane looks lost and miserable, her eyes huge and glassy.

I feel the sudden need to protect my friend, to keep her safe from her bad choices and her worst instincts. I grip the handle of the gas pump, sense the vibration under my palm. It's perverse, really: the hose, the pump, the coursing fluid. I almost laugh. Who is responsible for this? How is it that I've never, in all my years of filling cars with gas, realized it before?

The tank is full; the pump clicks off. I replace the gas cap, wipe sweat from my forehead, and reach for the Twinkies, take them from Jane's thin fingers, her loose grip. We get back into the car, doors slamming shut simultaneously.

Is it as simple as this, then? Is this love? "I won't tell," I say to Jane, certain as anything, unwrapping the indestructible yellow pastry and biting off a hunk of it. "Don't worry."

chapter sixteen

Seth is waiting for me outside our apartment building when we get home from Marcy, lurking in the small lobby like someone you should probably call the police to report.

"Will," he says, hoisting himself up and nodding hello to Jane. "I need you." Seth is like the semi-tame deer that hangs around shyly in the backyard, and you want to feed it because you think that without you it will starve, even though it won't. But still, you approach slowly with your hands full of organic alfalfa sprouts. Even though I'm due at the flower shop in a half hour and all I want is a shower and a bagel, my answer is yes; it's always yes.

It's eighty-eight degrees out, and Seth lugs a big cardboard box as we walk, shifting it from arm to arm. His face is dripping, his breathing labored. Nina has asked Seth to meet her at the Bay Bluff School playground, near my apartment. It's equidistant from her lab and Seth's new place, and also, I think, she probably wants to see him on neutral territory.

"I can't do this alone," he whispers to me as we stand together on the edge of the grass, and I know that this is as close as I'll get to a thank-you. He cradles the cardboard box and squints, looking around at the throngs of happy, screeching children. "Do you know what all these little kids and babies make me think of?"

A swarm of gnats circles in the air close to my own dripping face; I swat them away, and they return like thugs to harass me. "What do they make you think of?" I ask gently. We wander over to a bench and sit down, and immediately the painted wooden slats adhere to my thighs.

"Sex."

"Um, Seth, guys who say things like that probably shouldn't be hanging out at playgrounds."

"Ha." He fidgets, moves his hands from the box and clasps them around the back of his neck. Two full moons of sweat darken the armpits of his gray T-shirt. "I just mean, sex. All these women chasing after their kids, they all had sex and made babies and now they're here, yelling, 'Good job, Isabella!' and 'Aidan, I said no biting!'"

I laugh. "You know, that's just . . . that's a weird thing to say."

"Well, this is a weird place to be."

"I guess."

"You have no idea." He turns to me. The past half year of his life is stamped onto his unshaven face: puffy bags under his eyes, a marshmallow jowliness rounding his jaw, a spray of pimples dotting his shiny forehead, and another small zit nestled at the corner of his mouth. He adjusts his baseball cap, pushes it back past his hairline, then forward again to shade his eyes.

I still don't know why he and Nina broke up, and Seth is a fortress against questions. Whatever it was, a drunken one-night stand with a waitress at Rags or a drawn-out, angst-ridden tryst with a friend's almost ex, who knows? But I'm pretty sure Seth sabotaged his own happiness.

A hot, moist breath of wind stirs the trees. It feels like we're in a sauna. In the sandbox in front of us, without warning, a blond girl in a pink gingham sundress dumps a bucket of sand over a small boy's head. He presses his fat hands to his face and screams. The boy's mother, who had been sitting on the edge of the sandbox in a droopy daze, stands, scoops him up, and glares at the little girl. "Where is your mother?" she hisses, then shoots a lightning bolt at me and storms away with the little boy. The girl in gingham immediately starts wailing—loud, wretched moans, the anguished yowls of a dying animal—and then, a few seconds later, just as abruptly, she stops. She surveys the now-empty sandbox as if she has just witnessed a natural disaster, then looks over at Seth and me, eyes wet and blinking, face somber.

I nudge Seth. Am I supposed to do something, to fill in for her absent mother like a substitute teacher? I spot a cluster of women across the park, absorbed in conversation. One of them looks over toward us and waves. "Hi, Caiiiitlinnnn, hi, *sweeeetie!*" she calls.

Well, okay. Caitlin waves back slowly. Then she turns her attention to her bare feet, poking at her toes with a small stick.

I watch her for a little while. She seems to straddle a very fine line between self-sufficient and neglected. Or maybe there is no line, only the long, tricky road to adulthood that starts sooner for some than for others, and way too early for us all. "I like your dress," I say.

Seth, next to me, startles. He lets out a little whimper, and I follow his gaze: it's Nina, jogging toward us, impervious to the lethargy that grips everyone else. She's wearing a green T-shirt, cutoffs, and waders; they thwap against the blacktop as she nears us. She's carrying a cardboard box, too, and she looks both determined and slightly crazy.

"Hey," she says. "Oh, hey."

She drops her box on the bench next to Seth and leans in for quick hugs, one for Seth, not returned, then one for me. She's bony against my body, slight as a bird. She smells a little swampy, but she looks pretty, her hair pulled away from her face in a messy ponytail, wispy strands softening her features; her skin, which is prone to the blotchiness of the redhead, is perfect. On a good day, Nina looks like sunshine, like dew, like the angels gathered at her conception and danced on her mother's womb. Too bad for Seth, this is a good day.

"Hey, you," I say softly, aware that any expression of affection is a betrayal of Seth, but I miss my brother's ex-girlfriend, not the kind of missing you do late at night, alone in your bed, aching, but the kind you forget about, the kind that only hits you when you see a person you have loved, her physical self a reminder. The way she laughed so hard at your dumb joke about a talking snail that tears streamed down her freckly cheeks; how she once spent a full day without realizing that she had a speck of arugula trapped between her two charmingly crooked front teeth until her boss actually reached over and plucked it out. *Lettuce agree never to speak of this again,* I said that night, over dinner at the apartment, and she nodded solemnly in agreement.

"How are you?" I ask now. I can't help myself.

"Good, I'm good," she says briskly. She nods at Seth. "I brought your stuff." She stands above us in her ridiculous getup. "And you have mine. Obviously." She crosses her arms over her chest. The sun shines behind her. Even with my sunglasses on, I have to shade my eyes to look at her.

"Hey, Nina," Seth says, a fake, tense cheeriness knifing through his voice. He's sitting up very straight. "Look at that. That old beach ball." He points to a deflated red, green, and yellow plastic ball lying in the box Nina has brought for him. "I didn't know that was *mine.* I thought that was *ours.* I thought we bought that together, last summer. But hey, hey, Nina, that's cool, that's, like, a great metaphor right there."

"Oh," Nina says, surprised by Seth's icy rage, flustered, her face blushing fast and dark. "Okay. I'm sorry." She looks around, any-where but at Seth. "Well, I have to go. Back to the river. Back to work." Her voice catches on "work."

Seth doesn't say anything for a minute, and Nina doesn't move. "Wow, this must be really good frog weather!" I say. I have no idea what I'm talking about. After all this time apart, they are still this raw with each other, unable to act normal together for even three minutes, to pretend that their hearts, their beating frog hearts, haven't been removed and dissected and left for scraps. I find that I am, perversely, envious. Envious! Of their ungovernable connection.

Seth stares hard at Nina. "This is pretty fucking twisted."

Nina shakes her head. "I have to go." She motions toward the box with her chin. "There's a cactus in there. That one you bought. So be careful. I watered it last week. It should be fine for a while. I have to go."

But Nina still doesn't move; silence hovers over us again like a storm cloud about to burst. Am I the only one who can feel the pressure? I extend my arms in front of myself and do jazz hands. "Herpetology waits for no man!" My God, what's wrong with me?

Nina laughs a little and relaxes her shoulders. She bends to retrieve her things. Seth holds his breath and looks away as she leans over him, her loose shirt exposing the freckles on her chest and a thin slice of white cotton bra. "I really have to go," she says.

And, finally, she does. We both watch as she walks away, red ponytail swinging slightly. From behind, she could be anyone. Except for the boots.

Seth rifles through his box. "Awesome," he says. "I wanted that cactus back."

"Come on," I say, peeling my thighs from the bench. I take

Seth's hand and pull him up. "We need to leave. This is not a good place for you to be."

Seth rises, pulls his shirt free from where it was glued with sweat to his back and his stomach. "That is very true. That is a very astute observation."

"Ass toot," I say: our favorite, our only, joke left over from our shaky, shared adolescence.

He hoists the cardboard box into his arms and takes a weird, long sniff of it. "Oh, motherfucker," he says tenderly, as if he were cooing at a baby. "Mother*fuck*." We begin to make our way to the edge of the playground, toward the street where his car is parked. "I'm sorry to say this to you, because you're my sister, but I wish I'd been paying better attention the last time Nina and I . . . you know."

From nowhere, Ben's face flashes in my mind, Ben's face close to mine, its familiar planes and new, rough edges, his breath in the hot car, our one, ill-fated kiss. "I know," I say. If Seth and I had any precedent for physical affection, for the familial comfort of a hug, I would throw my arms around him now, squeeze him tightly, and rest my head on his wide, damp shoulder. Instead I just keep up my pace next to him, my flawed big brother, brought low by his miasmic regret. If he hadn't cheated on Nina, none of this would have happened. It seems like his longing should have a gravitational pull or the magnetic power to heal fractures.

"Hang on." Seth veers suddenly toward a green garbage can near the public bathrooms a few feet away. He sets his box down on the grass next to the bin and shakes out his hands, rolls his head to one side, then the other. "Okay," he says. "I'll walk you to the flower shop." He leaves the box there, by the garbage can, cactus and all, the detritus of his life with Nina, unnecessary now. He walks back toward me, swatting a mosquito away from his face, first with his right hand, then with his left.

chapter seventeen

Jane had finally called Ben when we were on our way back from Marcy. I was driving, and she was talking and applying mascara simultaneously. At first I was impressed.

"Hiya," she said. "I missed you." Her mouth was turned down in the putting-on-eye-makeup frown. "I said I missed you!" They chatted for a while, and she switched the mascara wand into her left hand and the phone into her right. "Yes," she said, "tonight," and "I love you." I caught a glimpse of how she examined herself in the mirror and then smiled at her own reflection. For the first time I saw what an overabundance of confidence looks like, how it accumulates like snowdrifts over the rocky landscape of complexity, of ambivalence, of guilt.

"When are you two getting together?" I asked her. "I'll call Declan. Let's make it a double date." I'd wanted to prove something. Who knows what? That I could have what Jane had? That I would never do what she had done? That I could if I wanted to?

The sun is setting when Declan meets us on the sidewalk in front of our apartment building; the sky is a nine-year-old girl's bedroom, decorated with puffy clouds and streaked with dusky pinks and candied purples. The heat has finally broken; the breeze that coughed hot exhaust all over the city for two weeks is cool and dry now. Ben folds his arm around Jane as if he hasn't seen her in three months instead of three days. Their fight the night before we left is ancient history. Declan stands in front of us, near the street, and rocks on his heels.

Jane bumps Ben with her hip. "Let's go dancing!"

Declan shakes his head, holds out his hand like a stop sign in front of him. "Irish men don't dance."

"Okay, let's stay home, then," Ben says. He unwraps his arm from Jane's waist and looks at her, takes her in. "I'll cook."

My breath catches. I glance at Declan, who is still bouncing gently, gazing at passersby. "Irish men don't stay in!" I say quickly. Maybe they do; maybe they don't. We're not staying in tonight.

So we wander over to Blue Roses, the café down the street, and commandeer a table outside. The place is busy, the sidewalks crowded. People have emerged from their air-conditioned caves, giddy and relieved.

Declan orders a bottle of wine for the four of us. I sit next to Ben and notice how Jane rests the back of her hand lightly on his neck, brushing it across his skin. He closes his eyes for a second and then turns to her. She smiles, her chin tipped toward him, her teeth naked and white. I feel like I'm witnessing a precursor to something private and enviable. She laughs delightedly at nothing. Is this all calculated? I'm seeing Jane differently now, after Dougie; I can't help it.

At the table next to ours, two girls hug each other and squeal. Declan pours wine for us, then, as soon as anyone has taken a few sips, he pours more.

"Are you trying to get me drunk?" Ben asks. They've only just met each other.

He winks. "You bet I am, baby." They're hitting it off, the two of them, and Jane is relaxing into the evening. Not me. I have to plant my palms on my thighs to stop my legs from bouncing under the table.

"What was it like, growing up in Ireland?" Ben asks, and Declan launches into a story from his scrappy Dublin childhood: how he and his friend Johnny used to steal underwear from the neighbors' clotheslines and switch them around, so that tiny old Mrs. McCormack ended up with beer-bellied Jack Fahey's graying skivvies. We all laugh, loud yelps that ricochet off cars and buildings.

"My daddy was a poor milkman," he says, shaking his head sadly, "and me ma raised fourteen wee ones in a two-room shack."

"Your father is an architect," I remind him, "and your mother is an ophthalmologist. And you're an only child."

He slaps his forehead as if he's just remembering this. "So, you two," he says, tipping his wineglass toward Ben and Jane. "How long have you been the happy couple?"

Ben pushes back in his chair a couple of inches, the wrought-iron legs screeching against the sidewalk. "My uncle Walleye used to say, 'Aunt Rose and I have been married for five wonderful years.'" He hooks his fingers into the holes in the table. "This was when they'd been married for almost fifty. We always thought he was kidding. Then one morning last year, Aunt Rose told him she'd put a week's worth of meatloaf in the freezer and that she'd filed for divorce."

Jane claps her hand over her mouth. Her fingernails are painted all different colors, red for her thumb, orange and yellow and green and blue for her fingers, a jaunty synthetic rainbow.

"That is a lovely romantic story," Declan says.

"That's a Hallmark Hall of Fame movie," I offer.

Jane moves her hand from her mouth. "You have an uncle Walleye?"

"His real name is Walter," Ben says, "and he also does have a wonky eye." He nods, as if that's the point of the whole thing.

"The next generation," I say, "is going to tell their stories about Great-aunt Brittany and Grandma Ashley."

"And Grandpa Jaden," Jane says, running her hand up and down Ben's arm, her fingertips fluttering like small flags.

"Remember old lady Tiffany, from down the block?" Ben stares at Jane's moving hand and grins. "She died an old maid."

"Six months, by the way," Jane says suddenly to Declan, emphasizing the number like it, too, was *fifty years,* or as if she's surprised by it herself. "We've been together for *six months.*"

"So it's serious, then?" Declan asks. The combination of his age—he's five years older than we are—and his former position as my boss gives him a tinge of experience, the aura of someone who knows things.

"Well," Jane says, "last week, after some discussion, we agreed on the names of our future children. Ella for a girl, Sam for a boy."

Ben holds up one finger. "Sam and Ella."

Jane giggles. "So it's back to the drawing board on that one!" She leans over, pulls Ben's face toward hers, and kisses him.

Are all of our jokes and conversations just the scaffolding for our physical desires? Are we just rabbits with well-developed frontal lobes? Three days ago Jane was wetly kissing Dougie in a smoky bar in Marcy. Now here she is with Ben, fingertips to skin, mouth to mouth, laughing about the names of their unborn children.

"Imagine yelling that on the playground," Ben says.

"Or in a crowded restaurant," Jane adds. "Look out! Sam-and-Ella!"

The table rattles, and I realize it's me, my left leg bouncing again, banging against the edge. It's too much, their treacly happiness, the warm gluey syrup of it filling my lungs. I feel as if I might be catapulted out of my chair, like a machine, spring-loaded and wound up. "Ha," I say, under my breath, tracing my finger around the rim of my glass. "Sam and Ella." I think about the prediction Seth made, months ago, that Ben and Jane's relationship would become serious and that I would be left behind. For the first time I understand that I am living in the midst of something that I might lose.

Under the table, Declan lowers his hand onto my thigh and squeezes.

Declan pays the check, refusing money from the rest of us, smiling at me. I glance away, suddenly shy. As we make our way back to the apartment, my head is full of cotton. I have the buzzy, fuzzy, not unpleasant sense that I'm barely touching the ground—that we're moving forward more than just physically. We're on a conveyor belt to the future! Or maybe it's the wine. On the narrow sidewalk, I hook my arm through Ben's. Behind us, Declan and Jane are chatting.

". . . since college," she says. I strain to hold the thread of their conversation while maintaining my loopy focus on Ben. ". . . nobody in the world like Willa. But you already know that." She's my advocate, my best friend and protector. *You hurt Willa, you'll be sleeping with the fishes!*

"So, what can you tell me about Marcy?" Ben is saying to me. He's grown more subdued as the night has worn on. "Jane hasn't given me much."

"She's a great girl," Declan says. My back is to them, but I'm picturing his long fingers, his confident smile, *oh, yes.*

"Well," I say to Ben, "you know." He doesn't; that's the problem. "Her dad acts like he's just, I don't know, misplaced a sock or something. Like, oops, where did my bank account go? Her mom is self-medicating with massive doses of retail therapy. It was a lot to take in. Jane . . . wasn't quite herself."

I could choose this moment, right now, to pull closer to Ben, to whisper in his ear, *Here's what I can tell you about Marcy: Jane kissed her old boyfriend.* But maybe it's true that Jane just wasn't herself. Maybe her family crisis turned her into someone else and then threw that other girl, the unJane, temporarily into Dougie's beefy arms. How can I blame Jane for the ill-advised actions of the unJane?

I feel the sudden, complicated relief of someone who has just convinced herself via the logic of tipsy reasoning. I tilt my head back to catch the breeze. It's delicious to be outside, to not be sweaty and enervated. My body belongs to me again. I could climb a mountain! But we're in Milwaukee. Yes, Jane kissed Dougie. But it's not always obvious, what's right. I turn my hazy thoughts back to Declan.

"I like my apartment in Chicago, but, sure, it's never really felt like home," he says, behind me. Well. I'll take that to mean that he's home *now*, with me, because of course that's what a nostalgic Irish immigrant who briefly dated me three years ago would mean. Have I forgotten something important? I shake off the strong feeling that I have; I let myself be propelled by my ambitious lust.

Ben presses his arm against mine. "I'm just trying to understand everything," he says, turning to me, his brown eyes watery and serious as a basset hound's. "So, thanks."

When we walk into the apartment, the air is still warm and muggy, in spite of the cool breeze outside. The wood floors are sticky with humidity, the furniture disconcertingly damp.

"That was fun!" Jane says. "Really fun!" She flips her hair with both hands and looks at each of us for confirmation. It *was* fun! Was it *fun*?

Declan nods gamely. "Yep," he says, after a minute. "Sure was fun!" We're standing in a clump in the middle of our living room, Jane and Ben and Declan and I and our new friend, awkward conversation.

"What a fun night!" Jane says again. The word is beginning to sound strange and foreign to me, like a kind of exotic stew or a great beast of the African plains. *Fuhn? Pfunn?* Ben is newly fascinated with a bit of string on his sleeve: in the time it's taken us to walk home, he's gone from subdued to sullen. Jane is ramped up and tipsy, unaware that the mood has shifted. She tickles Ben's ribs. She seems not to notice that he has stopped laughing. I close my eyes against an awful flash of insight: that unless I snatch the reins right now, my life is going to be a series of random decisions and diminishing returns, door after door slamming shut in front of me, a narrow hallway of yeses and noes. *Enough of this,* I think, or maybe I actually say it; I'm too tipsy to be sure. I grab Declan's hand and pull him into my room. This is our slow seduction.

I place my hand on his chest and push Declan down onto the bed the way they do on the TV shows Fran watches, about morally ambiguous lawyers who argue ripped-from-headlines cases and then have hot sex with each other. In seduction, I'll have to take my cues from prime-time television; I don't quite know what I'm doing.

I climb on top of Declan. He looks up at me, one eyebrow raised. "I'll be honest, Will, I wasn't expecting this."

I kiss him to prevent him from discussing it in any more detail, the unlikely chain of events that has brought us here. He tastes like wine and cigarettes. I could slow things down right now, just like this, with the taste of ashtray on my tongue. But I want him. And also, once I commit to a project, I like to see it through.

His body is solid underneath mine; we fit together, Declan and I, two warm, breathing mammals, arms to arms, chest to chest. We kiss some more and roll around on the bed, and after a while I feel I should let it be known that I'm enjoying myself. So I let out a soft moan and then, just in case he hasn't heard, a much louder one.

Declan stops what he's doing, which is something strange to my belly button. "Are you all right?"

"Absolutely!" I say. The word strikes me, suddenly, as the unsexiest word in the English language. *Absolutely!* It's a word for motivational speakers and preschool teachers. *Can my four-step confidence-boosting program change your life overnight? Absolutely! Boys and girls, these are absolutely the best hand-turkeys I've ever seen!* I laugh a little, then cover it with more ambiguous moaning. I sound like a dying lamb or a seal reuniting with an old pal.

A few weeks ago, Jane sent me an e-mail (she was in her bedroom and I was in mine). *Can you teach me how to talk dirty?* she wrote.

Mud! I wrote back. *Motor oil!*

Seriously.

Why do you think I know? I typed.

You have more experience than I do. You're more slutty.

Let's roll around in a pile of sewage, baby.

Seriously, she wrote again. *I would like to know what it entails.*

Entrails! I wrote back.

Jillian said you're supposed to, like, describe what you want. Jillian was a girl we knew in college who worked part-time at Hooters. She had a worldly quality about her. *Like, "Take me from behind," or whatever.*

This was the point in the e-mail exchange when I started

screaming, and then Jane and I convened in the kitchen and tore into a bag of chocolate chips. For the rest of the night, one of us would say, "Take me from behind, or whatever," and we would double over, laughing, the mysteries of talking dirty unsolved.

But here in bed with Declan, our bodies smashing together like a sandwich, alternating layers of desire and embarrassment, I'm wondering if maybe guys *do* find it incredibly hot, *Take me from behind, or whatever,* the "or whatever" tacked on not as an admission of cluelessness, but as an invitation to unimaginable kinkiness.

Declan whispers something that I don't quite catch. I remind myself that I want to be here with him; I've wanted it for three years. I think about Jane and Ben and wonder where they are. Declan shifts his attention from my belly button to my right knee.

I take a deep breath. "That drives me crazy!" I say.

He stops, looks up at me, his eyes squinty and intent. "Oh! Sorry!"

"No, no! In a good way." I pat his head, and then immediately regret it.

He nods and returns with great focus to my leg, his fingers stroking and squeezing, a lusty orthopedist. I lean back and consider the night we've had—how, since Marcy, Ben and Jane have begun to seem to me a single, warped entity, a creature at odds with itself. Ben and Jane. I want them to know something, to understand . . . I'm not sure what. I take a deep breath. "Oh, that's so good!" I say, like I'm calling to someone in another room, as if I'm eating a hot-fudge sundae someone made for me in the kitchen. "Yes! Yes!" I sit up and pull Declan toward me; he's on his knees, smiling and familiar. I have a twinge of guilt for this mild subterfuge, but it's all in the service of a greater good. "Yes!" I say again, and then the thesaurus in my mind slams shut, and I resign myself to more moaning.

And then, and then, he pulls me on top of him again, his arms around me, our rhythm improving, and suddenly I'm deep in it, in the sweetness of another body; it all takes a turn for the better, like a movie that gets off to a slow start but picks up toward the middle, and all the awkwardness that came before was just an unimportant prelude to this: the two of us. Lost. Absolutely.

And so. Here we are, resting together in the graveyard of my dignity. Declan is naked from the waist down, his long toes curling off the edge of the mattress; from the waist up, he's wearing a white T-shirt, a big black wristwatch, and a pie-eating grin. My purple sheet and green down comforter lie like wrapping paper on the floor.

"You are . . . surprisingly expressive, Willa," he says. He shakes his head, smiling, runs one hand up and down his stubbly face, and pulls me close. I nestle into the soft cotton of his shirt, breathe in the musky smell of him: lavender-scented laundry detergent and sex.

"So tired," I mumble, which would be true if the prickliness rising from my spine to my neck were the woozy hum of fatigue instead of the hot cringe of embarrassment. I squeeze my eyes shut.

"Mmm," he says. "Me fluhhh."

I wait awhile, silent and still, listening to the shallow whisper of his breathing. It grows slower and more even, and it doesn't take long before it's safe for me to lift his heavy arm from my body and roll away. I sit up and swing my legs off the edge of the bed, tap my heels gently against the mattress, and examine my hands, disembodied and ghostly in the whitish moon glow of the room. I glance over at Declan. His mouth hangs open slightly; everything about him is long and pale and slack. He looks more like he's switched off than asleep now, except for his penis, odd little accessory, friendly lapdog curled in repose. *You're welcome.* In the half-light, it winks at me.

I grab my robe from the back of the door, wrap it around myself, and sneak out of my own bedroom. The worn fleece is velvety against my body; being touched exposes nerve endings, and my skin feels like it's softly humming. I tiptoe through the hallway, on my way to the kitchen for water, but the flickering blue light of the television stops me in my tracks. I place my palm against the wall to steady myself. The rush of adrenaline feels as much like horror as delight.

"Well, well, well."

"I'm sleepwalking," I whisper. "Never wake a sleepwalker."

"That didn't sound like sleeping to me, toots." Ben points the remote at the TV; the blue light goes black, and for a second I feel like I might, in fact, be sleepwalking, dreaming about being naked in the hallway of my high school, and there's Ben, short, chubby, fifteen-year-old Ben, witness to my humiliation. "Sit down, luv," he says, doing a credible imitation of Declan. I make my way to the couch.

"What are you doing up?" I say.

Ben snorts. I hear, but can't see, him scratching his head, a sound like mice scrabbling through drywall. "Don't change the subject." He leans over and clicks on the lamp. "That was quite the commotion."

Like the heat wave, I feel myself shift without warning, become melancholy and regretful. "Don't tease, okay?"

"I like Declan," Ben says.

"Good."

He plops his feet onto the coffee table with a thump. "Not as much as you do, obviously." It's almost unbearably intimate, being here with Ben, naked under my robe, postsex, so near to the warm, sleeping bodies of Declan and Jane, Ben's long, hairy legs stretched out in front of us. "Sorry," he says. "Couldn't resist."

"Okay," I say. "But stop. I mean it."

He pulls a bag of potato chips out from behind the couch, offers me one. I shake my head, lean back. The rickety chair I'm sitting in wobbles and creaks. We're just playing at being adults here, in this apartment furnished by Ikea and the curb. I pat down my bed-hair. Ben flicks the TV back on, and for a while we watch a rebroadcast of the local news. The reporter has a Wisconsin accent so powerful it sounds like she might actually be speaking German. "Oh, *ja*," she says to the weatherman. "That break in the heat today sure felt *fein*."

"You know what I love?" Ben says.

"Hmm?"

"Those teasers they do before the commercials. *Will tonight's rain bring massive flooding to the area?*"

"*Is the carpeting in your home trying to kill you? Stay tuned!*"

"*Is there a mass murderer on the loose in your neighborhood? We'll let you know after the break!*"

"*Should you lock your doors and windows right now? We'll tell you, after sports.*" The plastic chip bag crackles. "Actually, I'll have one," I say, reaching for it.

Ben hands me the bag. "*Are those chips you're eating deadly? Find out, after traffic and weather!*"

"They are stale," I say, crunching. "But probably not lethal."

Ben grabs the bag back from me. "I like Declan," he says again.

I raise my eyebrows at him. "You know, I'm pretty sure he likes girls."

He throws a chip at me. It lands in my hair. I eat it.

"It's just, he seems like a good guy," he says.

"Yep." I think about Declan's hands on my waist, how they

hovered there lightly, and a little shiver runs up my spine. It's the ghost of women everywhere, reminding me that sex does not equal love. "He is. He's a good guy."

Ben scratches his head again, rearranges his legs on the coffee table, cracks his neck: a game of charades, and the word is "fidgety." "When I liked you in high school," he says, "it wasn't just a crush." My brain explodes, splattering the walls with goo. Ben scratches his ear, cracks his knuckles, crosses his arms. *One word, three syllables.* "I mean, I feel like I can tell you this now, now that I have someone and you . . ." He stops himself, grins at me. "Well, you *had* someone." He holds out his hand before I can jump in. "Sorry, sorry! Anyway, it seems silly," Ben continues, "with all that's happened since then, but I really thought I was in love with you. I saw us together. Married, kids. The whole package."

I'm glad for the dim light, for the bag of potato chips, for the TV on softly in the background. "You and Jane are my best friends," I say.

"Well, exactly."

Neither of us says anything else. After a while, I start to feel my customary urge to cure an awkward moment with a balm of weirdness. I stuff a huge handful of chips in my mouth, fill my cheeks like a salt-addicted squirrel, chew slowly, swallow. Ben shakes his head and laughs. I'm imagining, again, my life ten years from now; we're in the backyard of that small white house, Ben and Jane and *someone* and me, and those happy, romping, low-maintenance background children . . . only this time the someone belongs to Jane, and it's Ben with his arm around my shoulder, Ben's dream and mine coming together in a strange, bright, impossible collision.

"I've gotta go to sleep," I murmur finally, muddled and exhausted, pushing myself up and out of the half-broken chair.

Ben yawns and gets up. We're almost the same height, inches from each other. His face is stubbly, his gray T-shirt inside-out.

"One more thing," he says. "As long as I'm on a roll. I'm not going to ask you what happened in Marcy. Because I've decided that it doesn't matter." I'm wishing for another mouthful of potato chips as Ben clicks off the light, mercy-killing the conversation. "So good night."

"'Night," I whisper, retying my robe and turning back toward my room.

Declan opens his eyes as I climb into bed. "I thought you'd gone home," he mutters, and he rolls onto his side, his back to me, as, in the silence, I think about what Ben said, that what happened in Marcy isn't important. And I am drifting off to sleep, wondering why.

chapter eighteen

"Does anyone really know how to pick out a cantaloupe?" Ben lifts a leathery melon, strokes it gently, brings it to his face. "Are you ripe?" he whispers.

Jane pushes her sunglasses up onto her head and squints as the cloud that was obscuring the sun blows away. "They are the most inscrutable of fruits." She presses her sunglasses back down onto her nose. We're wandering around the farmers' market, past stands of Swiss chard and kale, snap peas and sunshine squash, okra and chutney: locally grown ingredients for recipes none of us will make. We move forward empty-handed, en masse, the four of us, toward a stall that sells only tomatoes, neatly arranged baskets of small yellow and orange and purple orbs bright and jolly as Christmas ornaments. As if any of us would have a clue what to do with a tiny, purple, veined tomato, what kind of complicated pasta dish would welcome such a thing. In fact, I pride myself on not knowing.

Declan taps his index finger on an oblong orange heirloom. "Where I come from, tomatoes are pink and swollen and tasteless, and served on a bed of iceberg lettuce." *To-mah-toes.* "I miss the old sod."

"The Irish are famous for their fine cuisine," I say.

Declan nods. "Accept no substitutes." I pretend that he's talking about us and reach for his hand. I notice Ben noticing, then quickly looking away. "We used to eat cabbage at every meal," Declan says, directing the statement at all of us, like a stand-up comedian. "Breakfast, lunch, and dinner, plus of course the three o'clock cabbage break." I have the sudden urge to draw Declan as a talking vegetable, round and green and leafy.

It's been three weeks since we first slept together, and I'm teetering on the brink of something, a shift in perception, a significant revelation. Could I be falling for Declan? My heart is running after my body, panting, trying to catch up. Our connection seems to be rearranging my chemical balance. I find myself thinking about him all the time, drifting off into gauzy fantasies about our future.

A sweet, fruit-scented breeze kicks up. A family pushes past us on the path, two disheveled parents—an unshaven father and a mother who looks strangely unshaven herself, blurry around the edges—and three children dancing around them, chanting a chorus of "I want, I want."

"Sebastian," the mother says, "I am not buying you broccoli right now. If I have to tell you again, I'm taking away that cookie." I look around to see if anyone else has heard. Jane and Ben and Declan are a moving triangle in front of me, absorbed in a conversation about a particular Irish delicacy made of pork sausage and boiled potatoes.

"I'll tell you about fish pie," Declan says. "And blood pudding!" Jane cringes; Ben laughs.

How easy would it be just to subsume myself to this, to Declan's big personality, to his hunger? Maybe part of desire is just knowing that you're desired. How enticing to give myself over to the idea of love.

"Blood pudding!" I say. "A dessert and a bodily fluid, all rolled into one!" Declan shakes his head and starts to tell me that blood pudding is not a dessert, but I wave him away.

Jane takes her glasses off, twirls them around her fingers, then fixes them on top of her head. She falls back with me, the walking triangle morphing into a square. Looking at her, I see, for a second, only the ways that we don't resemble each other at all. She's glowing and clear skinned, her hair loose to her shoulders, her eyes wide and brown. And it's true, my hair is loose and to my shoulders, my eyes wide and brown, but I feel furrowed in a way that Jane isn't, crimped, blemished, flawed.

"Wouldn't it be great if you could just Google your future?" she says. I twist my hair up into a bun and then let it fall back, the coiled strands tickling my neck. "You would type in *Where will I be in ten years?* and the Internet would tell you."

"Psychic Google!" I say.

"I had a job interview," Ben says, half turning toward us, "before I started working at the library." He takes a bite of the chocolate croissant he just bought and offers a piece of it to Jane. "For Citizens Rallying Against Pollution. And the director said, 'Where do you see yourself five years from now?' and I said, 'In my living room, eating a bowl of spaghetti in front of the TV.' I did not get the job."

"I would have hired you, mate."

"Thanks, mate."

Ben is getting ready to apply to graduate school for social work, here and in Chicago and Madison. He may not know exactly where he's going, but at least he's picked a general direction.

"Ben," I say. "There is no such organization as Citizens Rallying Against Pollution."

He grins, waiting.

"Oh! CRAP!" Jane says gleefully, clapping her hands. She takes her sunglasses off again, even though the sun-to-cloud ratio hasn't changed. For no good reason, this irritates me.

I grab her wrist and snatch the sunglasses from her. "Jane!" My voice comes out snappish and scolding. "Make up your mind about those glasses!" Ben, Declan, and Jane all stop suddenly and stare at me. Ben's mouth drops open slightly; my cheeks go hot. I shove Jane's glasses onto my face. "Well, you've proven that you can't handle the important responsibility of sunglasses," I say lightly, trying to cover for myself.

After a second, Jane laughs, a high musical sound, like a chime: her immediate forgiveness, unpondered and lovely.

"Right," she says. "I can't be trusted!" And now those sunglasses are riding heavily on the bridge of my nose, the frames slightly too big for me and the lenses, as it turns out, an annoying shade too dark. I suppress the urge to take them off.

We wander for a bit and then pause at the artisanal cheese booth. We huddle around it, piercing our selections with toothpicks: Mango Gruyère. Sicilian truffle.

"You all worry too much," Declan says. He pauses to chew. "Things have a way of working themselves out."

"Easy for you to say." I shake a hunk of apricot Gorgonzola at him. "You owned your own company when you were twenty-four."

"Which has now officially gone belly-up," he says, popping another lump of Tuscany cave-aged pecorino into his mouth. It's just like Declan to turn a momentous announcement into an offhand remark spoken through a mouthful of cheese. Although it's true that my freelance assignments had petered out, he's never mentioned that the agency was going under. He shrugs, preempting concern. "What can you do? I'm not bothered. Especially now that I know I can get free brunch on Saturday mornings." He skewers three more hunks of cheese on his toothpick like a shish kebab as the cheese lady behind the makeshift counter plants her hands on her hips and glares at him. He's clearly gone one cube too far.

Nobody knows what to say. We've never owned our own failed advertising agencies; we've never lost our livelihoods. We've never had livelihoods. So we stand there, ruminating like cows, as herds of people trudge past us, until Jane finally slings her arm around Declan. "Come on. Poor thing. I'll buy you a loaf of stale bread, and we'll see if we can find you a nice bowl of gruel."

They lope off together, Declan and Jane, and Ben turns to me. "He's one of us now."

"Holy Citizens Rallying Against Pollution," I say.

"Yeah."

"Is it weird that he didn't tell me?"

"I suppose so." Ben puts his hand on my back and leads me to a bench off to the side of the crowded square. He sits, pats the seat for me to join him. "Want to know something else weird?" A ball of Camembert congeals in my stomach and threatens to bounce. *No,* I think. *No no no.* I suddenly and completely do not want to know something else weird. I don't want to hear what Ben has to say. I don't even want to sit down next to him, in the proximity of something else weird, but he takes my hand and pulls me down onto the bench. "I'm thinking about asking Jane to marry me."

On the patch of grass in front of us, six small children run after each other like a dog chasing its tail. A soft lake breeze blows in, carrying the faintest whiff of something rank, dead fish or the septic-tinged odor of *Cladophora algae,* reminders that Lake Michigan is a living, belching organism. One of the toddlers on the grass splinters off from the game and runs toward his mother, flings his arms around her neck, and kisses her; she closes her eyes and sniffs his hair with such naked pleasure that I turn away.

I want to say something to Ben, I'm not sure what: *Mazel tov*?

Or *WAIT!* Okay, yes, *WAIT!* because all at once I see it, as clear as the peeling paint on the bench we're sitting on: This is the time in our lives when mistakes are made. And not just *What a bummer it would be to end up at the wrong college* or *Should I pass on that interesting volunteer opportunity,* but the big mistakes, the ones where you say yes and you walk down the aisle and you become my parents or Jane's. Or Ben's, who have been happily married but pleasantly distant from each other for thirty years, the kind of parents who take separate vacations. But none of this seems like the right response to my best friend telling me he's going to ask my other best friend to marry him. I edge toward him and lean in, throw my arm around his shoulder in a quick hug. "I call best man *and* maid of honor."

A little blond boy twenty feet from us screeches suddenly, and then they're all screeching, like an air-raid siren. "You don't get to call it, Willa," Ben says, over the din. He squeezes back. "It's not like shotgun."

"Too late," I say. "I already called it." I rest my head on his shoulder for a second, move away.

And then, on this perfect summer day, clouds skittering around the sky, children testing their lungs across the grass, we just sit for a while, next to each other, quietly, waiting for Jane and Declan to reappear. Ben reaches into the white paper bag and feeds me a piece of his croissant; with the back of his hand, I wipe crumbs from my mouth. I close my eyes to the shrill whistle of the children and to the image of Jane in a wedding dress and to my own psychic vertigo, a lurching befuddlement of emotions. Maybe this dizzy feeling is just my heart, adjusting to a new reality. Or maybe it's the mad, contagious confusion of those toddlers on the grass in front of us, spinning wildly before they fall.

· · ·

The next morning. My bed. A fleeting feeling, too vague to pin down. Something, somewhere, has shifted.

A trapezoid of light peeks through the blinds, captures the dust in the air, and makes it beautiful. I hear my own breathing, slow and deep; my eyes blur and focus against the day. Up close, a loose purple thread pulls away from the quilt. My elbow itches. The pillow is smooth against my cheek.

Someone is next to me, a lump under the covers, broad back, rumpled head of brown hair. A vague *yes* moves through me; I like this brown-haired lump. It mutters, moves.

If I could stay like this I would, in these pleasantly muddy seconds when I haven't figured it out yet, when I'm not yet the sum of my parts. But even while I'm thinking it, it's coming back to me: I'm piecing together who I am even as I'm trying to keep myself at bay. My room, my bed, Declan, me. Don't think about elephants! It's too late. I run my tongue across my fuzzy teeth, find a cool spot on my pillow. Declan will turn over, say good morning, say good-bye; I'll eat breakfast with Ben and Jane and go to work. Oh, but if I could, I would live in that other, newborn space for hours, fearless and observing. Because before I'm myself, I'm not the Willa I am: desperate, hungry, plumbing the depths of my own treacherous psyche and capable of unpleasant surprises. In that blissful, disoriented blankness, I could be anyone.

I move through the next few days like a stunt double of myself. There is a proposal, an acceptance, a celebration. We all go out for dinner and splurge on wine. I drink a little bit too much and let my giddiness stand in for genuine happiness.

I make them a card, a sketch of Ben and Jane holding hands on a sun-dappled beach, beaming, only instead of writing *Congratulations!* on the inside, I write *You're welcome!* and when they open it, they both look at me confused, like I am their strange, special little niece. I bake them a batch of celebratory chocolate chip cookies, but I forget to put in the sugar. I'm off-kilter, myself and not-myself, a simulacrum Willa with no other options than to act normal. I have the vague sense that this is life: the long, slow, doomed attempt to become the person you're trying to be.

At the kitchen table one afternoon, I make a list of new names for myself. Could I possibly be a Maude? An April? A Debbie? Change your name, change your life. I want to do something both radical and risk-free, but nothing comes to mind. I consider a tattoo, but I'm afraid of needles, as well as alcohol, pain, and strangers with tattoos.

I decide, finally, to chop off my hair. But then Jane reminds me that my head is a funny shape. "Tell you what, conehead," she says, raising her hand protectively to her own hair. "I'll give you a haircut. Just a couple of inches. That's something, but it's not everything. And it's free. And if you don't like it, Debbie, you can schedule an appointment and get it all hacked off. You have nothing to lose!"

How can I argue with "nothing to lose"?

Jane drapes a towel around my shoulders and spritzes my hair with water, running her fingers through the curls. "So, doll," she says, snapping her pretend gum. "Ya interested in a permanent wave today?"

"Bouffant," I say. "Lots of Aqua Net." We're quiet for a minute. Jane tugs gently. If hair is made up of dead cells, then your scalp is a graveyard. "So," I say, a chatty lady in a beauty shop, casual as anything, "are you thinking about the actual wedding yet?"

She tries to pull a wide-toothed comb through my hair, but it gets caught halfway down. "All I know is I want something very, very fancy, obscenely expensive. Perhaps a destination wedding."

"Jamaica," I say, "and eight hundred of your closest friends?"

"Hawaii, and nine hundred."

"With an ice sculpture and seventeen bridesmaids."

"An ice sculpture *of* seventeen bridesmaids." She gives up on the comb, kneels down in front of me, and stares intently, first at one side of my head, then the other, pulling hunks of my hair straight. I can smell her, minty breath and apple-perfumed shampoo and, underneath that, an unmistakably Jane-ish scent, two parts carrot cake, one part wood chips. She slips a hand under my chin and tilts my head up. "I'm going to take a good two inches off," she says.

"A good two inches." I try to nod, but her hand holds my head still. "Okay," I say, "and after the marriage vows are spoken, one hundred white doves will be released."

"And then after that," she says, "one hundred colorful balloons."

"Pieces of which will get caught in the throats of the hungry doves, who will then, tragically, come plummeting to the earth."

"Ah, perfect." Jane straightens and walks slowly around me, like a bride circling her groom at a Jewish wedding. I would mention this to her, but sometimes it's just too much effort, trying to explain these things to Jane Elizabeth Weston from Marcy, Wisconsin, whose parents never thought twice about her initials.

"The bride wore tulle," I say instead.

"The bride *was* a tool." She starts snipping. I close my eyes to the slicing sound of it, surrendering to Jane's warm nearness, her knuckles occasionally brushing my cheeks, my ears.

"The dress was hand-beaded by tiny fairies," I say. My eyes are still closed.

"The groom rode in on an elephant."

"Shrimp!"

"The groom rode in on a shrimp?"

"No. For dinner. Nothing says classy like shrimp cocktail at a wedding."

"Ben hates shrimp," Jane says.

"No, he doesn't."

"But he does." She's behind me now, clipping away, and then tugging the hair straight to check for accuracy. "Whoops!"

"Whoops?" She's silent. "Whoops?"

"Nope, it's okay. I fixed it!"

I shrug. This is the secret of curly hair: you can't really mess it up. "I've known Ben a lot longer than you have," I say. "I think I'd know if he hated shrimp."

"He loathes them. He can't stand their pink, veiny, curled-up bodies." Snip. Tug. "Says they remind him of maggots."

"Wow. I find this very hard to believe. Maybe you're confusing Ben with someone else who hates shrimp." *Dougie*, I think. *Maybe Dougie hates shrimp.*

She's quiet for a while. I crane my neck. She's behind me, motionless, scissors poised above my head. "You have."

"I have what?"

"You've known him longer. But I know that he doesn't like shrimp." She walks around me again, her bare feet softly slapping the floor, then squats down in front of me, close. She has a freckle just above her lip, a tiny smudge of mascara underneath her right eye.

"In lieu of gifts," I say, "the bride and groom request donations to the Anti-Crustacean-Defamation League."

She cups my chin again, her fingers cool, her face so close her humid breath moistens my cheek. "Damn," she whispers. "I'm sorry. I really should have put in my contact lenses before I did this." She tilts her head and squints. "Kidding! It looks great." She brushes off my neck, my shoulders. Curls of hair carpet the kitchen floor like tiny crescent moons—like shrimp!

I will help them plan their wedding. *We wouldn't be here without Willa. She brought us together!* I will wear a pretty dress. I will toast

their happy union, their joyful years. My rotten heart thuds a protest. I can't meet her eyes. What about me? I take a deep breath
through my nose. *What about me?* Jane is staring hard, scrutiniz-
ing, and suddenly I'm about to implode from it, from the pressure
of the closeness; you can tolerate a thing for a long time before
it reveals itself to be fatal, and it's been fatal all along. Jane rocks
back on her heels. "All done." She licks her lips, smiles. "You, my
friend, are ready for your close-up."

chapter nineteen

A few days later, Seth calls. There is a loud whooshing noise in the background. It sounds like he's standing on the shoulder of a highway or inside a washing machine. "So guess what, little sister? Mom's coming!" His phone cuts in and out. *Ssswhat, ister? Mom's ing!*

"That's hilarious," I say. "You're hilarious." Seth and I manage our relationship, or lack of relationship, with Fran and Stan by visiting them just once a year, at Thanksgiving—first Mom and Jerry in the morning, for the traditional Thanksgiving bagel brunch, then Dad and Tan Lesley for dinner. Conveniently, although my parents haven't spoken in five years, they live within ten minutes of each other, in adjacent gated communities with abutting golf courses. Once, my mom said, she thought she saw Lesley from the sixth hole and waved; it turned out to be a small dead tree.

"It's not a joke. She's worried about you." *Not a oke. rried about you.* He pauses. "Okay, she's worried about me. She's coming to help me move into the new apartment."

"Oh, Seth."

"Oh, Willa."

. . .

"Oh, kids!" A week later Fran sits in the rickety folding chair in Seth's kitchen, which makes it, I guess, the kitchen chair.

When I left my apartment this morning, Jane and Ben were sitting in the kitchen, filling out "Save the Date" cards. *Save the date! Save the date!*—the wildest and most elusive of the endangered tree fruits. The pile of cards grew into a stack on the table as they worked.

Fran takes a sip from her Styrofoam cup of tea and waves her hand toward us. "That couch needs to be moved back three inches toward the wall, and then to the left about, oh, five feet, and then out the door and into the Dumpster." She chuckles at her own joke. "It's *disgusting*!"

It really is: it's yellow, but a mustardy sort of shade that looks like it started out as something closer to ketchup on the color wheel, and threadbare in a way that makes you think of butts.

"Where did you get it, Sethie?" she asks. "Not from your old place. Nina would never have . . ." She shakes her head. "Oh, sweetie, I'm sorry." She shifts her attention back to the apartment and rearranges her expression. "Let's hit some yard sales tomorrow," she says. "See if we can't scare you up a nicer sofa."

Mom loved Nina. Just like I did, she loved what Nina did for Seth, how she softened him, settled him, smoothed his rough edges. His squalid new life seems to be causing her physical pain—which is having the fun-house mirror effect of distorting Seth's own emotions. In the face of her overwhelming sympathy, my brother is confused and defensive. He swipes a sleeve across his sweaty forehead, glances around his grimy new apartment, and lets out a little sigh. He peers down at his couch, personal failure in the form of a sofa, then looks at me like a trapped bunny. I recognize that look, and the sorry lift of his shoulders, as the secret language of two people who survived the same childhood:

it's a last-ditch apology, preemptive but meaningless, for how he's about to hang me out to dry. "Hey, Mom! Godzwilla has something to tell you. She has a new boyfriend!"

In the bathroom, just five minutes ago, as we were rummaging through a box full of towels and, oddly, canned soup, I asked Seth not to say anything about Declan. "You know how she is," I whispered, appealing to my brother's empathy, that underused muscle. "You know how she'll be." She'd be overly invested in my personal life, I meant; she'd manage to be both eager and concerned in the same breath. It's her talent, forged in the fires of her crappy marriage. When I was in seventh grade, she used to sit down with me after school, pass me a plate of celery and peanut butter, and fix her maternal gaze on my face. "Was anyone *not nice* to you today?" she would ask, her eyes boring into mine. "Did any of your girlfriends behave badly toward you? Because I will call their parents if you want me to."

Now, she claps her hands in glee and scowls at me simultaneously. "A boyfriend!" she says. "Is he someone special? Is he *one of the ones*?" I sense that divorce and remarriage have made her flexible, in a strange way.

I smile at Seth and pick up the scissors we've been using to slice the packing tape on his cardboard boxes, brandish it at him and then stab a hole in the seam of a box labeled PLATES, CUPS, SHOES, TWIZZLERS. *All right*, I think, trying to rally. *This is not so bad.* I hadn't planned on collapsing these two particular emotional tent poles, but what the hell. I'll introduce my irreverent, used-to-be-my-boss, dumped-me-three-years-ago-for-another-girl Irish boyfriend to my mom. So what if he interprets it as a move toward serious-relationship status and runs for the hills? So what? Why not? I'll do it! Yes!

"Uh, *no*!" I say. "I do not have a boyfriend. Seth! What a weird thing to say!"

Seth mouths *Sorry*. He lifts his shirt to rub his pale, hairy, newly chubby belly.

"Why are you still single?" I say.

"If you have a beau," my mom says, "I would like to meet him."

I fold back the box flaps and start pulling out badly wrapped, mismatched plates and bags of red licorice. "Seth, seeing as all the furniture belonged to Nina, why don't we just keep a few of these boxes so you can turn them over and use them as cute, portable end tables. Martha Stewart Living in Squalor!"

"We could go to Will's apartment right now," Seth says. He squats down next to BATHROOM & CANDLESTICKS & SOME SOCKS, rips the tape off with a *phhhlrrtt*. "See if he's there."

"And, hey, maybe Mom has an old coat in storage," I say, "that you could use for a bedspread. It's a *good thing*!" I wave air quotes at him.

"Oh, and your roommate's probably there, too, with her fiancé, right? We can say hello to them, see how they're doing, your roommate and her fiancé."

"Because Nina kept the bedspread, right? Along with the sheets and the pillows and the bed? When she kicked you out?"

Seth gives me the finger, and I think, *We've gone too far*; and I think, *Why do we even pretend to be friends?* And then he laughs.

"Kids," Fran says. She takes another sip of tea. "Why don't we get out of this apartment, hop in my car, and hit those rummage sales right now?"

Fran's shiny silver rental car smells like secondhand smoke, which probably comes with the contract: choose a midsize sedan for its extra legroom and the lingering odor of tobacco.

"I never cared for Milwaukee," Mom says, honking at the car

in front of us as it sits at the green light, unmoving. "Scene of the crime."

"Scene of our childhood, too," I say from the backseat, surprisingly offended. "Scene of that time when we were little and we tried to make you a birthday cake out of pancake mix and you pretended you loved it. Scene of your daughter winning the regional spelling bee when she was in fifth grade. Scene of practically our entire lives." I pull on the seat belt's shoulder strap, which is digging into my neck.

"You're so sensitive, honey." My parents moved from Chicago to Milwaukee in the seventies for my father's job, just after they got married: ninety-two miles, but a continent of culture shock for my mother and, apparently, light-years of regret. "I love you and Seth, I just don't like this one-horse town." She lays on the horn again as the old lady in the car in front of us, her gray head barely visible above the seat back, finally guns it through the light just as it turns yellow.

"The feelings associated with a place can become an emotional crutch," Seth says, "a habit that, sometimes, can only be broken by physically moving away. Paralysis can come in many forms."

"The self-help section at Barnes and Noble is still working for you," I say. Seth nods.

"Look!" Fran says. "A sale!" We've been cruising up and down Lake Drive and its side streets, trawling the city's tony east side for good rummage sales, most of which have closed down for the day. But one or two football field–sized front lawns are still strewn with the flotsam of the wealthy—last year's chrome-and-steel espresso machines; racks of brightly colored Ingrid Södersstrøm children's clothes; once-pricey, roughed-up Woodley end tables; and Ashford and Holt chairs in need of reupholstering. My mother is the queen of spotting diamonds in the rough. (Jerry, she likes to tell us, had a comb-over when she met him and was wearing Transitions lenses.) She'll end up in the headlines someday for buying that funny-looking, paint-splattered canvas that had been stashed for sixty years in someone's garage. *(Gosh, we didn't know Grandma's old friend Jackson was famous!)*

Now, she swings a left turn from the right lane and pulls onto Kenwood. "I see a love seat," she says, peering out the window. "Looks spendy. Let's see if we can't Lutheran them down." Fran wasn't kidding about not liking it here, and she's sharpened her blade since the last time I saw her.

Seth gets out of the car slowly. A cloud of melancholy and regret has been hanging over him for months now as he's been embarking on this crummy new chapter of his life. It's so heavy I can practically see it, can almost smell it. In fact, if melancholy and regret smell like hummus and a sweaty T-shirt and some kind of unfortunate masculine body spray, I *can* smell it. He slouches against the car. "Great," he says, his voice vaulting toward cynicism but landing on surrender. "A love seat."

Our mother is already furiously negotiating by the time Seth and I make our way over to her; we stand back and elbow each other, let her do her thing. "I understand that this piece has been well maintained," she says to a woman in a linen pantsuit, "but I also see a small rip in the fabric here and several scratches near the base. I'll give you two hundred dollars for it." She plants her hands on her hips and waits for the inevitable nod.

The expansive lawn is crowded with bargain hunters. A pregnant lady is lugging a high chair to her waiting minivan, leaving a long trail in the grass: the tracks of the nesting human in her native habitat. A little way across the lawn, a couple examines a table stacked with china and kitchenware. I notice the woman with her back to us, her red hair twisted up in a messy, pretty ponytail, her small frame in a flowy green sundress. Thin, freckled arms; canvas sneakers. And then I register who she is. The man she's with is tall, dark haired, in a crisp purple shirt and jeans that say *I'm a young lawyer and it's the weekend*. They're leaning into each other, his arm around her resting just above her hip. I gasp before my brain catches up with itself, before I can tamp down my surprise, and I hop in front of Seth, trying to position myself in his sight line. "Bamboo!" I yelp, heaving an umbrella stand up toward my brother. "Look, Seth, it's *bamboo!*"

Sure as I'm not actually a connoisseur of home furnishings and gardenware, Seth can tell something's up. He taps my shoulder, shoves me gently to the side. "Oh, shit," he says, craning his neck, as Nina's companion—boyfriend, obviously—turns to her and whispers something in her ear. "Shit. I need to leave. Tell Mom we need to leave. We need to leave right now. I need to get out of here."

Fran walks toward us with a triumphant smile, high stepping across the long grass in her pink espadrilles. "Mission accomplished!" she says, tipping an imaginary hat at us. Sometimes that's all it takes: a new expression or funny little quirk to remind me that, emotionally, Fran checked out of our lives ten years ago. And, sure, I've spent plenty of time with her since then. But in the deep and fundamental way daughters are supposed to know their mothers, I hardly know mine. And then I feel it all over again. The loss of it.

"Mom," I say. Seth is standing still next to me, staring straight ahead. A giant wasp buzzes past, close to his face; he doesn't flinch. "Great job on the love seat. We'll come back for it later. Let's go."

She shakes her head. "But I'm just getting started!"

"Nina's here," Seth says, his voice a dull, defeated monotone.

Fran lifts her face, pricks up her ears like a hungry cat who's just heard the whir of the can opener. Our mother wants so much for Seth and me to be happy, to find our footing where she lost hers. But to her, our happiness is a home improvement project, only she's never had the right tools for it. Before either of us can stop her, she's beelining over to a table stacked with small appliances, toward the petite redhead with the boyfriend at her side and, now, the blender cradled in her arms. Seth slumps even slouchier and covers his eyes with his hands.

"Nina!" Fran calls.

"Oh, crap," Seth mutters. "Oh, Christ."

I jog over to Fran, my sneakers smacking the grass, the thighs of my cotton shorts shooshing. "Mom! Fran! Mom!" I call again, louder, outrage bubbling up in my voice: *"Mother!"*

And then, just then, Fran stops short, a few feet from Nina, tiny redheaded rummage sale shopper who has finally turned to us, who has pivoted, still holding on to her handsome man, and now he turns his body to us, too, both of them curious, anxious to see what all the commotion is about, Nina's wide face a question, *Who are these people, Josh? Oh, Brad, honey, what are they doing, what do they want? Tim, why is the older one calling me Nina,* and my mother puts out her hand to stop herself and she shakes her head, "I'm sorry, I'm so sorry," because, good God it's not, thank heavens it's not, it's not Nina after all.

And then, with a swiftness of purpose and a clarity of mind that will shock me later, I hustle us all out of there, away from the rummage sale of quality furniture and mistaken identity and over to Braun's Bagels and Lunch, home of the worst deli food in the Great Lakes region, and the place that Seth and I have referred to, for as long as I can remember, as Eva Braun's Bagels.

We make our way with our food to a small round table in the corner of the empty restaurant. Seth chomps down on a big, pale, puffy bagel—more of a bread doughnut, really, than a bagel.

"Oh, Sethie," Fran says, squeezing a tube of dressing onto her salad. "I just wish I could fix this for you."

"We are the masters of our own destinies," he says, chewing and nodding, and I can't figure out why he's not more annoyed with Fran, why he's suddenly cheerfully spouting his personal-improvement aphorisms. Maybe it's the carbs, lulling him into submission.

"I can't eat this," I say, gnawing on a doorstop slathered with strawberry cream cheese—inexplicably, the only kind they have. Eva Braun's Bagels is where we used to come for lunch on the weekends, the three of us, after Stan left, and so it holds a certain place in our hearts, a room in the house of our collective memories—if not the cozy living room of nostalgia, then maybe the foyer of endurance.

Fran nibbles on a wilted piece of lettuce and nods. "Your father told me just the other day that he misses this place. Unbelievable!"

"Just the other day," Seth says. "Good one!"

"Right!" I slide my bagel over to Seth, who begins to demolish it. As far as I know, our parents haven't spoken in years.

Fran looks at us. "Well, isn't it funny the way things work out, but Jerry and I have gone out for dinner a few times recently with your father and Lesley." She dabs at her pink lips with a napkin and nods to herself. "I really like that Lesley."

This is the part in the movie where the main character—restless, drifting, sensitive girl trying to find herself, a coming-of-age story for our time!—does a double take and spits out her water all over her mother. Unfortunately, the only thing in my mouth is the aftertaste of strawberry cream cheese.

Our mother locked herself in her darkened room and didn't get out of bed for three months after the divorce. For six months after that, she didn't go grocery shopping, cook dinner, pick me up after school, or drive me to my piano lessons. So I made my own way. The day before I left for college, a FOR SALE sign freshly planted in the lawn in front of our house, my mother looked me up and down, patted my head, told me that I needed a haircut and never to get married. She is the source of my primal knowledge: that the death of love is a small black hole that sucks your soul right out of you. I narrow my eyes at her.

"Your hair looks nice," she says. "It could use a trim."

"This is . . . fucking crazy," Seth says, laughing.

"I know," I say. "I just got it cut!"

"Well, what can I tell you?" Fran plants her hands flat on the table, blue veins mapping the terrain to coral-tipped nails. "Your father had some tax questions a few months ago, and he made an appointment with Jerry. They hit it off. Jerry suggested the four of us go out, and I thought, *Why not? Why not?*"

Just last year, Fran sent me a thick brown envelope filled with photographs and love letters my parents had sent to each other before they were married. *You can throw these out if you want to,* she scrawled on her note to me. *I HAVE NO NEED FOR THEM.*

"I mean," she continues, "life is too short to be so angry. To hold grudges."

Darling, my dad had written in one of those long-ago letters, blue ink on a scrap of white paper. *We're out of milk.* She had saved this note.

I heard them arguing once, late at night, in their bedroom. I'd had a bad dream and was about to push open their door. I must have been about nine or ten; I remember the pajamas I was wearing, soft pink fleece with a poodle on the front.

You were supposed to take care of me, my mother was wailing, *but you . . . you're a thief. You are the thief of my happiness!*

Somehow I knew even then that it was a melodramatic thing to say, and I snickered to myself. The thief of her happiness!

And then, from behind their closed door, I heard my father

laugh, too, a loud, mocking, derisive hoot. And suddenly we were allies, the two of us, in our cruelty. Immediately I felt the stirrings of a complicated remorse, a clattering misalignment of my affections. I turned and went back to bed.

Seth stares at our mother. His mouth is hanging open, a bit of chewed bagel visible. "Would you please close your mouth," I whisper; he winks at me and opens it wider. What is Fran offering us, with this new information? What is she hoping to give us? Maybe just this: evidence that your mistakes may not be the end of you. I feel a surge of forgiveness—for my parents and Seth, for Ben and Jane, saving the date without me, for us all.

Fran tips the last of her water into her mouth. She chews an ice cube and looks from me to Seth and back again. "We tried Thai last time. Cajun the time before that." The ice crunches against her teeth. "Turns out we all get along quite well."

chapter twenty

It's Ben's idea to go camping. "Because who can say when any of us will ever be able to afford a real vacation?" he argues from his perch on our sofa.

"I think you have to have a real job before you can take a real vacation," Jane says. She's not just talking about Ben; she means all of us. She's sitting cross-legged on the couch; Ben's head is in her lap. I'm sprawled on the floor. It's hot again, and we've sunk back into a torpor. We haven't moved in hours. Maybe days. I fan my face with a magazine.

"We could drive north," Ben says. "Somewhere cooler than here."

"I . . . don't . . . know." Jane speaks slowly, as if simply moving her mouth requires all of her limited energy. "The Amsters might need me."

The Amsters are a family she has just started babysitting for, to earn extra cash. We love talking about them as if they're actual rodents: *Those Amsters keep such a messy house! That little Amster really loves nuts!* I have the vague feeling that babysitting for the Amsters isn't going to be a good move for her, that with every extra hour of part-time work, with every new bathroom or toddler's butt she cleans, she's sliding farther into a fate she won't be able to climb out of. She's teetering dangerously close to the edge, to that elusive but irreversible moment when a person tips from full-of-promise to never-quite-lived-up-to-her-potential. But who am I to talk?

"I want to go camping!" I yell, surprising everyone, including myself. In fact, I hate camping. I hate, hate, hate it. The few times I've been—once during my short-lived involvement with a temple youth group when I was fourteen, once on an overnight, the culmination of a miserable summer at day camp when I was ten— were exercises in itchy discomfort, mosquito-riddled, sunburned days full of forced marches and lanyard weaving, and long, stuffy, sleepless nights in smelly tents. I've never understood the allure. I'm indoorsy.

But Jane's reluctance has jostled something inside me. I don't want to be a person who hates camping. If I feel so adamant now, at twenty-six, what will thirty-six look like? Or sixty-six? Will I be one of those old ladies who writes angry letters to the editor and calls things "newfangled"? *I can't figure out this newfangled voice mail!* Jane doesn't want to go camping? Well, I do.

Two days and a four-hour drive later we arrive at Wood Lake State Park (which Jane and I, from the backseat, dubbed Wood Tick State Park), and it is cooler here, in the shade of the tall pines, and it is better.

Declan, squinting, looks up at the twilit sky. "Ah, did anyone check the weather forecast?"

"No."

"Nope."

"Well," Ben says, "it hasn't rained in a week. So it's not going to rain tonight. Isn't that how it works?"

"In Ireland," Declan says, "you don't have to check the weather. Even if the sky is a brilliant blue when you start out, and the sun is splitting the heavens, you know to bring your rain gear. Because in ten minutes, it'll be lashing."

He's gazing at the big Wisconsin sky, pinking toward evening, but he's seeing something else. Lately he's been talking about Ireland as if it's a fond relative, a dear, slightly demented great-aunt, the one who makes jewelry out of uncooked macaroni and then gives it to you for your birthday.

We're sitting around a campfire that, with the help of a whole book of matches, an entire newspaper, and no skill at all, is burning brightly. We've set up our tents, and we lit this fire, and now none of us knows what to do next. In fact, none of us knew what to do an hour ago; I don't have high hopes for either of our rent-a-tents surviving a light gust of wind. There were so many stakes! We need an expert, but among the four of us, there is none. I look at Declan, balancing precariously on the two wobbly back legs of his canvas chair. "I mean," he says, "just lashing. Pounding rain. Soak you through and through." He turns to me and winks. Almost everything he says sounds dirty to me, stained with sex. I feel a familiar lurch, low in my gut. Like learning to play the piano, practice has improved us.

"In Ireland," he says again, his cigarette dangling, "would you believe, there are corner shops that sell nothing but umbrellas and Wellington boots."

"Nothing but umbrellas and boots," Jane says. "Yes, I've heard that. I also heard that there was some controversy over whether these stores could legally refuse to serve leprechauns." Jane has a way with Declan.

"Anti-leprechaun sentiment is unfortunately rampant in my country."

I look down at my lap at the pencil sketch I'm doing, of the four of us gathered around the fire pit. For fun, I've been drawing us without looking at the paper. Nobody looks like they're supposed to: Ben's head is a half inch away from his body; Jane's left eye floats near her ear. Declan resembles a praying mantis.

Ben heaves himself up. Bits of leaves and pine needles cling to his jeans. "Maybe we should collect some more of that, what do you call it, wood? To keep the fire going?" He and Declan wander off. When they come back, they toss some twigs into the fire and high-five each other.

Declan sits back down next to me. "Being outside always makes me crave a smoke," he says, lighting a cigarette. "Then again, so does being inside."

We sit for a long time, staring at the campfire, mesmerized. Ben and Jane roast marshmallows, Declan tears one of his special cheese-mayonnaise-and-butter sandwiches in two and gives me half. Minutes drift by in silence. Ben takes out a map of the campground and marks an easy trail along the lake for a hike tomorrow. "The local flora promises a riot of color!" he reads out loud. "If you're lucky, Wood Lake's very own beaver family might make an appearance!"

Jane rests her head on Ben's shoulder. I stretch my feet toward the fire. The sun sets slowly, fireflies pop out of the darkness, frogs awake and start calling out to each other, a beautiful, prehistoric bellowing. We say things, like "It's getting late" and "I wish we'd thought to bring more than just marshmallows and one sandwich" and "How long do you think we'd survive after an apocalypse?" And nothing touches me except the heat of the fire on my legs, my face. I'm in a pocket of glowing light, protected from complicated relationships and huge mistakes, past and future. The night feels perfect. Maybe I don't hate camping!

The first drops of rain aren't enough to send us into our tents, but the next ones are: a sudden, heavy downpour that comes in sharp little knives. Declan looks pleased as he grabs my hand and pulls me toward our tent. Ben and Jane duck into theirs. The rain falls hard on top of us, all around us, as if we're being stoned. It seems like a miracle that our tents are holding up, an honest-to-goodness little miracle.

"Are you guys okay?" Jane shouts.

"Tell my mother I love her!" I call back. Declan flicks on our fluorescent lantern, and a bright, artificial, greenish light fills our tiny tent. It looks like an office in here, a little cubicle in the woods. It feels like old times.

We're sitting on our big rumpled sleeping bag, knee to knee. Declan smiles at me and shakes his head like a puppy; droplets spray my face. Why are we in these tents, in these configurations? Why am I not laughing with Ben, or helping Jane find a dry shirt? Because humans couple off, slaves to biology, helpless under the vice clamp of desire. I reach my hand out, rest it on Declan's arm for a second.

He inches over to a dry spot on the sleeping bag and stretches his long body out. "I've decided to go home for a visit in the fall," he says. The top of his head touches one end of the tent; his feet skim the other. "For a visit, or maybe longer."

I'm cold, all of a sudden; goose bumps rise on my arms and legs, the back of my neck. "'For a visit,'" I repeat, "'or maybe longer.' . . ." What is he telling me? *Come with me, my darling? Good-bye?*

"Well," he says. He seems to have grown a reddish shadow of stubble in the last few minutes. I've never noticed this in Declan, this tendency toward ruddiness. I lean forward to touch it with the same hand that brushed his arm. "Well," he says again, "the agency. And my apartment in Chicago. I feel . . . untethered. I don't know." His accent lulls me for a moment, with its quick, sharp *t*'s, and those lovely, rounded *o*'s like music.

"Of course," I say. Of course. It smells like mold and feet in here, that particular musky blend that brews inside a tent, and we're breathing in each other's exhalations. I pat my hair, thick as a fur coat in the humidity. "So, what, then? September?" I'm try-ing to sound breezy, carefree, like a girl who has just been told that the bakery is out of scones: *It's okay, I didn't really want a scone! A muffin will be just as good!* But my voice comes out weird and tremu-lous and loud. *Fuck your scones!*

"Maybe," Declan says, looking at me now, studying me with a wrinkled brow. I have the notion that things are easier for some people. Declan sits up and takes my hand. "You could come," he says. "For a while?"

"Um." The phrase echoes in my brain, changes shape, mean-ing, a noncommittal alloy of syllables. *Furrow Isle.* Could I come *4-0-aisle*? Maybe I could. Yes?

He's still gazing at me, full of concern, the stepchild of affection. "Will, I really, really like you. But I don't want to mislead you."

"No," I say. "Yes. I get it. Of course." My heart goes numb, but underneath that, underneath its Novocained throb I can feel the stirrings of an ancient sorrow trying to thrash its way to the sur-face: a wretched thing, a blind, albino fish. Who am I in this world? What am I doing here, all alone? All alone forever, or only *for a whale*? It's not that I haven't asked these questions before, or that I'll ever be able to answer them sufficiently. It's just that a particu-lar loneliness has been napping for a few weeks. And now, all of a sudden, it's been zapped awake. The rain stops just as suddenly as it started, and laughter comes from Jane and Ben's tent.

"Will!" Jane yells. "I have to pee!"

"Okay!" I lunge for the tent flap and unzip it, wriggle my way out. "Here I am!" The ground is black and soggy; fresh mud squishes underneath my sneakers. The fire pit is charred and siz-zling, and the night air is cool.

Jane unfolds herself from her tent and comes over to me, smil-ing. "What was *that* all about?" She means the fierce rain.

"Yeah." I'm stunned, dizzy, flung away from myself and snapped back. I grab her hand. There is a reeking public bathroom a few hundred yards away, and we head for it. As we walk, water from the trees drips onto our heads. Halfway up the stony trail I let go of Jane's hand. "I think Declan just broke up with me," I tell her. The words come out of my mouth, and just like that, they're true.

"What?" Jane whispers. "What the? *Just now?*" As if the timing of it were the unforgivable sin. She stops to hug me, and I let her. Her sharp chin digs sweetly into my shoulder. "I never liked him," she whispers. "Especially after he killed your puppy." It's our running gag, what we say to each other after the demise of every relationship, the first Band-Aid on the wound of every failed date. *I never liked him, especially after he tried to poison those babies . . . especially after he stole your nana's wheelchair . . . after he had sex with that donkey.* Usually it makes me feel better. Now it just makes me feel hopeless.

She's still hugging me in the middle of the path on the way to the outhouse when something nearby moves, scrabbles, a sound like newspapers rustling, and in the dim light of the moon, a hulking shape emerges from the brush, squat and huffing, red eyes flashing. For one weird second I think that it's Declan. Jane grabs my elbow and screams. Then I do, too.

We stand there for a few seconds, petrified, all three of us. Jane is still screaming, and I might be, too, and the thing is staring at us with its demonic eyes, and then I close my mouth and I'm thinking, *That fat badger is going to kill us.* Although I don't know if it's a badger. It could be a sloth or a possum. Or an opossum. I wonder, briefly, what the difference is between a possum and an opossum. Is an opossum Irish?

Jane, finally finished screaming, clutches my elbow and tries to pull me away, back in the direction of the tents, but I'm rooted, so she lets go and skitters a few feet to the left, and then she stops, and the warthog stares and seems to contemplate its next move, and then we are a silent triangle of scared animals.

In what feels like ten minutes but is probably less than ten seconds, Ben is rushing up the path, Declan behind him. "What is it?" Ben yells. "What's wrong?"

"Fuckit!"

Someone takes my arm; it's Ben, pulling me away, pushing me aside; he waves his arms wildly and yells, "Go away! Get out of here!" in a low and menacing voice to the hippopotamus, who snorts and snuffles and then turns around and nonchalantly strolls back into the brush, as if that was all he was waiting for, someone to tell him what to do, and he didn't want to come to our party anyway.

"Fuckit," Declan says again, hopping over to us, clutching his foot. "I stubbed my fucking toe on a fucking rock."

I look at him: tall, useless, too late. *Especially after he didn't quite love me.* "That was some big bunny!" I say. My hands are shaking. My knees feel like water.

Ben hurries over to Jane. "Hey," he says, breathing hard, half laughing. "Honey. You okay?"

"I'm fine." Jane's voice scares me. It's brittle, hard as the fucking rock Declan stubbed his fucking toe on. She shoves past Ben and walks fast up the path, toward the bathroom, away from us all, and in a flash it's clear to me. Yes, Ben saved the day, hero in the epic battle against a benign and lazy raccoon, but he saved my day first; Jane was wide open and he left her there, vulnerable. I'm the one he took care of.

Ben stares after her. "What?" he says. "What just happened?"

That night at the campground, nobody sleeps. Declan, insensitive enough to casually break up with me on a camping trip in a tent in the woods in the rain, is sensitive enough to stay on his side of the sleeping bag, leaving as much space between us as he can in this cramped hothouse of mildew. Throughout the night, he tosses and turns, sighs and grunts and occasionally whispers to himself. *Oh,* he mutters, *ohhhhh,* and *Christ, this is insane,* and *What was I thinking?* And I'm awake to hear it all, to wonder if he's full of regret or just trying to get comfortable while a rock digs into his kidneys. I lie rigid on top of the damp sleeping bag in my jeans and long-sleeved T-shirt, tensed against another invasion, animal or human.

There is murmuring from Ben and Jane's tent and then silence. It's only the next morning, when I crawl out and see them sitting at the picnic table, that I know we were all awake to our demons in the night. Jane's dark hair is matted like a nest, as if the babies of that nocturnal creature found a place to sleep after their mother wandered off. Her eyes look sunken, the skin around them puffy. Ben, across from her, elbows on the table and head in his hands, looks like a digitally age-progressed image of himself.

"Oof," I say.

"Ugh," Jane says back.

"Glarg." Ben gives a little wave and yawns.

I pour myself a cup of weak, cold coffee from a Bugs Bunny thermos of indeterminate origin. "Whose idea was this, anyway?"

"Yours, I think," Ben says. "Definitely not mine."

Declan emerges from the tent after I do, rubbing his face. "This is worse than the morning after that piss-up in Glasgow in ninety-seven." He might as well be speaking another language. And, boom! What was delightful yesterday is revolting today. I decide to take this as a good indicator of my mental health. He straightens his spine slowly, his hands clutching his lower back, and he looks at me, sees me smiling to myself, and smiles back. *And . . .* I'm over him. I can't wait to tell Ben and Jane.

If there is a Ben and Jane. My heart sinks, or leaps, I can't tell, as everything clicks into place, Ben and Jane sitting across from each other looking ruined, looking like an Edward Albee play. This is the end of things, and the beginning. This is perfect timing. This is fate. This is the way things are supposed to be. Now we can all move forward. The morning is bright and cinematic, sunlight lacing through the branches, touching down, light and shadow shifting with the breeze.

"We have something to tell you," Ben says, not looking at me. His tired face betrays nothing. I sit down next to Jane, close, ready. Declan slurps his coffee loudly.

"We've decided," Jane says, playing with her cup, "we've decided..."

"We're not getting married next fall," Ben says, and there's my heart again, punching against my chest.

"We don't want to wait."

I turn to Jane, confused, and she's gazing at Ben, and she's smiling, her face crinkling with happiness, and Ben, who still hasn't met my eyes yet—why won't he meet my eyes?—reaches across the picnic table for Jane's hand; she elbows her cup of coffee out of the way, and some of it sloshes onto the table, some of it splashes onto me.

"Hey," I say. *"Ow!"* Indignant, even though it's yesterday's cold coffee.

"We're going to have the wedding next month," Ben says, still gazing only at Jane. "Smaller."

"Sooner," Jane says.

"More *intimate.*" Ben rolls his eyes, mocking himself for his own sincerity.

Jane nods. "More *us.*" She slips her hand out of Ben's. A squirrel chitters in the tree above us. "We were just thinking. About my parents' situation. We can't afford a big wedding, and anyway, the truth is, we never really wanted one." She scratches her head, twirls a strand of hair. She does this when she's nervous, fiddles with her ear, rubs her neck, twists her curls. "We'd rather have a small gathering, just family and a few friends."

"If we're gonna do it," Ben says, "let's do it."

Declan holds up his little plastic cup of coffee. "Congrats, you two. Cheers." If he's aware of the inherent discomfort of the situation, of him breaking up with me while Ben and Jane decide to add just a little more time to their eternity together, he's not acknowledging it. But he won't look at me, either.

"Next month!" I stretch my mouth wide to imitate Jane's big grin. "Wow!"

"Willa," Jane says, suddenly serious. "Will you serenade us with a love song at our wedding?" I'm known for my singing voice, which is so off-key and unpleasant that our snarky downstairs neighbor James once asked me if we'd gotten a new dog, and could we please train it not to howl so horribly.

"Yes," I say, with an exaggerated nod. "Yes, I will. If you will accompany me on the ukulele."

Declan laughs and pours more coffee into everyone's cups. I glare at him.

Ben gets up abruptly and walks over to his tent, starts yanking the pegs out of the ground. Jane bustles at the picnic table, crumpling the empty marshmallow bag, and Declan heads back into our tent.

My stomach growls. I'm ravenous, suddenly, hungry in a way that feels gaping and sad. I make my way toward Ben. He's humming to himself tunelessly. He used to do that in high school when he was particularly absorbed in a task, sometimes during tests and quizzes. It didn't add to his social standing.

"Nice song," I say, and I accidentally step on a tent peg, jabbing the soft side of my foot. "Shit!"

"Careful," he says, waving a mosquito away from his face. "You really ought to be more attentive." He looks at me, finally, and raises his eyebrows. "A-*tent*-tive." He pulls at the loop around the last stake as the yellow tent falls in, deflating slowly, like a parachute.

"Yes, I get it." I grab one of the pegs from the pile and hold it up to him. "I hope marrying Jane isn't a mis-*stake*." And immediately I cringe. Like so many things, this started in my brain as a sort-of joke, then took a wrong turn on its way out of my mouth.

Now Ben stops what he's doing and straightens.

"I didn't mean . . . you know I didn't . . . I'm sorry." I hug my arms around myself and laugh, *Huh huh, huh*.

But Ben doesn't say anything. He just looks at me. His jaw is tight. His wavy hair stands up in peaks, like whipped cream. There is a rip near the bottom of his T-shirt that threatens to colonize the whole shirt; I have the strange urge to reach out and yank it.

"Easier coming down than going up!" Declan calls, as he dismantles our tent. Jane, twenty feet away, is shoving puffy sleeping bags into their tiny nylon bags, punching them down.

And Ben just stands there, his hands in his pockets. It's just the two of us right here and the sun and the birds and the clean smell of damp earth, and maybe I'm wrong, but I think I see a dare in his eyes, a challenge: *Tell me, am I? Am I making a mis-stake?* The years of our friendship telescope in front of me. The warm spring day when we cut school and went to the beach, but still, straight-arrows that we were, spent the day studying; the Thanksgiving after Fran and Stan separated when Ben begged out of his own family's celebration and ate turkey sandwiches with us at Ma Krugman's All-Day/All-Nite Diner. I think, now, in his familiar brown eyes, that Ben is offering himself up to me, that he is asking me: *Willa, are you brave?*

And I don't know. Am I brave?

. . .

Ben's hike is the only thing standing between me and the end of this emotional disaster. "It's okay, Will," he says to me quietly, as we load the car. "We don't have to hike."

Jane wanders over. "Really," she whispers. "Let's just get you out of here."

But I don't want to be that person. I don't want to be the sobbing drama queen who forces her friends to leave the party early. I bend and retie my sneaker. "Are you kidding?" I ask. "I've been dying to meet that beaver family."

Declan zips the fully disassembled tent into its bag: shocking, in a way, that last night's shelter is this morning's backpack. "You three go," he says. "I'm going to stay behind and read my book," and I nod, grateful for this small kindness.

When we finally make it home, after the hike and the long drive, it's almost dark. Declan helps lug my backpack and sleeping bag up the stairs to the apartment. He stops at the door, leans toward me, his fingers lightly circling my wrist. "Can I stay tonight?" he asks. His voice is low and hoarse. "Please?" And despite an off-the-charts reading on my bad-idea-o-meter and a raised eyebrow from Jane, I nod. Because in spite of it all, he's still Declan: the man who cheats at Scrabble so that I can win, who smiles at me when we're alone like he wishes he could rent a room in my head. So I say yes; I let him.

We unpack and shower and fall into bed. I don't know what I'm doing; I feel like a rag doll, limp and defenseless. My skin is cool from the shower, but the night is hot, the air in my room an entity, close and still. A car outside honks; someone yells. This is all practically a memory even as it's happening, a cautionary tale I will tell myself about the time I slept with that Irish guy the day after he dumped me: *I said yes, but oh, boy, I should have said no.*

Under just a sheet, Declan sidles up close and slings an arm around my waist. His knees knock into mine. I realize that I'm holding my breath and exhale slowly.

And then, to my surprise: nothing. He sighs, his breath near my face a slow, swishing whisper. He doesn't make a move. His arm just stays where it is, heavy around my waist. He doesn't even try for breakup sex, that ramped-up cliché, the head-on collision of misplaced emotions. "I'm sorry," he murmurs, "I'm sorry," and I think, *Thief of my happiness,* and I laugh to myself and blink hard.

"You suck," I say.

"You're great," he says, and my heart congeals into a giant blob of blood pudding.

The next morning he clears his few possessions—a pair of jeans, a toothbrush, two shirts, his iPod—out of the apartment and hugs me good-bye.

Jane finds me a few minutes later standing in the middle of the living room, unsure about what to do next. She leads me to the couch and makes me tea; Ben brings me a huge blueberry muffin from the bakery. Jane sits next to me and rests her head on my shoulder and we watch mindless TV for a while: a sitcom from the nineties about a gorgeous but quarrelsome group of friends who are all teachers at the same high school; another one about a gorgeous but quarrelsome group of friends who own a restaurant together. Everyone assumes the headwaiter is gay, but he's not!

Ben and Jane are careful and quiet with me all day, gentle, as if I have the flu, but their kindness can't hide the giddy energy that buzzes around them. The two of them. Their plans. They think I'm mourning this breakup, but it's something more than that. I look at them, and suddenly all I can see is a big hole in the middle of my own life. Every time they touch each other I feel itchy. *I think I caught a case of poison envy in the woods,* I would say, if I could admit it to them, which I can't.

. . .

Two days later, Jane's mother calls.

"Willa, how *are* you?" Mrs. Weston asks. Five minutes later I'm still talking.

"And then he broke up with me," I say. "In the tent. In the middle of a storm. With another day of camping ahead of us."

"Oh, honey," she says, her maternal voice a blanket of sympathy. "You'll be all right. You're a gorgeous girl. You'll be fine."

"Mrs. Weston," I say, "when Jane and Ben get married, will you come be my roommate?" I sort of mean it. It makes my stomach hurt to think about Jane moving out, moving in to a new place with Ben.

She laughs, and it sounds like a yelp, as if she's just burned herself on a hot stove, and I recognize it as the sound a person makes when she's bumped up against someone else's insatiable need. "Oh, honey," she says again. In the background, water rushes, dishes clink. I imagine her standing at her kitchen sink in a green apron patterned with those geese. "Say, Willa, do you remember Dougie Tyler? Janey's friend?" I tell her that I do. *Vaguely.* "He mentioned to me that he's going to be in Milwaukee tomorrow on a sales call, and he wondered if he should surprise Janey with a visit. And I thought, *Wouldn't that be nice for her?* Shall I tell him to stop by?"

And I hear myself saying yes. I find that I can't say no.

"Dougie! What are you doing here?"

The next afternoon Dougie Tyler peers at me from underneath his baseball cap and grins. "I was in the neighborhood," he says. "Passing through on my way to the Midwestern Annual Fishing Rod Convention. In Oostburg!"

I step aside and usher him into the apartment. "I thought it was the North American Turnip Enthusiasts Conference in Crivitz." I plant my hands on my hips. "Or, no, was it the . . . Summer Yodeling Festival in New Glarus?"

"Ha, ha! I'm on my way to the . . ." He pulls his cap down and gazes behind me at the living room. "The People Who Have Living Rooms . . . Meeting." He looks back at me. I have the urge to scratch him behind his ears.

"Janey's not here," I say. "She'll be back in a few minutes."

Dougie's blond hair peeks out like hay from the back band of his cap. A floral overnight bag that I hope his mother lent him is slung over his shoulder. "It's awesome to see you, Willa," he says. He nods. I nod.

I point to his suitcase. "Did you get that for your bar mitzvah?" He looks at me and tilts his head, probably thinking, *Jerk.* Probably thinking, *Piss-poor substitute for the real thing.*

I bring him a glass of water, and we sit, we wait, because it's Jane he's come to see, his old friend, his old flame, his ex-girlfriend, the one who's getting married next month, the one he kissed just a few weeks ago in a bar in Marcy. I smile at Dougie, conscious of the way my lips pull, my cheeks shift: how an insincere smile is really just a squint.

In the awkward moments, as he sips his water and I try to avoid eye contact by pretending fascination with objects around the living room—the worn blue-and-green rug, a candlestick, my feet—I begin to have the strange sense that Dougie is a mirage. I think that he may be a fuzzy hallucination, and not just of himself but of all the men who have wandered through my life: Declan; Ben; Ed-who-dated-Jane-and-then-me-and-then-wrote-a-poem-about-us; Ryan Cox, fantasy boyfriend; even my father; even Seth. He's sitting across from me, the real Dougie Tyler, a hazy stand-in for all those boys, those guys, those men. If I reach out and poke him, I believe my finger would go right through to the other side, to the back of the couch he's sitting on.

"I wonder where she could be," Dougie says, startling me with his human voice.

"Who?"

He raises his empty glass to his lips and then just pretends to swallow, clearly having decided at the last second that asking me for more water would be too much trouble for both of us. This makes me like him again and also believe that he's real. "Jane," he says, rubbing his thumb up and down his glass. *"Jane."*

After I got off the phone with Mrs. Weston, I tried to convince myself that I was doing something good, or if not actually good, then at least benign, or if not benign, then possibly neutral? Aside from the moment, at the gas station, when she made me promise not to tell Ben, Jane has spoken to me only once more about what happened in that smoky, polka-throbbing German bar in Marcy. "It's water under the bridge," she said.

When Mrs. Weston suggested the surprise visit, I told myself that Jane would actually be happy. I told myself she would appreciate an unexpected hello from her old buddy, but I knew that I was dipping my feet into an ocean of ambiguity. *(Or was I?)* This would be an experiment, a test. I would be there when Jane laid eyes on him, and I would see the answer on her face, not to the question of whether she should choose Dougie over Ben—that was no question at all—but to a different one altogether. *Is there a person-sized space between Jane and Ben?* I look at Dougie, finally. He's taken off his cap and has placed it, oddly, on the floor next to his feet. His blue eyes are spaced far apart, his blond hair receding just a little bit, his mouth narrow and pink. The trick to drawing faces is finding just the right balance between light and shadow. Dougie's, I realize, is mostly light, practically no shadow at all. He clears his throat and runs his fingertip around the rim of the empty water glass, producing a low, vibrating murmur.

"Very talented," I say.

"I know, hey?" He stops. "So, Janey's getting married."

"Yeah."

"Weird, right?" He glances at me, sad and hopeful, as if I might save him.

"No, not really."

A minute later, the door to the apartment bangs open. They're laughing about something: Jane's head is thrown back, and Ben is leaning in, as if he's about to bite her on the neck. *I can't believe you did that! Well, he was staring at me!* They take a few steps into the room, Jane with a brown paper bag in her hands; she veers toward the kitchen with it and then stops short as she sees Dougie. Her face does a twitchy thing, her nose wrinkling as if she smells something odd, and she gasps, then quickly covers her mouth with her hand. She turns bright red, fast and furious, a chameleon taking refuge on a ripe tomato.

"*What the?*" she says, through her hand. "I mean, *What a,* what a surprise! Dougie!" She elongates the *-ie, Dougeeee!* She shakes her head and turns to me now, takes it all in, eyes wide, and she juts her chin toward her bedroom, the farthest in this small apartment from the living room. *Follow me,* she laser beams to my mind, *and explain this.* She's still holding the paper bag.

Ben, for his part, extends his hand to Dougie. Jane pivots and presses the bag into Ben's other hand, then pulls me up and drags me behind her. "Be right back," she mutters. "Gonna go change." In her bedroom, she clasps her hands to the sides of her head as if to hold her brain in, then turns around in a circle, the slow dance of the utterly confused. "What is he . . . how, what?"

"I know," I say. "I mean, I didn't know. I mean, your mom called, but you were out." I hear myself fudging the chronology of it. *Yeah, your mom called . . . yesterday.* But once the fib jumps out of my mouth, I can't reel it back in. Jane's room is stifling, lacking ventilation or any kind of cross breeze. An Andy Warhol poster on her wall, a cluster of pink and red and orange lips, is curling under its cheap frame. I cross my arms in front of my chest and look down at my bare feet. "He's on his way to a conference." I feel like sitting, like collapsing under the weight of my own ill-considered machinations, but the only piece of furniture in the room is Jane's unmade bed, a rumpled, cozy nest I used to crawl into with my best friend—a onetime haven that has become, since she and Ben got together, the focal point of my unhappiness, has come to exert a reverse magnetic force on me, flinging me away with its aura of grossness, of what they do there, the physical embodiment of all that is wrong with my life. The bed of my friends is my enemy. So, okay, I'll stand.

"Couldn't you have called me? Warned me?"

"You were out."

She looks at me as if I'm crazy. "My cell?"

I smile weakly. "Um, whoops?"

She rolls her eyes. "And my mom arranged this?"

"Well, yes, but you can't be mad at her, Janey. She doesn't know what happened between you two."

"Nothing happened," Jane hisses, with so much force that I think she almost believes it.

The low sounds of two voices reach us from the living room, indistinct. "What do you think they're talking about out there?"

She turns and practically leaps out of the room, but then she pauses, her hand on the doorknob, and says, "Please help me get him out of here. Please?"

The windowpane rattles with the slightest breeze. Someone in one of the downstairs apartments coughs—with all the windows open, we can hear everything, every detail of the lives of people we hardly know. "That's my egg," I heard someone say this morning, in a normal tone. "As you can see, it has my name on it." I remember what Ben told me, in the dark of the living room, weeks ago: that whatever had happened in Marcy did not matter.

Ben and Dougie are sitting across from each other at the table laughing like old friends when we come back into the room. "She used to give free popcorn to all of her pals." Dougie is telling Ben about how he and Jane worked together at the Marcy Multiplex when they were in high school and for a couple of summers after college. I've heard these stories. I pull up a chair between them. Ben listens, rapt. "Late at night, after we closed, Jane and I would go out and change the movie titles on the marquee." Dougie laughs, a surprisingly girlish giggle, and turns to Jane. "Remember? *Planet of the Grapes*? *O Brother, Where Fart Thou?*" His face is wide open, his blue eyes big.

Jane, in spite of herself, laughs. "*A Beautiful Behind.* God, we were idiots."

Dougie flinches, but keeps smiling. "It was fun, though."

"That's funny," I say, for no reason. "Take your stinking paws off me, you damned dirty grape!"

Ben stands. "Hey, we brought some dinner home. Just some sandwiches, but there's enough for everybody. Doug, will you join us?" I can't tell if he really wants Dougie here, or if he's just being polite. Or if he's offering the sandwiches as a consolation prize: *I got Jane, so you can have my tuna salad on whole wheat.* I can't read him at all.

"Sure, man. Thanks." Dougie leans back in his chair and looks up at Ben, grateful and searching.

"I'm just going to run out for beer," Ben says.

Jane fidgets, bends to scratch her shin, and makes a face at me. I try to convey powerlessness in the look I return. The truth is, I want to know how this will all play out.

Ben leaves. Dougie crooks his arms above his head, immediately taking up more space. "Did you hear about Brad and Angelina?" I know not to laugh at this: Brad and Angelina Muellerhueber are friends of Dougie and Jane's who got married right after college. "They just had a baby," Dougie says. "Skye. *S-k-y-e.*" He shakes his head at the strangeness of it. What will they think of next?

"I love it," Jane says, a defiant edge in her voice: proof that she has moved far beyond Dougie's provincial small-mindedness. She grabs the edge of Ben's vacated chair with both hands; the five silver bracelets she's wearing slide down her arm and jingle together at her wrist, like a Slinky.

Dougie clears his throat. His arms are still bent awkwardly behind his head. "I'm not here to try to . . . convince you of anything." He clears his throat again. "But you and I—"

"Wait," Jane says, suddenly steely. "I'm really sorry, but this is actually not a great time for a visit." She shifts her weight, still gripping Ben's chair. "It's just . . ." Her eyes dart down and around, as if scanning the room for an excuse, then settle back on Dougie. "It's just not."

Still half tipped and leaning, Dougie lets the front two legs of his chair fall back down with a bang. He pushes himself away from the table.

This will be his defining moment, the humiliation he will return to; the pit in his stomach late at night that, years from now, he will trace back to this day, this moment, this rejection. Suddenly, and with my own hot flash of regret, I wish I could disappear.

"Really?" Dougie says. He stands, a step too close to Jane, face to face. My body is tense, recognizing before my brain does the way some men hide their anger under the surface, bubbling so softly you don't even know it's there. "Because, I mean, I didn't just drop in on you, Janey. You might even say I was invited."

Jane does a gangly, startled little half jump backward, wrapping her long arms around herself, an adjustment of feet and legs, a realignment of limbs. "Dougie," she says, "I don't know what to say."

"Me, neither." He looks both disagreeable and ridiculous standing there in his red baseball cap, his pressed white shirt, his casual-Friday khakis, back straight, shoulders squared, a few inches shorter than Jane. He reaches out and lays a meaty paw on Jane's shoulder—as a reminder or a last-ditch effort or maybe just for balance. It doesn't matter. By the time Ben comes back home, carrying a gallon of Rocky Road and a six-pack of beer, Dougie's gone.

I draw in my room for hours that night, trying to make sense of things. The high school misfits from our old comic book return to me: The Overachievers plan a low-budget wedding, champions of thrift! The male Overachiever marries a beautiful princess, but first they must battle the evil villain Ex, ineffectual but persistent foe bent on ruining them. The Overachievers go their separate ways.

Afterward, I rip up the drawings, the thick paper shredding like cloth, pencil grease smearing my fingertips.

I feel like I'm trudging through melting slush. But underneath, there's a river raging.

Declan has dumped me; Jane, imperial ruler of her own life, has disposed of Dougie. Ben and Jane's wedding is moving forward fast. As a favor, my boss, Molly, is supplying the flowers— she's giving them a hefty discount on the stems and she's letting me put together the arrangements at no charge. The wedding will be in three weeks, at Alewife Park, north of the city, on the lake.

"We really don't need much," Jane whispers to me a few days later at the flower shop, her hand on my arm, as I lead her around the store. "Just a few nice bouquets for the tables, something for me to carry, something for you to carry." She squeezes. "I don't know! You're the expert!"

I narrow my eyes. My name tag today says SULLEN. I made it this morning. If anyone asks me, I'll say my name is Suellen. *What, you've never seen a fucking typo?*

"I like these," Ben says, pointing to a bucket of garish yellow lilies.

"Nobody likes those," I say. "They're for funerals."

Jane nods. "Funerals, not weddings."

Ben touches the petal of one of the lilies. "For the funeral of my bachelorhood!"

Jane removes her hand from my arm and swats him. "This is so nice of your boss," she says to me. "And of you! We'll have the prettiest wholesale flower arrangements decorating the cheapest plastic fold-up tables at Alewife Park, picnic area number five, *ever*!"

"And the best darn potluck reception this side of the Mississippi," Ben says in a southern accent.

"Is your mom making her deviled eggs?" I ask.

"Yup, and her blue-ribbon sweet potato pie," he says, still in a southern accent; to my knowledge, Ben's mom does not make sweet potato pie.

"But seriously, Willa." Jane adjusts the bottom of her T-shirt, which is riding up. "We really do appreciate this. I mean, we're getting your expert attention, and we can actually afford it."

That's the second time she's called me an expert—an expert *flower shop worker*—in the last five minutes. I pull a gladiolus from its bucket and remove a few brown petals. "You realize I'm faking it, right?"

"Oh, I love those!" Jane says. "They're so . . . happy! Wouldn't it be awesome to carry a bouquet of bright pink and yellow gladioli down the aisle? Nobody really does that, do they? They're such tall flowers. But I'm a tall girl!" She smiles at Ben, then at me, and then her expression changes, which is when I realize I'm scowling. "But whatever! You're the . . ."

"I'm the expert."

Her hand flutters to her hair. "Anyway, we also thought that people could take the centerpieces home with them if they wanted to. We thought that would be nice. That's what we were thinking. Right, hon?"

"We we we," I say. "All the way home." Ben glances at me sidelong.

Jane tugs at her shirt again, self-conscious. "I have to go. You guys figure it out." She heads for the exit. "I totally trust you!" she calls, with a little wave, as the door jingles and shuts behind her.

"What a control freak," Ben says.

"Bridezilla." An unexpected wave of love for Jane rushes over me, for my friend who is planning her wedding with casual happiness, with a complete lack of narcissism, with nothing but easy joy and respect for the celebration of it. She amazes me. I shiver a little in the air-conditioned chill of the shop. "I'm going to make her something beautiful," I say to Ben. I ease three bright pink gerbera daisies from their bucket, my favorites, and vow to do better, to be better.

The store is quiet, empty now but for Ben and me, and I busy myself with the flowers, setting a white iris against a yellow tea rose, spreading a small bunch of lavender asters around the outside. Ben follows me around, pretending to have opinions, making fun of me. *Mmm, no, that one's all wrong, yep, definitely that one instead.* I pull out a fleshy, phallic anthurium and hold it up to Ben, its erect stalk bobbing lewdly against its dark pink base.

"Would this be funny?" I ask.

"Awesome," he says. "Nothing like a botanical sex joke at a

wedding." He grins and shakes his head. "*My* wedding. That's so fucking strange."

I nod.

Ben points to my name tag. "Why were you pissed at Jane? Is that supposed to be some kind of performance art?"

"I don't know. I'm sorry."

He plucks a pink chrysanthemum from a pail and studies it for a long moment. "She's going to apply to law school."

I feel like I've been stabbed. I look down and see that the thorn of one of the roses I'm holding has actually poked my palm. "That is not . . ." What is he talking about? It's impossible. Jane would have told me. "What are you . . . ?" I close my eyes against the feeling of my life spinning out of control, careening like a car off a cliff. There is no way Jane wants to go to law school: Jane, wearer of ill-fitting T-shirts from Goodwill, gimlet-eyed cleaner of suburban houses, poet of soap scum and toilet bowl ring. Ben has obviously misheard. She must have said something else. Perhaps she got angry and then told him she regretted her lost cool. "Ben," I say finally. "There is no way that's true."

He nods, and I get the fleeting impression that he's enjoying it a little, this slow, sadistic slicing. "We're considering the East Coast. D.C."

The thorn prick on my hand is bleeding a little, an occupational hazard. "Was anyone ever going to tell me this?" As if that were the problem. The withholding of information.

"I'm telling you now." And then he softens; I see it on his face, in the way his posture shifts, how he carefully slips the chrysanthemum back into its place among the other flowers, runs a finger slowly over the bridge of his nose. "I guess she's feeling—we're feeling—like we can't just stay here forever. Like our lives are in a holding pattern. You know?"

"But what about you?" Ben mailed his grad school applications just last week. We celebrated by making him buy us dinner; *You're going to be a social worker,* we said. *You'll be rich!* "What about you?"

He shrugs and smiles, the answer obvious. "I kind of want to wait another year. Maybe I'll work for a nonprofit for a while . . . find something, you know, meaningful. . . . Anyway, I hear there are some okay grad schools out east."

I suppose Ben is right, and if I'm honest with myself, I know it, too: that it's not exactly satisfying to work part-time jobs we're nominally suited for just so we can live in crummy, thin-walled apartments that we can barely afford; how old it's getting, eating cheap pasta or scrambled eggs every night off chipped plates; sitting on rickety, third-hand furniture and watching crappy TV because we can't afford cable and we definitely can't afford to go out. Pretending we like it this way. Attached to nothing but ourselves. If I could bring myself to admit it, I'd agree that we're stuck in a pleasant limbo of our own making. But I can't. And so all I hear from Ben is "We're moving on." All I hear is good-bye.

That night, Jane climbs into my bed, settles in next to me on my wrinkly purple sheets. Ben is at his apartment, packing the few things that are left there, the dishes he rarely uses, the clothes he hardly ever wears, the pots he never cooks with. He'll live here until the wedding—he basically lives here anyway—and soon after that, they'll get their own place. That's the plan—a plan that now includes the East Coast, I guess.

He kissed Jane good-bye after dinner, sighed deeply, and said, "Well, I guess I should go now."

They hugged, and Jane laughed as she pulled away from him, a rogue strand of her dark hair Velcroed onto his stubbly chin.

"You're going off to pack," she said, "not die."

Now, I adjust myself in my bed, roll onto my back, fold my hair under my head like a pillow. Jane lies next to me, quiet, breathing deeply. The smell of flowers is still fragrant on my hands. Headlights from passing cars flash across the ceiling, then the wall opposite the bed. Jane rolls onto her side, toward me. "Sorry if I got on your nerves at the flower shop today."

"God," I say, feeling small and shabby in the shadow of my bighearted friend. "*I'm* sorry. You didn't get on my nerves. Not at all. It's the breakup, I guess." I close my eyes for a moment, let that half-truth settle between us.

"Ben said he told you about law school, about us maybe moving."

"Uh-huh." Still on my back, I turn my face to hers. Her nose is shiny, her eyes dark in the lamplight.

"I don't know what to say." She furrows her eyebrows, little wrinkles trenching a familiar path, and I think about the million tiny ways Ben knows her now, how when you love someone, you take that person into your body, your fingertips predicting their angles and curves; how you smell like them in the morning.

"It's okay," I say, because it ought to be. There's a smear of face cream on her cheek, pearly white against her pink skin. "Do you really want to be a lawyer?"

"Maybe." The blanket on top of her rises and falls with her shrug. She licks her lips and sighs. Her breath is toothpaste-minty. "I'm tired of looking at blue toilet water."

"But what will I do without you guys?" What will I do? My throat is thick, suddenly: I'm bereft.

"I know." Her voice is high and thin. "I can't even let myself think about that." Outside, a motorcycle buzzes past, so loud it sounds like it's about to barrel into our apartment. "Anyway, it's months away. And you'll visit. Like, a lot."

"Yeah." It comes over me at once that I'm bone tired. My body is sinking into a presleep lull. I close my eyes again for a second, maybe longer. When I open them, Jane is right where I left her, staring at me intently. I imagine myself visiting Ben and Jane in their cute apartment in D.C., sleeping on their pullout couch, drinking their good coffee in the morning. *We're taking you to the best Ethiopian restaurant, right around the corner! Tomorrow, the National Gallery. . . . This was so great, you guys. See you soon, see you again soon.*

Jane fidgets and wriggles and arranges her body, ending up a sliver closer to me; we could touch noses now if we wanted to. She exhales, her breath a warm puff. "Okay," she says. "G'night." She rolls away to the other side of the bed, the soft mattress bouncing gently in her wake.

chapter twenty-one

The dim hallway of Seth's building is a dark and gloomy contrast to the sunny morning, and it takes my eyes a few minutes to adjust. My brother called me a couple hours ago. "Do you have any toilet paper you could loan me?" His voice was a low rumble on the other end of the line. "I ran out."

"Um, I guess so." Seth lives around the corner from Haber's Drugs, and two blocks from the Shop 'n' Save. "Sure." I cracked my neck and looked around my room. Jane had slept in my bed for much of the night; I remembered that she'd crept away just as the first dim light was sneaking in. There was still a head-shaped indentation on the pillow. I felt weird, like an abandoned lover or a sixth grader alone at the lunch table. I rolled over onto my stomach with the phone in my hand. "Do you need, um, anything else?" I couldn't imagine what he would say to that. A box of Cheerios? His dignity?

I got dressed and went to the grocery store for toilet paper, milk, bread, peanut butter, a bunch of bananas, and, on a whim, one pear. I thought it would be funny to hand Seth the piece of fruit and say, "I brought you *this pear,* but I see you already have it." I changed my mind about that and ate it in the car.

I smile at him now as he takes the paper bag from me. "We

need to get you out of here, Seth," I say brightly, standing in the doorway of his apartment, trying to both exude cheer and breathe shallowly at the same time. It smells like pot and wet towels and some other things, old and greasy and unidentifiable. "Oh, Seth," I say. "We need to open some windows and then get you out of here."

I peer around his dingy apartment at a tableau of dissolution: empty pizza boxes and beer and soda cans strewn about the living room, a tangle of wires in the middle of the floor, a pair of socks next to the TV, a full bowl of something wet and yellowish on the futon. He actually is using an upturned cardboard box as a coffee table, the idea I suggested to him—yes, meanly, but *jokingly*—when he was moving in. He hasn't even bothered to throw a dishcloth over it. The apartment is the physical manifestation of defeat, a glimpse into the psychic landscape of a man who can no longer be bothered.

Seth watches me looking around. He scratches his head and gives me a half smile. "Can I get you something to drink?" he asks, and we both start laughing.

"A nice dessert wine, if you have it?"

He heads toward the kitchen with the bag of groceries. "You're a good sister," he says quietly, so out of character that I gasp, then immediately decide that he must have said something else. *You're a shoplifter?*

"Thanks," I mumble, and follow him into the kitchen, where he is already guzzling milk straight from the carton.

"Do you know where I want to go?" he asks, wiping his mouth with his sleeve. I shake my head. "The Domes." The Mitchell Park Domes are a Milwaukee landmark, three huge, glass-encased botanical gardens shaped like breasts. They loom over the city, a fetishist's gigantic fantasy. Seth shoves a handful of Cheerios into his mouth. "The Domes," he says again, crunching, "because I like

the gift shop. If you want to. I guess.we could go anywhere, really."
He looks around. "I probably should go somewhere. . . ."

I turn my attention to a grease stain on the linoleum—luckily for me there are plenty to choose from. I see right through my brother's forced nonchalance. Nina told me: the Domes are where they had their first date, their first kiss behind the hibiscus in the Tropical Dome, their new love hatching in the steamy heat of the climate-controlled rainforest.

"We can go there," I say. "If you want to." A visit to the scene of the crime seems like a very bad idea for him, but I'll go along with it. Maybe I'll feign an interest in cacti and guide us to the Desert Dome, where plants bloom despite their parched surroundings. It could be just the thing for us both.

"I just can't seem to pull my shit together," Seth says to me, as we wander down the circular path in the Tropical Dome, vanilla flowers and orchids blossoming lush and thick before us, and a damp, sweet smell wafting—an odor, like so many things, somewhere between perfume and decay. "I feel so bleak. And then these spasms of fury come over me. One minute I'm okay, the next second I want to kick a bunny."

"Bunnies can be such assholes."

We're quiet for a minute as a woman and two babies in a massive double stroller roll up behind us. We have to step off the path to let them go by. The babies' big heads are inclined toward each other, bobbing in sleep. Their mother, in a pink tank top and yoga pants, walks by quickly, her face grim and resolute.

"My office mates probably think I have a bladder problem," Seth says. "I take so many bathroom breaks just to get myself under control. I'm a train wreck. I feel like a chick on the rag."

I run the tips of my fingers across the feathery edge of a fern.

"I have news for you, though," I say. "That is not how *chicks on the rag* feel." Sometimes my brother takes me by surprise, and before I know it I'm sucked into the vortex of his vileness.

"No," he says, shaking his head. "It *is*. That's how Nina was."

How have I lost this argument? But I have. "Um, well . . . how are you going to turn it around?"

"I've decided," he says. "I'm not going to." He pushes his hand through his hair.

"Oh, Seth," I say, any remaining annoyance consumed by a blaze of sympathy for him. "You won't feel this bad forever!"

"No, no, no. I mean, sure, I could, I could get back on track, but I realized recently that being so in touch with my emotions is kind of a good thing. It's left me with more to *give*." He puts air quotes around *give*, as if, even as he's saying it, he knows he won't be giving anything to anyone. He keeps his hands suspended in the air for a few seconds, demarcating nothing. "So at first I was thinking I could become a monk, although then I thought I would make a crappy monk. Like I'm going to eat rice and not have sex for the rest of my life." I'm a few steps ahead of him, murmuring *Mm hmm*, trying not to think about my brother having sex, before I realize he's stopped to read the description of a kapok tree. "So then, Wilford, I thought, what do people do who are, like, full of their own feelings? What do they *do*?" He looks at me intently, too intently. "They create! They write, they paint, they make music. . . . I mean, that's what you've been doing all these years, or whatever, feeling shit and then, like, drawing shit?"

"Why, Seth, I didn't realize you were paying attention."

"No, shut up. This is serious. I'm serious. I'm going to write a screenplay!"

"Okay, well . . . great!" I cringe, imagining the kind of script Seth would write: a little rom-com, where the redheaded girl-friend, Gina, is a merciless bureaucrat, or maybe a dental hygienist, someone who likes to use sharp tools and inflict pain, and Sam, our hapless hero, just can't see what a ballbuster she is, but then, after some complications, maybe an ill-fated trip to Jamaica or a futile quest to find the winning lottery ticket he accidentally threw out, he finally *does* see, and he ends up with the incredibly hot yet selfless kindergarten teacher. Or maybe an action flick, where the nerdy math geek rescues the planet from an attack of evil freckly, redheaded aliens, gaining the love of his incredibly hot yet selfless coworker at the lab. *Jessica loosens her wavy blond hair from its bun; it cascades down her back. She takes off her glasses. Sam reaches for her.* "*I never noticed how incredibly hot you were before!*"

"Great!" I say again.

"But, you know, all these years I've been exercising the other side of my brain." He taps his head. Seth works for the city's Department of Water Quality, analyzing data on microscopic organisms and contaminants. *Everywhere I look,* he likes to say, *I see shit.* He's been saying it since long before he and Nina split up.

"Yeah?" I haven't seen my brother this animated in months. So I'm trying to pretend that the bad feeling in my stomach is from too much coffee.

"And this is where you come in!"

"Ah."

"Will, seriously, listen. You can help me write it! You can, I don't know, cut your hours at the flower shop, that'll give you some extra time, and I'll give you an outline, a really detailed outline of what I want to happen, and we'll write it together! I mean, you could do most of the writing, and I'll have, like, creative control!" He looks at me with so much sincerity that I am, for a moment, tempted to say yes.

"No."

"Just like that?"

When I was fourteen, Seth told me that his best friend, Eric

Ackerman, captain of the swim team, had a crush on me. *Write him a note,* Seth said. *Tell him you're interested!* I was already five-eleven then, my boobs as big as my head, my center of gravity treacherously high. I hadn't met Ben yet. I had glasses and braces and hair that grew out instead of down, and I had not yet discovered the magic of a silicone-based antifrizz product. My limbs were too long for my body, like a marionette's, and I was in the habit of apologizing to the inanimate objects I bumped into—lockers, desks, lunchroom tables. *Sorry! Oh, whoops, sorry about that!* Still, I wrote that note. So, yes, there was a time Seth could convince me of anything. "Yep," I say now, bonking my hip against a bench at the side of the path. "Just like that."

Seth is quiet again, sulky. We've rounded half of the perimeter of the rainforest and are slowly making our way back to the entrance. I'm starting to feel sticky and overwhelmed by the humidity of this enormous greenhouse, a misplaced succulent, a cactus trapped in the wrong dome. I suck in a deep breath that doesn't quite do the trick, that gets caught somewhere partway down. The woman with the dozing twins is coming up behind us again, the stroller clacking as it gains on us.

"Hey!" Seth turns as she nears us, trying to edge past. "Hey, do you mind?"

She looks up, a little confused. "Sorry," she mutters, slowing slightly.

"Yeah, well, we're trying to walk here," he says, jamming his hands into the pockets of his jeans. "Why don't you get off the path with that double-wide of yours?"

"Jeez," she says. One of the babies stirs, squeaks, then settles. Their mother shrugs. "Guess they're not the only ones who need a nap today." She maneuvers her stroller off the paved walkway, crushing a few tiny purple flowers as she does.

"Seth!" I say, when she's out of earshot.

"Well, we had the right of way!"

"Oh, yeah. I forgot about that sign, BABIES IN STROLLERS MUST YIELD TO GRUMPY PEDESTRIANS."

He lets out a little huff and sulks some more, shoulders slumped, head down. "Hey," he says, after a few minutes, looking up and glaring at me. "I bet you're getting excited for Jane and Ben's wedding. That's coming up real soon now, isn't it? I bet that'll be fun for you." He takes his right hand out of his pocket and flicks the leaf of a flowering philodendron. "You brought them together, and now off they go without you. Happily ever after." He breaks the leaf off the plant, then tosses it onto the ground. "Must suck."

"Um, well. . . ." The wheels in my brain spin furiously before I realize that no answer is required. Seth will say whatever Seth will say. I understand with a sudden, sharp stab that I'm here to take it.

"No, seriously, Willa, you're so judgmental. You think I'm the loser and you're this . . . this . . . holier-than-thou princess good-girl martyr. It's pathetic. You think your life looks any better than mine? You think that by not *actively* fucking up you're not a fuckup?"

He stops to catch his breath and I turn and look at him, this grown man, my brother, who ruined his relationship with Nina and seems hell-bent on destroying ours now, too. A trickle of sweat runs down the side of his face. The earth tilts off its axis. Admiration and pity cannot coexist.

Two bright yellow birds swoop and squawk overhead and land in a rustle of leaves, startling me. I had forgotten about that, that there are tropical birds living in the trees here. They probably think they're in Borneo or Java or Botswana, somewhere hot and wet and real. But they're living out their entire tropical-bird lives in the Mitchell Park Domes in Milwaukee, Wisconsin. Idiots. Bird brains!

"Hey," I say. "I think I'm ready to leave now." Seth is still staring straight ahead, and for a second I'm not sure if he heard me. I pick up my pace as we near the exit. I drove us here; he has no choice but to follow.

When I get back from the Domes, a big package is sitting in the middle of the kitchen table, wrapped in shiny silver paper and tied with a red bow. Ben and Jane are scrunched together on the couch, reading the same book.

"Who's this one from?" For the past three weeks the UPS truck has been stopping in front of our apartment. I've gotten to know the driver. His name is Don. His daughter, Kate, is a freshman at the University of Iowa. His son, Evan, has been in and out of rehab. But he's doing much better now.

"Us," Ben says, smiling.

Jane nods. "Us!"

"Oh, cute," I say. They've gotten a present for each other. Maybe I'll get myself a present. Congratulations on losing your boyfriend and your best friends and your brother! You're really alone now! Maybe a tablecloth or a nice assortment of jellies. Or an egg spoon. Declan was always going on about egg spoons. *You can't get an egg spoon in this bloody country.* I really want to go into my room and lie down. I start down the hall with a backward wave. "Gotta get ready for work," I mumble.

"No," Jane says. "It's from us to you!"

I bounce back into the kitchen, excited in spite of myself. A present! "Why?"

"Just open it," Ben says, dog-earing their book.

I shove the bow aside and rip into the paper. I've never understood people who unwrap presents as if they're performing surgery, carefully peeling back the tape, delaying gratification until the last possible second. I tear the silver paper off with one satisfying yank.

END UP, it says on the side, and I wonder, for one fleeting second, if this box is trying to tell me something. *See, dumb ass? Here is where you END UP.*

"Oh!" I say. *Kaffeeautomaten.* A coffeemaker. But we already have one, a serviceable hand-me-down from Bonnie Weston. I look at Ben and Jane on the couch, Jane cross-legged, her left knee resting on Ben's right, both of them gazing at me hopefully. They're starting to resemble each other, like dogs and their owners. Ben's hair is longer than it was in high school, and Jane often wears his shirts; their expressions, I've noticed, mirror each other's more and more, those eager half smiles, the way they purse their lips when they're confused, forming the silent *wh?* of a question.

I get it, of course: this fancy coffeemaker, with its built-in water filter and its integrated bean grinder, this German brand my parents always made a point of not buying. It's for me, this *Kaffeeautomaten,* because they'll be taking the old one with them.

"It's programmable!" Jane says.

"For when you're just too tired in the morning to push a button!"

"Wow," I say. "This is amazing. Thanks." Tears push up against the backs of my eyes, the pressure building. "This is really . . . amazing." I'm imagining this state-of-the-art chrome-and-steel machine in the Dumpster out back, picturing myself dropping it off at Goodwill, unopened—*auf Wiedersehen*! What a deal for someone else, what a find. "Thank you so much."

Gratefully, I feel the tears recede, floodwaters that at the last minute do not breach the banks. In a flash, I see myself drinking coffee alone at the kitchen table before work. Someone else has moved into Jane's old room. Her name is Andrea. She hates coffee. She cooks with Hamburger Helper most nights and there is the

pervasive smell of beef in the apartment. She gives herself pedi-
cures on the couch; she uses those little Styrofoam toe sandwiches
to keep the bright pink polish from smearing.

"I was thinking about cutting down on caffeine," I say, pressing
my fingers against the edge of the box and smiling at my friends.
They look back at me, bewildered. "I mean, I won't, though. Yay!
Now I won't."

chapter twenty-two

All day long I've been either on the verge of tears or actually in tears. At the flower shop, while I was snipping the stems of a bunch of tulips, I nicked my index finger, and I cried so hard I had to close the store for ten minutes.

Later, just before my shift ended, an elderly man walked in. He took his time wandering around the store, then finally picked an assembled bouquet of barely open red roses and bursts of pink aster mixed with a spray of white daisies. He placed the flowers on the counter with a gently shaking hand. "These are for my wife," he said, with a small, adoring smile. "We'll be married sixty years tomorrow."

"Congratulations," I said as the tears spilled down my cheeks. I plucked a tissue from the box underneath the counter. "Allergies," I said.

The man nodded. I could see the bones of his shoulders through his thin cotton shirt. His blue eyes were watery and sympathetic. He paid for the bouquet and put his hand on mine. I don't appreciate strangers touching me, but I didn't pull away. I had the feeling that this man was going to say something kind and wise to me, maybe something about patience or the permanence of love.

"This place is very expensive." He patted my knuckles and scowled a little bit. "Next time I believe I'll buy my flowers at the Shop 'n' Save on Elmwood."

When I got home, I changed into a T-shirt and my last pair of clean shorts and collapsed onto the couch, floppy as a jellyfish. I haven't moved since then.

Ben opens a package of spaghetti and dumps the pasta into a pot of boiling water while I flick through the channels. Jane is babysitting for the Amsters for the evening. *(That little Amster never goes to bed! He's downright nocturnal!)* So it's just the two of us. The German coffeemaker sits on the floor in the middle of the room, squat and gleaming, like a tiny Prussian soldier.

After a few minutes of pots banging and cupboard doors opening and closing, Ben asks, "You hungry?"

"Sure."

He hands me a bowl of undercooked spaghetti with tomato sauce from a jar and a sprinkle of Parmesan. "Wow," I say, jabbing at the stuck-together noodles with my fork. "Fancy!"

"My uncle Al, from Sicily, gave me the recipe," Ben says. "Did I ever tell you about Uncle Al? Al Dente?"

"How long have you been waiting to use that one?"

"Just about"—he glances at the clock—"forty-five minutes." He sucks a noodle, loudly, then dabs at his chin.

Is this the last time we'll do this, Ben and I? Is this the last time we'll be easy together, just the two of us, single and unfettered, slurping spaghetti and watching TV? Jane hates eating on the couch; the possibility of getting stains on the fabric undoes her.

I probably knew, in high school, that Ben had a crush on me. I might have even known that he loved me. Why else would he have dropped out of his beloved Geology Club, with its weekend field trips, so that he could spend his Saturdays with me? Why would he have studied for my Spanish tests with me when he himself took French; why would he have bothered explaining continuous functions to me over and over again when we both knew I was never going to pass calculus; why would he have listened sympathetically to my endless rhapsodies about the unattainable track-star superhero Ryan Cox? He was my best friend, but best friends have limits, and Ben had none. He would have done anything for me, and I let him, again and again. I knew. Obviously I knew.

I glance at him, next to me on the couch, the sharp lines of his jaw, his face shadowy with a day-old beard, his long fingers close enough to touch mine, but not touching, ever. Lately we've avoided even the most incidental physical contact. If our hands brush when I'm handing him a plate, one of us recoils. If we accidentally nudge past each other in the hallway, we both practically leap to opposite walls. *Sorry! My fault! Sorry!*

He catches me looking at him and raises his eyebrows.

"You have a little . . ." I point to his face. He picks up his napkin and wipes off a nonexistent spot of sauce. A reality show about a family with seventeen children, all of whose names start with *T*, drones in the background. *After our sixteenth child, we weren't sure the Lord was going to bless us with another, but then along came Trystal!*

I can hardly swallow for the thick coil of sadness lodged in my throat. I have *screwed up*. I have headed down what looked to be the same road my friends were traveling, only to find myself lost in a thicket of dark and dangerous woods while they traipse off, hand in hand, into their clear, sunny future. I rest my bowl on my lap and take a deep, jagged breath. Declan's gone. Seth is gone, or maybe he hasn't been here in years. Jane is leaving. There is only one person who has ever saved me, and now he's going, too. Is this adulthood? Loss, loss, and more loss? There is no possible way I can reconcile it, no way at all.

"Ben."

He turns. "More sauce?" He dabs at his cheek, his chin.

"No, not that." I reach for his hand to stop him from more unnecessary face wiping, and my breath catches and I start crying, big heaving sobs that erupt from me, low and awful, suffering cow sounds, sobs that ought to loosen the mass in my throat but don't, shuddering quakes that only breed more and more weeping, until I'm pretty sure I'm about to start hyperventilating or give birth to a calf.

And tears are streaming from my eyes, and snot is rushing from my nose, and it's Ben, Ben who swabbed calamine lotion on my chicken pox sophomore year, Ben who sat next to me on the bathroom floor as I puked my guts out after eating sushi from the deli counter at the Fuel-n-Food (*Didn't I tell you, never, ever eat raw fish from a gas station?*), Ben who has seen me at my worst, my ugliest, and who is now just staring at me, tender and baffled, patting my hand like the old man in the flower shop. "Weeping Willa," he says softly, and as my sobs finally begin to subside, he gently touches the wet skin above my lip, where the tears have pooled. "Nice. You look pretty."

"Shut up," I say.

He offers me the sleeve of his shirt, and I wipe my face and nose with it.

"Will?"

I sniff. "I was just thinking about a really sad movie I saw a few years ago."

He pulls me toward him for a hug, and I let him. I rest my head on his warm chest; he pets my hair, working his fingers through the curls. Somewhere in the back of my mind is the idea that maybe there is a reason we've avoided contact for the past six months.

The word "don't" scrolls across the news crawler in my brain, DON'T DON'T DON'T DON'T, and then JANE JANE JANE JANE.

But then I just turn it off, *click*, and I tip my face up to Ben's. And once more, here we are, we're kissing.

. . .

There's only one thing worse than kissing your best friend when he's two weeks away from marrying your other best friend. And that is sleeping with him. If there's anything worse than that, I'd like to know what it is. Within the bounds of the law, of course. Certainly, murdering your parents would be worse than sleeping with your best friend, etc. Murdering anyone! All forms of abuse and probably some categories of theft would fall under the "worse" classification. But beyond that? I'd like to know.

Ben traces his finger across my cheek. "Oh, crap," he says. "Oh, boy."

I adjust my right leg, which is caught between the couch pillows, and pull my arm out from under his body. It's fallen asleep, a tingling stump. I shake it to try to get the feeling back, bang it against the edge of the couch. *Whap, whap, whap,* an unintentional echo of things. "Can't feel my hand," I say.

Ben props himself up on his elbow, staring so intently at me that I feel like I might be getting sunburned. I want to turn away. We're so completely squished together, chest against chest, thigh to thigh, nose to nose, there's nowhere else to look, so I'm forced to watch it pass over his face, all of it—the last half hour of lust and desire and, in the middle of it, sadness; his guilt and confusion and heartbroken remorse, and also, holy moly, the transformation, the face of my best friend altered, his eyelids heavy, his mouth edging up at the corners, the gooey vulnerability of Ben in love. With me. His feelings are so full-on true and irrefutable; he is so emotionally bare that, in spite of our actual nakedness, in spite of having just had sex with the boy I've known since I was fourteen, and with nowhere else to turn on this narrow, saggy sofa of truth we're resting on, I just have to close my eyes. I close my eyes to it.

"What we just did," Ben whispers.

"I know."

"We're really in it now," he says.

The TV murmured in the background while we made love, and I was grateful for the noise, as if the industrious sounds of the Hitchcocks and their seventeen children could drown us out, could somehow make it okay.

He licked my ear as two of the Hitchcock girls made their own laundry soap. I kissed him and moved my hands lightly down his back as the mom in her long denim skirt homeschooled the children. *How long did God take to create the earth?*

"Six days," I murmured, lost. Ben laid his hands on my hips as the boys prepared to go deer hunting. *The sisters are doing spring cleaning while the brothers go hunting,* one of them said. For a brief and confusing moment I thought that Ben and I might be related. I touched the side of his neck and thought about Jane and wondered if he was thinking about her, too. Had it been only an hour since she'd strolled into the living room wearing my second-to-last pair of clean shorts, bright yellow ones, and promised to do my laundry tomorrow, and then made little puppy dog noises until I said okay? Only forty-five minutes since she'd happily waved good-bye to us and said, "Smell you both later!"?

I considered how two people could devastate another with one ridiculous physical activity, the unlikely insertion of parts. How this would devastate her. How it would rearrange everything. And, yes: I was desperate to rearrange everything.

But the pressure of Ben's limbs, the heat of his body, reminded me that I was being rearranged, too. I loved him, finally.

I moved myself underneath him, felt the sofa cushions shift under the small of my back. He slid inside me with a shocking, irrevocable moan. They were making dinner. Someone, Theresa or Tristina, was using a mortar and pestle, energetically pounding and grinding . . . although now that I think about it, I might have imagined that part.

There was a commercial for car insurance and a promo for a very special episode of another reality show, about a family of giants who run a bakery. *Big People, Little Tarts.*

"Willa," Ben whispered. I folded my arms and legs around him and pressed my cheek against his. "You."

And then it was over. There was our fast breathing and the weight of Ben on top of me, surprisingly comforting; with the hand that was dangling off the couch, I patted around for the remote and turned off the TV. So long, Timothy and Tomothy, the twins. My own breathing slowed. I could feel Ben's heartbeat returning to normal.

I have known him for all these years, but I had never felt his heart before.

"Yes," I say now. "Oh, boy."

"What are we going to . . . I mean . . . God, what have we . . . ?" Ben pulls back, dislodges from me, and springs off the couch in a quick movement; he sits, his back to me, naked on the floor. "Dammit," he says quietly. "Goddammit."

My whole body goes cold. "Really?" I look around for a non-existent blanket as my arms and legs suddenly turn prickly and warm. I touch my hand to my forehead. My hand is freezing, my forehead hot. I feel like a broken oven. I grab a pillow and try to cover myself with it. "Because I know this is . . . but you can't just . . ."

Ben doesn't respond. He just sits there for a minute, and then he jumps up and puts on his clothes. He turns to me, the face that rested tenderly against mine a few minutes ago now pinched with anxiety. "You have to get dressed!" he says, gathering up my shirt and shorts. "You have to get dressed right now!"

I can't keep up with this, with the lightning shifts, the mad swings from contentment to panic, love to . . . whatever this is. I thought Ben and I just consummated our long and complicated friendship, and that together we would now deal with the repercussions. But did I just become the faithless slut who ruined him? I pull on my bra and underwear, trying to still my shaking hands, newly aware of the mole on my thigh, the shiny stretch marks on the sides of my breasts, the dark hairs below my belly button.

With a clatter, Ben clears the two bowls of now-cold pasta from the floor where we'd moved them, somewhere between the *That's a Lot of Hitchcocks!* theme song and the family's weekly trip to the grocery store for twenty gallons of milk and a cart full of ground chuck. He busies himself in the kitchen, stuffing our half-eaten dinners into the garbage, loudly washing the pots and dishes. He has the water on full blast, a monsoon; he's hunched over, arms working. Steam rises from the sink. He must be sterilizing those pots and dishes.

I'm dressed now, perched on the edge of the sofa, surveying the room. It looks the same as it did earlier today, the faded blue-and-green rug neat and centered under the gouged coffee table, the ancient yellow lampshade straight. It looks like nothing happened here.

Jane will come home.

She'll collapse onto a chair. *I'm pooped! How was your night?*

Good. Ben made spaghetti. We had sex.

He turns off the faucet and makes his way over to me, sits down next to me, takes both of my hands. His are damp. I think I've been here before, or somewhere like it. I stiffen, brace myself.

"I'm sorry," he says. I try to stay still, frozen in this spot, to keep my distance, to let it just happen; what an amazing thing, to lose even more. There is less and less of me. "I need to figure this out," Ben says. *Yes, figure it out. It was a mistake. Put the pieces back together.* He sighs. "I feel crazy and confused." *I'm not coming to visit you two in D.C., just so you know.*

For a long time, he doesn't say anything, just sits. My hands in his are starting to sweat. I have to scratch my nose. I can't be the one to pull away. There is a strand of hair tickling my face. My nose twitches. I might be going mad. *Just let go of my hands already.* "Well?"

"I love you," he says.

Oh. Relief floods over me, warm and liquid. "Good." For the millionth time in just thirty minutes, it all changes again. And everything complicated washes away.

Jane rushes through the door, a bright burst of color in a pink tank top and my yellow shorts. "I swear to God, he bit me! That little Amster bit me!" As predicted, she flings herself onto the living room chair. As she plops down, a tuft of stuffing bulges out of a buttonhole in the brown cushion; one of us pokes this same gray foam back into the chair at least five times a day. The strap of her shirt slips down her shoulder. Her hair is messy, and her face is flushed and beautiful. She looks from Ben to me and back to Ben—her head bobbing, arms folded, legs splayed. "I was putting him to bed, and he started crying and kicking, and then the little fucker bit me!"

Ben moves over to her, stands behind her, and starts rubbing her head, the way he stroked mine. He glances at me, pained, then turns his attention back to Jane's scalp.

"Look!" she says, holding out her long arm and examining it, then turning it over, wrist up. "Okay, there's nothing to see, but that's just lucky. The kid has sharp little teeth!"

Ben's hands move from Jane's head to her collarbone. "Poor baby," he says. His voice catches, and he clears his throat. He massages Jane's shoulders.

"Ouch! Ben! Too hard!"

"Sorry," he says, loosening his death grip.

"You always were *kneady*," I say. I make a little squeezing motion with my hands.

Jane says, "Oh, boo!" and Ben presses his lips together so tightly they disappear.

A pool of acid sloshes around in my stomach. "Are we going to tell her?" I asked, on the couch, before she came home. "Are we going to *not tell her*?"

"I think I should be the one to tell her," he said.

"I'm her best friend!"

"I'm her fiancé." *Fiancé*: it surprised us both with its strange effect, the self-conscious emphasis of a word that has no precise English equivalent. Her betrothed? Her intended? *We never intended . . .*

"You win," I said.

"Will." Ben moved so that his bare knees grazed mine. "How are we supposed to feel?"

"Like shit," I said, but I didn't; not exactly. I rested the back of my hand against his face.

"She's going to hate us," he said, and it took a minute for the quiet reality of that statement to sink in. *No*, I thought, *she won't*. He looked at me, stricken. She would. She would hate us. How could we live with that? We kissed again, an inoculation against it.

Now, still standing behind her, Ben glances around the room, his eyes darting. *It looks like you're playing pinball with your eyes, I* would like to say as his gaze bounces from ceiling to floor to rug to television. *Like you're playing eyeball!* Instead I swallow hard and observe how Jane begins to relax as the tension of the evening eases out of her while it simultaneously slithers up into Ben's spine.

"What did you guys do tonight?" Jane asks, her voice high and tired; she sounds like a little girl.

A noise comes out of Ben's throat, somewhere between a cough and the death cries of a strangled cat, and my own breath stops for a second, and I think, *He's going to tell her.*

He fake coughs a few times, one hand cupped over his mouth in a ladylike way. Jane's eyes are closed, and she's sunk deeper into the chair. Ben's hand returns to her shoulders. "I made spaghetti," he says, "and we watched TV." He keeps rubbing, calmly now.

I'm observing Ben's hands, his fingers digging gently into the skin just below Jane's collarbone, thumbs circling the knotty muscles. "The spaghetti was crap!"

"Mmm." She rolls her neck. "This feels so good."

"I mean, really," I say. "The spaghetti was awful. The worst!" Ben lets out an exasperated sigh, like the parent of a recalcitrant toddler. Is his shirt on inside out?

"We should take cooking classes after the wedding, honey," Jane murmurs. "We both suck."

"Yeah." Ben has found a spot on the wall above my head to focus on.

He won't tell her, at least not tonight.

Right here, on this couch, we took each other's clothes off; his hands lingered on my waist, and he laughed and said, "Twelve years. You really know how to play hard to get."

He won't tell her. He gets so much mileage out of being loyal Ben, unassuming and steadfast and true, but he just cheated on the woman he's supposed to marry in two weeks. How long will he keep our secret just to preserve the image, this idea of himself?

I stare at him, even though he won't look back. He's still massaging Jane, his hands moving over her broad shoulders, her upper arms, pressing and squeezing, and right here, right now, I give myself over to it, to the whole sordid, complicated mess; to this new, imperfect man; to the inevitable breaking of all of our hearts. Jane's, yes: shattered. But Ben's, too. And mine. *Love can be ruthless.*

Will they say good night to me like it's any other night, walk into Jane's room, and fall into bed? I wrap my arms around myself. A part of the far wall has begun to warp in the heat of this long summer, the white paint turning brownish. The kitchen faucet drips.

"God, I am so glad to be home," Jane says with a little contented shudder, and, in our dingy, warm living room that still smells of pasta, I know exactly what she means. She wriggles and adjusts herself in the chair, her whole grateful, deluded body at the mercy of Ben's moving hands.

chapter twenty-three

Ben stops cleaning the bathroom mirror for a second and stares at his reflection in the blurred, streaky glass. He's been wiping the mirror with a rag for five minutes, but the glass just keeps getting dirtier and dirtier. "Remind me," he says. "Who is Al?"

I'm on my knees, swishing the toilet brush around in the bowl. "A friend," I say, neglecting the part about how he's Jane's friend, too; how he was hers first. "A friend who throws excellent parties." The pretty blue toilet water looks like the ocean, but the New! Spring Fresh Scent! is making me nauseous. I've never noticed this before, how cleaning is the act of replacing grime with chemicals.

"Oh, look," Ben says, a little bit dazed. "I've been using Murphy Oil to clean the mirror. That's . . . probably . . . not right. . . ."

"I think we should get some ventilation in here."

Ben nods, exhales a small laugh. He reaches over me, heaves open the window, and the cool fall air floods in. I lean toward him and kiss his sweaty arm, a move that manages to feel simultaneously natural, premeditated, and horribly awkward all at once. Sometimes, even three months in, it still feels like someone died.

. . .

For four days after we slept together, the clouds gathered. Ben barely spoke to me. He slept in Jane's bed and he acted like Jane's fiancé, and I couldn't help but wonder. So I couldn't look at him— although I did think about him; I thought about him more in those four days than I had in twelve years: he had taken up residence just under my sternum, where it hurt to breathe. And sometimes, during those four days, it struck me that this was Ben, Ben I'd had sex with, Ben I'd gone cuckoo over, and I laughed when I shouldn't have: while I was brushing my teeth, while I was helping a customer at the shop. Even to my own ears I sounded weird.

I sat at the kitchen table with my soft pencils and sketched for hours. I was working on a series of drawings of our apartment, wide sweeps of the rooms and details—corners and radiators and half-open windows, a blanket thrown over a chair, a crooked rug, a doorknob. My brain didn't yet grasp what my fingers knew: I was trying to preserve what we had destroyed.

We both overcompensated with Jane. Ben touched her constantly, one hand somewhere on her body at all times, as if she were a helium balloon that would float away without him tethering her to the earth. I was attentive but rattled, falling all over myself, tripping over my shoelaces, arms flailing: sitcom Willa. And Jane was just on edge, like a rat in a cage who senses that the storm is about to hit.

"Fuck! I spilled my juice again!"

"Let me clean that up for you." I was already half out of my chair.

She opened her mouth in surprise. "Okay, wait a minute. Is something wrong?"

I froze, unprepared. "What? No!"

She reached across the table and touched her hand to my forehead. "Are you ill?"

"Ha!" I said, and I moved quickly away from her, got the sponge, and squeezed it out.

She grabbed it from me. "'Let me clean that up for you'? I don't believe I have ever heard those words come out of your mouth." She set the sponge on the orange puddle and watched the juice soak in. "Well, not in that order. Maybe a version of those words. Like maybe, 'Let you clean that up for me.' Or 'Clean that up! Me let for you!'"

"Ha," I said again. Ben wandered into the kitchen, scratching his face. He glanced at me and made his way straight to Jane, sat down next to her, and draped his arm around her neck.

"Morning." He ran his tongue over his teeth and then kissed her cheek.

"Here, want some juice?" she asked. She handed him the saturated sponge.

"Ha!" he said.

Jane got up and padded across the kitchen, her bare feet long and white and thwapping against the linoleum like flippers. She had on just a green sports bra and a pair of Ben's boxers. Ben was wearing only gray shorts; I was in a long T-shirt. It was hot again. We were all skin.

"You two have suddenly become, like, really poor conversationalists." Jane poured three cups of coffee. In one, she dumped the last of a carton of half-and-half and four teaspoons of sugar, then handed it to me.

"Thanks." I stared, entranced, as the white cream swirled into the coffee.

"It's the heat," Ben said, rubbing his face again, up and down, a scritchy, sandpaper sound.

Or it's that we slept together.

"Willa," Jane said, "do you have to work today?" I shook my head. "Because I don't have a dress for my own wedding, which, as you may recall, is in eleven days. And I just don't think I'm going to feel comfortable getting married in the buff." She hugged her arms across her chest and smiled broadly, held it there, a snapshot of herself.

"Yeah . . . okay," I said softly, wrapping my hands around my mug. "I guess we could go shopping." I thought about the day, just the two of us. *That one looks pretty! Ben and I had sex! Let's go get salads!*

She took a long sip of her coffee, then set the white cup down on the counter. She had given Ben and me the nice mugs and taken the small chipped one for herself. "Oh, don't make me beg!" she said, raking her fingers through her hair. "I hate shopping as much as you do!"

"No, we can go! I want to go. Please, let me go dress shopping with you!"

She laughed. "And you, my tall friend, you need something pretty, too. You're not going to my wedding in shorts and flip-flops."

"Definitely not," I said, "because those shorts are dirty, and you promised to do my laundry."

"That'll never happen," she said, and slurped her coffee. In spite of Jane's passionate love of cleaning, she hated to do laundry. Ben washed her clothes, and sometimes mine, too. He had a knack for getting the whites white.

Things felt ordinary for a moment. Music, heavy on the bass, boomed up from our downstairs neighbors' apartment. I looked at my friends. If I squinted, I might be able to convince myself that everything was okay, that we could remain suspended in this limbo forever, insects in amber.

"What are you going to do today, babe?" Jane laid a hand casually on Ben's shoulder and kissed the top of his head. It was an intimate gesture, stunning in its normalcy. When she found out what had happened, she would never do that again. My heart took wing, a soaring black bird of prey, a vulture.

Ben's shoulders slumped under the weight of it all. He looked at me, and I nodded. "Janey, can you sit down?" he said.

"Why?"

"We need to talk about something." He pressed his index fingers to his temples for a second.

"Uh-oh, you've decided to invite your crazy aunt Betty after all?" She rinsed the orange-juice-soaked sponge in the sink. "You're dead set on having a parade of monkeys lead the processional?"

He looked at her tenderly, and because I knew what was coming next, and because I was so accustomed to empathizing with Jane, I felt a surprising flash of rage at him. He was about to dismantle her. But so was I. "Honey, can you . . ." he pointed to the chair between us.

Jane looked at Ben, and then at me, and her eyes grew wide, and she slid into the chair, her long body loose. "Gulp," she said. "This can't be good."

Sitting on the kitchen floor, rag in hand, I swipe at a smudge of dirt an arm's length away. I've cleaned myself into a corner. The entire floor in front of me is wet and gleaming, and I'm trapped, back to the wall, on the only dry part of the linoleum. I see that I should have started here and worked my way out, but a belated understanding of the tricks of the trade doesn't help me now. "I didn't think I wanted to wear a costume," I say. "I thought we would just go in our regular clothes. But now that seems kind of pretentious, weirdly, like we're too cool for Halloween costumes, and I think I want to dress up!"

Ben stands in the doorway. "The party is in an hour, right?" I nod. "I think, if you want to go in costume, we need to make use of the tools at hand." He sets his spray bottle of generic shower cleaner down. "I'm done, by the way." His brown hair is wet with sweat and curling up at the ends. He wipes his forehead with the back of his hand. "I mean, Christ!"

One thing you get used to when your roommate is cheerfully compulsive is a clean apartment. Also you get used to: the way she mumbles to herself and then laughs, as if she's telling herself an excellent joke; how she rarely closes the bathroom door all the way; how she weeps during movies that aren't even that sad; the way she hums while she eats; the exact way she calls for you when she needs you to kill a spider, half name, half scream: *Willl-AAAH!*

The day Jane left, Ben and I held each other on the floor, and he said, "Is it okay if I tell you I'm going to miss her?" The first time I went to the grocery store without her, I walked down the cleaning supplies aisle, and I thought about how we joked about inventing a bathroom cleaner just so we could call it Muck-Off! and I almost cried, right there in aisle 8.

"For example," Ben continues now, pulling the mop out from behind the kitchen door. "We can just pop the head off this sucker, affix it to your body, and then you, with your hair, are a mop!"

"Funny." I pretend-squirt him with my bottle of floor polish. He might have said the same thing to Jane. For all I know, this was one of their jokes.

"Well, I'm going as me, but showered." He peels off his shirt and turns toward the bathroom.

"Wait!" I say as he heads down the hallway. "I'm trapped here! Come rescue me!"

"Oh, poor Will," he says, mock serious. "You'll just have to rescue yourself."

. . .

"Okay." Jane rested her arms on the kitchen table, extended her legs past the sides of her chair. Her bare foot bumped into mine. "What is it?" No matter what she was imagining, I thought, it was not as bad as what we were about to say. "What could make you both look so distraught? Just tell me."

Ben looked her straight in the eye. "I am so, so sorry," he said. She took a sharp breath. "Willa and I . . ." He reached for Jane's hand. "We, um . . ." He looked down. He was losing his resolve.

"Janey," I said. I had the weird feeling I used to get sometimes when I was little, lying awake in my bed: that my arms and legs were growing enormous, while the rest of me, my head, my torso, was shrinking. I glanced at the clock. It was 9:38.

"Willa and I, we, the other night, we . . ." He shook his head as if to clear it and made an odd, snuffling noise. A shaft of weak light slanted in through the kitchen window. "We slept together."

"I'm so sorry," I said quickly, knowing it wouldn't mean anything, hoping that she would remember, someday, when she pieced together the shards of this conversation, that at least I had said it. My mind flashed to the morning my dad moved out, to my mom's explanation: *It's not as if you didn't see this coming.* But of course, no. I hadn't.

Jane yanked her hand from Ben's like it was diseased, but she stayed where she was at the table, between us. The music from downstairs had stopped, but now it started up again, a low drumbeat and then a wailing guitar solo. "This is not funny," she said softly, almost a whisper. "This is really not funny, you guys."

Once in a while it was surreal, being with my old friend after we'd so drastically changed the terms of our attachment. Sometimes the unwelcome image of high-school-Ben would come to me; we would be kissing, sheets crumpled at the edge of the bed,

227

his lovely body entwined with mine, and from nowhere my brain would offer up the memory of my short, round, eminently dorky pal sitting on his desk in Ms. Barnum's classroom, talking to her about an upcoming issue of the magazine, his shirt missing a button, his stumpy legs swinging against the chair. Soon those images stopped coming, though; he stopped being the strange amalgam of teenage-Ben and adult-Ben, and, somehow, when I wasn't expecting it, he magically became himself.

In the beginning, we killed our guilt and sadness, squelched all the confusion and regret with sex. And it worked for a while. I wanted him with my whole body—thighs, tongue, elbows, toes: parts I didn't know were capable of wanting.

When we were away from each other, I drifted into reveries about what kinds of new, creative ways we might fit together. *Could that leg go there? Oh, maybe if his hand went here.* We would find out. I was always, always ready to drop everything and fall into bed with him—or fall onto the couch again, or the floor. All he had to do was look at me.

And anyway, I didn't have much else going on. My schedule was clear.

"It feels strange to wake up in the apartment, but in your bed," he said, running his hand over my stomach.

"I can imagine." We had agreed to tell each other everything we were thinking and feeling, a strategy I was already regretting. He leaned over and kissed me. I squeezed my eyes shut. I wished I had woken up before he had, to sneak out and brush my teeth. His lips pressed against mine. I could feel that he was smiling. But I missed Jane. I missed Seth. I may have even missed my parents, although not the parents I had now, nor the ones who'd been drifting in and out of my life since college, but possibly the parents I'd had when

I was ten, the ones who picked Seth and me up from school one day at lunchtime and took us to a matinee, just for the hell of it. I flung my arms around Ben and arched my neck toward his mouth. *Hello, hello, come in. You are always welcome here.*

We formed a third being to replace her, a thing made out of sex and euphoria and constant surprise. I was like a three-year-old on an airplane playing games: endlessly delighted that every time I peeked out from behind my hands, Ben was still there. Well, maybe I could have been more careful with my heart. But we had crushed Jane's, and so that's how we got through those first weeks without her. That's what we did.

We tiptoe through the front door of Al's apartment, two scared mice. The living room is warm and bright and loud and packed with people, which, come to think of it, is the only way I've ever seen it. Maybe Al's apartment only exists if there's a party going on, like *Brigadoon* with a keg.

"Well, here we are." Ben looks down at his shoes. "Can we go now?"

"Remember that party we went to in high school?" We had, in fact, been to only one party in high school—a pregraduation senior class bash thrown by Jake Pizorkski, whose parents owned Pizorkski's Sausages and Fine Meats. We arrived early at Jake's house—a glass-walled, seventeen-room compound with a long, lit path that sloped down to the lake, a mansion known locally as Liverwurst Manor. We were the first people there. Jake didn't know who we were, although he pretended to. "Um, so, you guys psyched about college and stuff? Gonna have a great summer?"

"Oh, gee!" Ben said. He was so short back then that he had to crane his neck to meet my frantic eyes. "This is so embarrassing, Jake, but we have another soirée to attend this evening!" Jake handed us each a cellophane-wrapped variety pack of minisausages at the door and politely thanked us for coming, as if we were good friends of his parents.

"I think I still have some of that turkey jerky," Ben says now, grabbing my hand and squeezing.

"Well, we're staying for at least fifteen minutes this time." I squeeze back. We're at our best like this, two misfits shoring each other up against the terrifying swell of normal human interaction. We both know that it's a better thing to face your fears bravely, to talk to an acquaintance at a party, to sit down next to a stranger and smile, but even in high school we'd been content to rely on each other, and so we had never even tried.

Al lists toward us, clearly already a little bit drunk. He hands me a big plastic cup of his famous neon blue-green potion. "Heyyyy," he says, engulfing me in a hug. It's only been four months since we last saw each other, at Amy and Rafael's wedding in June, but he hugs me like it's been years. "Happy Halloween! Where's your twin?"

I smile and take a sip of my drink. I thought that, when a tornado touches down in a small town, people heard about it. "Huh," I say, over the din. "I don't know!"

Ben pulls me into the room and leans toward my ear. "Do you think Jane could show up here?" he hisses.

"I don't know. Probably not. Maybe." I offer him my cup. The thought has, of course, occurred to me.

That morning in August, after we told her, Jane pushed back from the table and walked slowly into her room. She kept her spine straight, her posture dignified, but she couldn't stifle the choked sob that escaped her throat. Ben and I sat, silent, immobile. We heard objects moving around, hangers jangling together, zippers unzipping. After about ten minutes, she walked out the front door, carrying two suitcases and a fat backpack. She didn't even turn around. She didn't yell or scream or shriek that she despised us. She just left. A few days later, I got an e-mail from her, requesting that we leave the apartment the following Saturday so that she could retrieve her things. Saturday! It would have been her wedding day. She included in the e-mail a list of objects that belonged to her—the blender; the chair with the stuffing poking out; the coffeemaker, of course—and a few things she wanted that we'd bought together. "I will leave a check for you for half the value of those items," she wrote, formal as a contract.

That Saturday morning, we left the apartment and went to Rock River, our coffee shop. After a while, Ben headed to the library for an early shift. I didn't have to work that day. I didn't know what to do with myself. I loitered. I sat in the big chair near the window, where I could watch people walk by, and I peeled my eyes for Jane, for the dark head that rose above the crowd, for the long legs that propelled her quick stride. I didn't expect to see her. Why would she stroll around her old neighborhood and risk bumping into the two people who had betrayed her? I paid for a refill and made my way up the block, edging closer and closer to our building, until there I was, lurking in the alley, peering around the moldy mattress that was still propped up against the wall, waiting for Jane.

She showed up just fifteen minutes later. At first I didn't recognize her. She was wearing a baseball cap, her hair in a ponytail and pulled through the back of it, and she seemed somehow shorter than she actually is. I flattened myself against the wall of the building next to ours, and she didn't see me as she jiggled her key in the front door. Her mother's blue Dodge Intrepid waited at the corner, Mrs. Weston square shouldered and grim at the wheel. I felt like a spy—like the worst spy ever, a spy who had just dreamed up her mission twenty minutes ago, one who was dressed in yellow shorts bright as a banana and pink sneakers, still clutching a to-go cup of lukewarm coffee. A spy who, if she had to escape, would undoubtedly spill her drink and then trip over her shoelaces as she ran.

I took a deep breath. When Jane exited the building, not long after she'd gone in, she was hauling her lamp and the blender. Our neighbor, James, held the door for her, and she smiled her thanks. I noticed, then, that she was dressed in a pair of Bonnie Weston's pants, the pink floral leggings Mrs. Weston had worn on our shopping expedition, way back in June, three lifetimes ago. On Jane, Bonnie Weston's leggings were capris.

"Mom!" Jane called, and motioned with her head for her mother to pull up to a newly vacated parking space right in front of the building, a premium spot. She tugged at the waistline of her pants and adjusted her grip on the lamp. I pressed myself harder against the wall. That was the moment I realized what we'd done, Ben and I. It wasn't that I hadn't known before. But seeing my best friend in her mother's ill-fitting leggings, lamp and blender in hand, that was the moment I understood that we'd changed her—not just her future, but her past, too.

Now, Al's living room is a crush of people. "I don't think she'd show up here," I say to Ben. Why would she go anywhere we might be? But as I look around at the throngs of grown adults in silly costumes—a lion, a sexy nurse, Spider-Man, a marshmallow—and then at Ben, in his shirt and jeans and furrowed brow, I realize: I have no idea what any of us are capable of.

"Willa?" A chubby witch in a long black dress taps me on the shoulder. "Willa! Hi!" Amy flings one arm over my shoulder and presses down for a second, the half hug of the noncommittal. "We're here with the baby!" she announces. "Can you believe it? *The baby!*" She looks delirious, her pretty blond hair matted, her face blotchy, purple smudges so dark underneath her eyes I think it must be makeup, until I lean in closer and realize it's not. She's wearing a pointy black hat that has tipped precariously to the side of her head, but she doesn't seem to notice. "You don't have any gum, do you?" She covers her mouth with her hand. "I didn't have a chance to brush my teeth tonight." She laughs, then blinks hard. "The baby never, *ever* sleeps! It's insane." For a second I think she means the baby is insane, and I nod sympathetically. How terrible to give birth to a baby, only to find out that it's insane!

Rafael comes up behind her, the tiny, wet-mouthed baby strapped to his chest in a pouch. Rafael is wearing regular clothes and, in a nod to the holiday, a headband with wobbly, bobbing antennae attached. The baby, wobbly itself, its arms and legs flailing, looks larval, like something alien-insect-Rafael might decide to snack on later.

"Wow," I say to them, peering at the pink-clad infant, her little tongue lolling, big brown eyes gazing past me and then crossing, as if, overwhelmed, she prefers to stare at herself. "Congratulations!" Amy and Rafael both look like they're going to cry.

"Her name is Liliana," Amy says. "After his great-grandmother." She jerks her head toward Rafael. "Apparently she never slept, either. Just four hours a night, right up until she died at ninety-six. Nobody told me that before we named her, though." She narrows her eyes and glares at Rafael, then at me.

Ben, next to me, bends toward Liliana. "She's beautiful," he says, as Amy takes it in, the tall, handsome man she has met before as Jane's boyfriend, here now with me, holding my hand.

Amy tilts her head; her black witch's hat slides down to her ear. "Huh," she says. "I mean, oh, yes, thanks. We think so." She rests her hand on Liliana's round, fuzzy head and walks away with Rafael.

"I think it's been fifteen minutes," I say, deflated, somehow demoralized by the whole interaction. Ben nods.

And then the door swings open and she glides in—tall, graceful, face powdered, lips blood red, her hair streaked and sprayed stiff: the bride of Frankenstein, white robe trailing like—oh, yes—a wedding gown.

"Oh!" Ben says as together we realize that it's Jane, and my heart thumps fast, choosing flight.

Jane surveys the place, looking past us, smiles, and waves at a group of people near the kitchen, conspicuously far from where Ben and I are standing. She drifts across the room, stopping briefly at the big bowl of candy on the coffee table, and heads over to the group (an evil ballerina; a nun; Van Gogh, a splash of red where his ear once was; a glowworm), bending to receive an eager round of hugs. From the way Jane is enveloped and embraced by this group, I can see that the troops have rallied, that most people do know what has happened, that our betrayal has made headlines.

And as they circle their wagons around her, I know, too, that Jane will replace me, if not with one of these solicitous friends, then with someone else, and soon. Our hearts are like starfish, regenerating what we've lost. We move forward, regroup, reconfigure; people find ways to be happy. I try to make out what Jane is saying, but the room is too loud and full. All I hear is music and laughter and the occasional excited screech.

"Should we go over?" Ben asks. If the background noise weren't so loud, I'd think my ears were playing tricks on me: he sounds almost eager.

"No way."

"I think we have to. Preemptive strike."

"And I think a jump from a second-story window probably wouldn't kill us."

"Come on, Will. I promise to protect you from the completely innocent woman whose life we ruined."

I take a huge, fortifying sip of my disgusting drink as Ben, his hand on my back, guides me toward the island of misfit toys that surrounds Jane. And if my ears weren't still playing tricks on me, I'd say a hush falls over the room.

"Ah." This comes from the glowworm, Bridget McCarragher, the poet who, according to Jane, writes only florid iambic pentameter about her ex-boyfriend, punctuated with emoticons. Bridget plants her hands on her plush, stuffed green hips. The nun turns to Jane and whispers, close in her ear. Jane shakes her head in response, her helmet of white-streaked hair immobile.

Van Gogh, aka Larry Hirsh, rotund confessional memoirist, places his hand protectively on Jane's arm. "Well," the evil ballerina says. "This is awkward."

I will Ben to put his arm around me, but he doesn't. He stays close, though, even as he takes a half step toward Jane. "Hey," he says to her, and I raise my hand in a little wave.

Jane swallows hard and pulls herself even straighter. In the split second before she opens her mouth, I understand that we are all here for a reason: Ben and I to find out whether or not we have destroyed her, Jane to let us know that we haven't. And then I realize something else, something fully detached from this moment, from the clear answer she is giving us with her impeccable posture, her sublime costume, her imperious gaze. I hear the echo at the depths of me, the baleful howl from the darkness beneath my darkest heart. I didn't want my best friend to have what I didn't have. So I took it from her. I took it.

Jane looks us both up and down. "I see you came dressed up as human beings," she says. "How clever."

Ben turns away; I see the tears in his eyes, and the surprising shame of that makes me turn away, too. I take his hand and head for the door, and as we stumble down the long hallway of Al's apartment building, Ben lets out a little moan, a despair that almost exonerates him. But I'm silent, a cold wind blowing through me. *What did you expect?* I think, but do not say.

chapter twenty-four

I haven't spoken to my brother since August. We've had longer dry spells, but none like this—three months swollen with mutual pride, our silence so obviously spiteful and pointless. I've started dreaming about him, vague, gauzy, increasingly disconcerting dreams of Seth in various situations and permutations. We're walking along the beach together when suddenly he turns into a seagull and flies away, squawking; Seth as the superintendent of my apartment building, plunging my overflowing toilet; weirdest of all, Seth and Ben, interchangeable, Sethben, Benseth, my dark-haired companion, his arms open, running toward me across an expanse of meadow, eyes misty with affection and concern and, oh, yes, there it is, lust . . . but who is it? Ben? Seth? This last of which is why I woke up this morning, curled around Ben, intent on making contact with my brother, finally determined to patch things up.

His phone rings seven times before he picks up.

"Hi," I say. "It's me. Will."

"Will Shulman, from college? Your voice sounds different. How *are* you?"

"Shut up."

"Oh, Wilma MacIntyre, from the Department of Public Works. Listen, I'll have that report to you by Monday."

"Seth, stop it."

"I'm just surprised, is all." His voice is gravelly, as if I woke him up, although it's almost noon. Clearly, nothing has changed in his miserable life.

"So, do you want to go get coffee or something?" My heart races; I feel like I'm asking him out on a date, and I brace myself for a stinging rejection.

He pauses for a full fifteen seconds, plenty of time to come up with a good excuse, then clears his throat. I hear rustling in the background, imagine him sitting up and throwing his grimy blankets off, flinging his pale, hairy legs out of bed. He'll tell me to fuck off; he'll tell me he's gotten perfectly used to his miserable life and doesn't need me to try to help him. And I never could. *Well, no. I'd rather not get some coffee or something,* he'll say, mocking, *but thanks so, so much for calling.* He clears his throat again, and I realize that I'm holding my breath. "Nah," he says, and the disappointment leaks through a shoddy dam in my chest. I'm about to hang up. "But I could go for some ice cream. Are you in the mood for ice cream?"

We meet at Lakeside Licks—like Braun's Deli, another relic from our youth. The ice cream isn't very good: is, in fact, frequently freezer burned and often downright crystallized, possibly morphed into some other substance entirely, but the flavor options are endless, which made it our favorite when we were growing up. Bubblegum Blowout was my top choice until I was eleven, neon pink and studded with real nuggets of gum—a delicious choking hazard of an ice cream flavor. Seth usually went with Sweet Cotton Candy (as if "cotton candy" alone wouldn't be quite cloying enough). He nudges me and points to it in its brown tub, still exactly where it was fifteen years ago, quite possibly the very same tub.

We take our ice cream (adult flavors now—one scoop of coffee fudge for me, vanilla almond and rum raisin for him) to a small orange Formica table. Seth hunches over his cone and opens his mouth onto it, sucks down a third of the top scoop with one enormous, loud slurp. He licks the corner of his mouth and juts his chin at my ice cream, which is starting to melt a little bit, a drop of beige dribbling down the side of the cone. "I'll have yours if you don't want it," he says, smiling, and I realize how much I've missed him.

"Sorry I've been so out of touch," I say, as if that's all it is: *I've been crazy busy!*

A very tall man and an extremely short woman step into Lakeside Licks, the heavy glass door whooshing behind them.

"That's okay," Seth says. "I've been really *swamped* at work." He winks. I think that this bodes well for us and points toward reconciliation. He wipes his mouth with the back of his hand, then licks the back of his hand. "Plus I've been playing a lot of high-stakes Internet poker."

Uh-oh. "Really?"

"No." He vacuums up another half scoop of ice cream and swallows it without any evidence of enjoyment. He looks at me again, his brown eyes tired and slightly unfocused.

"So, guess what?"

He raises an eyebrow, waits.

"I'm with Ben now."

The tall man at the counter peers down at the top of his tiny girlfriend's head. "I know what I saw," the man says, under his breath.

"But I told you already," she says, her voice a girlish whisper, "he's just a friend."

"Oh, fuck you," the man says, still quiet but suddenly ugly and threatening, like a thundercloud rolling in.

"Fuck me?" the girlfriend says softly, quizzically, without rancor, as if she's contemplating which ice cream flavor to order. "Oh, no . . . fuck *you*."

Seth glances at the couple, who is about to plunk down at the table adjacent to ours. "Huh?" he says, distracted. "Ben's with what, now?"

"Jane moved out. Back in August. Ben and I are together!" The story spills out of me. I've been waiting almost three months to tell him. For eleven weeks it's been just Ben and me and our swirling fog of guilt, and I've been living the strangely lonely life of the girl who got what she wanted. "So we, you know, we got together," I tell Seth as ice cream drips down my hand, "a few days before their wedding, or, I mean, a few days before they were supposed to get married. But they didn't." My heart is pounding. Out it comes, all of it—the surreal mix of pleasure and shame of being with Ben, the way I've begun to suspect that the shame might be part of the pleasure; the terrible emptiness of the apartment without Jane; how I never thought I'd do what I did; how easy it was, in the end, to do it. If anyone will understand this, the ugly underbelly of friendship, the way the worst of a person sometimes just wins, it's Seth. "So we told her. We sat down at the kitchen table and we told her, and it was awful," I say, "for everybody."

Seth is quiet. I sit back and perform triage on my collapsed scoop as it melts down the soggy cone. "Really awful," I say again, and I wait with relief for my brother's reaction, for support from the one person I know whose path is littered with the detritus of the relationships he himself has ruined.

He tips back in his chair, as Fuck-me and Fuck-you decide at the last minute to take it outside. The door jingles as they leave. "Fuck me?" the woman whispers. "I don't think so."

Seth watches the door shut behind them and then swivels back to me. "Wow," he says finally, and I think he's referring to the unhappy couple, and I nod. "This must be really, really hard for you and Ben. Really tough."

I look up at him, my coffee-fudge-flavored lips stuck in a hopeful smile. "What?"

"Oh, I mean, just, it must suck for you that you *destroyed your best friend's life.*" Seth's voice is a taut whisper now, and he's breathing hard, almost panting. "Damn, Willa, you make it sound like you were in the path of a natural disaster. I'm so sorry about it, this you-sleeping-with-Ben-behind-Jane's-back thing, this thing that just *happened to you.*"

"What?" I say again, my mouth slackening out of its frozen grin. This is not what I expected. I swallow, try to regain composure. "How can you be judgmental about this? You of all people?" *Nora,* I think. *Libby. Shelly. Nina.*

He leans in and slaps his right hand onto the Formica, his left hand gripping his ice cream cone so tightly it cracks. "What the hell is that supposed to mean?"

I tilt my head at him, narrow my eyes. "You, you're like the, the president of two-timing. The emperor of infidelity!"

Seth exhales and relaxes just a little. "The chairman of cheating?" he says.

"The . . . sultan of straying?" I'll always, always follow his lead.

He examines his broken ice cream cone and then looks around the empty shop. "Trust me, Will, you have no idea what you're talking about."

I get up and walk over to the counter for napkins and notice that the ice cream-scoop guy has been listening intently to our discussion. He's leaning on his arms on the glass counter, staring at us, his paper cap riding high on his head, his mouth slightly open. I eye him, decide I don't care.

"Enlighten me," I say to my brother, sliding back into my seat. "Please."

"I don't know that I need to fill you in on the details of my personal life, but I will tell you that I didn't cheat on Nina. I did not ruin my relationship with her by cheating."

I swipe at a blob of melted ice cream on the table between us. "Oh."

"Yeah, *oh*. It wasn't like that." He cracks his neck, tipping his head to the left, then to the right. "Nina got pregnant."

"Seth. God."

"And believe it or not, your asshole brother wanted to marry her." He takes a napkin and wraps bits of his broken cone in it. "But she didn't want to marry me, and she didn't want the baby." A ceiling fan clatters above us, and in the back room, tinny music from the oldies station starts playing, Elton John. *Good-byyyye Yellow Brick Roooaaadd.* "She, um . . ."

He blinks, and I finally see what the last ten months have done to my brother, how they've altered him, how his newly discovered penchants for self-help books and sugary indulgence have been not the desperate pursuits of a man sunk in his own useless remorse, nor even the wild graspings of an aching soul trying to conquer its pain, but Seth's futile, his utterly futile, attempts to defeat the bitterness. To not let it win. "So she got rid of the pregnancy, and then she got rid of me," he says, shrugging. "And I really, really hate her."

There have been times that I have thought, *I do not love my brother.* There have been times that I've longed so hard for his absent approval, his distant, wavering affection, that my longing hardened into dislike, into a solid mass of ill will, and I have thought, *I don't care if I never see him again.*

Only now, I realize that all of that was nothing, my disappointment just a drizzle, my anger a cloudburst compared with this, this cyclone of sympathy, this hurricane of love for Seth that knocks me down, leaves me breathless and soaked and clinging to a branch: this knife-pain I feel is his own heart, beating inside mine.

"I didn't know that," I say. My voice is thick and clogged. I reach for his hand even though we don't, as part of our unwritten sibling contract, touch each other. "I hate her, too," I say, my eyes filling, and Seth nods and lets me rest my hand on his for a moment before moving it away, and yes, I understand what it means, to feel the pain she caused, to hate Nina: the woman who did what she thought she had to do.

I saw it yesterday, when I came home from the store. I set my bag of groceries down on the counter. Ben was at work. His computer was open on the coffee table, the screen blank. I wanted to look up pictures of sea cucumbers. Are they fish? Are they vegetables? I didn't think twice about turning the computer on. I thought twice about opening the document on his desktop labeled "Letter to Jane—draft," but then I did it anyway.

Dear Jane,

If you're reading this, then you've seen my name in your in-box and you haven't hit "delete." For that alone I'm grateful.

I know I have no right to say this, after everything I've done, but I miss you. And I'm so, so sorry.

I thought I'd have a million things to say to you, but I find myself at a loss. I'm afraid of saying the wrong thing—which I know is a little bit beside the point. Jane, I don't know how to tell you how sorry I am for hurting you. If I could somehow change the way it all happened . . . well, that's beside the point, too, isn't it?

I heard from Amy that you got accepted into all of the law schools you applied to. That's great news. I'm a little surprised you've decided on Marquette, especially since that wasn't on the original list. But things change. Obviously. So you're staying in Milwaukee, close to your family. They must be pleased.

   Write to me, if you want to. I'll understand if you don't.
Ben

I shut the computer down, tiptoed away from it as if it were a sleeping skunk. I went to the bag of groceries on the counter and unpacked slowly: four bags of pasta, four jars of sauce. Some oranges. An onion. A tub of strawberry yogurt. I waited for the squeeze in my gut, the twitch of jealousy or anger that never came. There was only a jolt of eager anticipation: could we somehow be friends again, the three of us?

I figured Ben would come home and tell me. I was sure he would.

But when he walked in the door he had other stories to recount: about the woman on the bus who'd grabbed his hand as he walked by; about Spencer, his coworker at the library who got high during his lunch break and then ate an entire birthday cake meant for Margo, the children's librarian. "It said HAPPY BIRTHDAY TO A SPECIAL LADY on it," Ben said, "in pink frosting. And Spence downed the whole thing. He said he thought it was, like, public property." He peeled an orange and imitated Margo's reaction: "'Goddammit, I'm seventy-two years old today. I thought I might have a piece of my own goddamn birthday cake.'"

I laughed and said, "I didn't know children's librarians were allowed to talk like that," and Ben smiled at me. And then he noticed that his computer was sitting there, on the table, and he picked it up to move it, carefully clicking it shut.

. . .

Ben peers over my shoulder, munching on a waffle. "I like the way your mermaid is wearing a business suit," he says. "You don't usually see that."

"Mermaids have a reputation for being slutty. But this one is a corporate executive." I'm drawing a template for a mural that we're going to paint in Jane's old room: her final, colorful exorcism. In three months we've done our best to erase her physical presence from our lives. We've moved furniture, painted the walls, bought a replacement lamp and armchair from a cheap second-hand store. We still don't have a blender. But we can live without one. Some absences are easier to abide than others.

Ben watches now as I sketch the mermaid's jellyfish cell phone and clamshell briefcase. "She's in trouble," I say.

"Huh?"

"Her company's underwater."

With little fanfare, Ben moved into the apartment as planned: but into my room, my bed. Jane's old room is empty except for a few boxes. The door mostly stays closed.

"I like her chest," he says. He raises his eyebrows and points to the sunken treasure chest I've drawn in the background. "But what the hell is that?" He crooks his finger toward the menacing gray creature swimming near the mermaid, dorsal fin slicing the water, a thick wad of money clamped between its sharp teeth.

"A loan shark," I say. A few waffle crumbs sprinkle down onto the table, onto my drawing. I brush them away.

"You are a very strange person, Willa," he says. "Very." There's the slightest key change in his voice, a sharp note, a barely discernible shift, and I hear, in that one sentence, how things can swerve off course without warning: not that they have, but that they could.

"Yes," I say, "well, you have to respect the artistic vision, even if you don't understand it."

He's silent for a long minute.

"What?"

"Nothing." He runs a hand from the top of my head lightly down the length of my hair; it makes me shiver.

"You can tell me."

"I'm thinking how Jane would like this. Your weird drawing. A mural in her room." He leans down close, his chin on my shoulder, breath on my neck; I can smell it: warm and sweet, like bread. He watches as I put the finishing touches on the spiny ray of a starfish, then begin to sketch the wriggling arms of a sea anemone.

"With friends like us," he says.

I stop drawing for a minute and lean into him. "Yep," I say.

The mural template is not quite finished. I grip my pen and hold it over the paper, arcing a few small circles in the air. Ben is still next to me, still breathing in my ear.

I love you, I think. *I can't believe how much I love you.* I lower the pen and begin to ink the fleshy, intestinal curves of a shrimp, its long, groping antennae and stumpy tail. I draw another one, as veiny and disgusting as I can make it.

Ben straightens and moves away.

"Not a big fan of the shrimp?" I say.

"Ugh," he says and laughs. He turns and heads out of the room. "Did you not know that about me?"

What do you want for your birthday? I type.

A robot guinea pig, Ben writes back.

Oh, but all the kids want a robot guinea pig. What if they're sold out?

I don't care. Find one! It's my birthday and I WANT A GO-GO GUINEA PIG.

Ben will turn twenty-seven in two weeks, just before Thanksgiving. After everything that's happened, it feels momentous, an occasion we need to mark, if only because: here we are.

Do you want a party?

Yes. I do. A princess Barbie dress-up party.

We're sitting next to each other in bed, blankets scrunched down at our feet, laptops resting on pillows. A tree branch bangs against the bedroom window. There's the low howling sound of wind outside and, inside, the tapping of our fingers on the keyboards. I press my thigh against Ben's. *You can have a princess party,* I write, *or a Barbie party, or a dress-up party. Not all three.* The familiar little note dings on his computer.

He presses back against my leg. *Screw that, then. Let's just go clubbing and get high on E.*

Okay! Yes! But we've never gone clubbing, and I don't exactly know what E is, and neither do you.

Last year, Ben's birthday was a month before our high school reunion: before he and I had reconciled, before I introduced him to Jane. He celebrated at a bar downtown with a group of friends from the library and a girl named Lydia who, he found out that night, did not return his budding affection. He ended the evening alone in his dingy apartment, a little bit drunk, eating Doritos and watching *Starsky and Hutch* on the Retro channel. He told us this sad story on our first three-person date at the bowling alley. "God," he said to us then, "that was a depressing birthday," as if he could finally breathe, because depressing birthdays were behind him forever.

He starts typing now, then stops and sighs. "To tell you the truth, Will," he says, "I'm not really in the mood for anything big. How about we go to that new vegetarian restaurant, I can't remember the name, the one that opened up near the theater?" He shifts his body on the bed, his hands still resting on the keyboard.

It's called the Vegetable Garden. *Tempeh Tantrum?* I write.

Ha. Good one, he writes back.

He hasn't said anything to me about the note to Jane. Did he think better of it? Did he send it? Has she written back? *I don't mind,* I would tell him. *I'm glad.* But I can't tell him that, because then I'd have to admit that I was snooping. Even though I wasn't, not exactly—it's more like I stumbled on it. Or tripped right over it, and then picked it up and examined it closely. *No, wait, it's not Tempeh Tantrum,* I type. *It's called Soy to the World.* .

He clears his throat and looks at me. "No, it's not."

The Lentil-men's Club? I hit return.

"Willa." He presses his finger and thumb against the bridge of his nose. "Enough puns now. No more. Do you know the name or not?"

Sorry. I falafel about this. Return again.

"Jesus, Willa, *stop!*"

My face goes hot. When did my cute, annoying jokes stop being cute? Tears prick up behind my eyes. I have no arsenal for this. Ben has always been able to see right to the core of me, only now sometimes he doesn't like what he finds there. I turn my head toward the wall for a second, then back to the computer. *Gluten-berg Bible.*

He makes another noise in his throat and shakes his head. "I don't even . . . that doesn't even make sense." He snaps his computer shut and sets it on the floor next to the bed, and then he rolls over, his back to me. He got his hair cut the other day, and there's a half inch of tender, pale skin visible at the nape of his neck. "I'm sorry, Wildebeest," he murmurs. "I'm just really tired."

"It's okay," I say. *I really don't carrot all.* I could shut down my own laptop and inch over to him, curve into his body. I could close my eyes and slow myself to the rhythm of his breathing. But instead I sit here and keep staring at my computer screen.

Ben stretches, sighs again, arranges his pillow. After a while, his breathing becomes regular and deep, his back rising and falling. Then, in the dark and for the millionth time, I type *Jane Weston* into the search engine: not sure what I'm hoping for, knowing I won't find it.

chapter twenty-five

The flower shop in early November is a bleak place. Halloween, with its rush on lurid, not-found-in-nature orange lilies, spider mums, and curly willow, is over; Thanksgiving, a cheery, bustling long weekend, is still around the corner. It's two weeks of dull anticipation now, two weeks of a chilly, empty store enlivened only by the occasional customer looking for a quick bunch of boring roses. As autumn fades and the gray clouds gather, maybe people are too blue to believe that a pretty arrangement of flowers might cheer them up but not so accustomed to the low light of winter as to have developed coping strategies.

That's my theory, anyway, born of too much time behind the counter at the store, staring into the distance and thinking about my life. Molly is in Las Vegas for the annual meeting of her feminist entrepreneurs support group, Businesswomen Against the Longstanding Legacies of Sexism, so I've been working a lot of hours and passing the time by making inappropriate signs that I don't put up: LIFE MIGHT GET BETTER ONE OF THESE DAYS, BUT IT PROBABLY WON'T. SAY *THAT* WITH FLOWERS! And NOTHING TELLS HER "I'M SO SICK OF YOU BUT WE'RE TOO STUCK IN A RUT TO BREAK UP" LIKE DAISIES.

Ben kissed me good-bye before I left for work this morning, a lingering kiss at the door, his mouth on mine, the taste of corn-flakes and toothpaste, and as he held me a strange, small shiver moved through me, a filament of regret, a thread of something electric and dire. "See you later," he said softly, his hand still on my back, and I knew that we would, but nothing, to my ears, had ever sounded so sad.

I'm concentrating so hard on this memory and how that one kiss held, in its peculiar moment, every deeply imperfect connection I have ever made in my life that when the door swings open and Declan hobbles in, on crutches, I'm hardly even surprised. I'm magical! I knew it! I can conjure my thoughts! I close my eyes for a second and picture a hot-fudge sundae, then open them.

"Hello there," Declan says. Everything about him is sheepish: his longish hair; his scruffy, unshaven face; his bowed head; the tone of his voice, somehow both apologetic and yet aware of its own appeal.

"Hello there to you," I say, smiling in spite of myself.

"Ah," Declan says, relieved, and looks up at the ceiling. "She'll talk to me."

"I thought you'd be in Dublin by now."

"Well. That." He shrugs, as best he can while still gripping his crutches, and I understand, all of a sudden, the secret of his success: the little golden parcels he hands out that pass as information, as answers. *Well, that?*

I raise one eyebrow, drum my fingers on the glass. "Did you want to buy some flowers or something?" I think how Jane would love this, the story I would tell her, how she would tilt toward me, hands clasped, an evil smile on her face. Is it even happening if I can't tell Jane about it? I've been wondering that lately.

Declan makes his way over to me, one slow tap-step-swing at a time. He's wearing the green Trinity College sweatshirt that he used to stash in my closet sometimes. Blood suddenly rushes

FRIENDS LIKE US

from my head, or to my stomach, or near my pancreas; somewhere, inside me, blood is rushing like a river when it should be, I don't know, rolling gently like a stream. Declan! How is it that we can live in this world, love people, and then say good-bye to them?

When he reaches the counter, he's breathing hard. He stabilizes himself for a second and then looks at me. There's a thin sheen of sweat on his forehead, on the skin I used to touch, and I realize how much this little visit is costing him. "As you can see, I've a broken ankle," he says with another half shrug.

"Let me get you a chair."

"No." He raises one shoulder. All of his gestures are newly confined to his upper arms. "I'll be on my way in a moment." *On me way.*

"Your accent's gotten thicker."

"Well, it does when I'm nervous."

"I thought you'd be long gone by now," I say, bringing the conversation back around to *Well. That.*

Declan pauses and adjusts himself. "No, not gone yet." He looks away from me with a skittish dart of his eyes, glances at the back wall, then down at the counter. "The thing is, after you, after we . . . I, I met someone."

Is he here to confess? Is that it? Did he think he needed to break the devastating news to me in person? I cover my face with my hands and pretend to sob. *Ooooowaaaahhhh!* and then I peek out through my fingers to enjoy the stunned horror on his face, watching as it shifts, in a quick minute, to relief, to Declan's customary good humor. "Willa!"

"Hi!"

"Well, I didn't know. How was I to know? We haven't spoken! You kicked me out, you'll remember."

I nod, thinking of the camping trip, of the sharp, surprising pain of his rejection. "So, you met someone."

"Yes. Well, and as a matter of fact, that's over."

"You're not here to—"

"No! I mean, not that I wouldn't. And now that you mention it, if you're interested . . ." He winks.

"Maybe just a quickie in the storeroom," I say, my hands on my hips. "I've always had a thing for men on crutches."

"Right," he says, winking again. "I'll get to my point." And then he just stands there, in front of me, for a full thirty seconds, until I start to think I'm the one who's supposed to say something. "Okay," he says finally. "Well, it's come to my attention that I may behave, in certain situations, with women . . . I may . . . I may not, ah . . ." He puffs out his cheeks and lets out a long, whooshing sigh. "I may be, well, you know, just . . . I don't know." He stops abruptly and looks at me with big, hopeful, puppy dog eyes.

"Wow."

"I was in a minor bicycle accident," he says. "You Americans really ought to drive on the left, as God intended. Anyway, I'm fine. But I broke my ankle, and Emma, lovely girl, that's her name, Emma, she wanted to care for me, to nurse me back to health."

"So you broke up with her."

"Yes."

"Well, that's understandable."

"She read me the riot act. And I suppose she made me understand a thing or two." I wait. Declan squirms. "And then I got to thinking, Willa, did you . . . were you . . . did *you* want more from me?" For a second he is wide open, right here in front of me, sadness and hunger, bones and breath.

"You mean like more mustard on that sandwich you made me that one time?"

"That is what I mean."

I could make a million dollars writing the official rule book for this: how to behave when your ex-boyfriend tries to make amends.

If only I knew what the rules were. I think about how, years ago, he chose someone else over me. And that, if I'm honest, eventually I would have done the same thing. I flick my thumb across my cardboard signs. FLOWERS WON'T FIX IT. "I think maybe I wanted more, but not necessarily from you," I say. Declan looks, unaccountably, hurt. "That came out wrong."

"Nah," he says. He scratches his face by tipping it to his shoulder, hands-free. "I think I know what you mean." A car radio blares. A woman pushing a stroller hurries past the store. A bus slows down as it passes and lets out a hiss of exhaust. There are all kinds of lives being lived around us.

"Oh!" I say, just remembering. "But I'm with someone new, too!" Sometimes when I think about Ben, it's like he's been waiting in the wings of my mind for the past twelve years. And now here he is, in his starring role. "Well, not new, exactly," I say. "It's Ben. And it's a long story."

Declan shakes his head, disbelieving. He smiles with half of his mouth. "The cheeky bastard!"

"Cheeky," I say, shoving my hands into my apron pocket. "I suppose so." I'm remembering how, with Declan, the way his words sounded could sometimes compensate when I wasn't sure what he was saying.

"I probably shouldn't ask about Jane, then," he says.

I still can't hear her name without wanting to dive under a piece of heavy furniture. "Yeah," I say. "That'd be the 'long' part of the long story."

We stand around in silence for a few minutes, smiling uncomfortably at each other. Chapter 1 in the rule book: It's the moment you've been waiting for! He's come back, tail between his legs. He's finally realized what a jerk he was! You care, but not as much as you thought you would.

"Listen," he says finally, "I should be off." I nod, relieved. "It's *really great* to see you, Willa." He sounds so sincere I almost laugh.

"Okay," I say. "Feel better." He looks at me, confused, and I point to his ankle.

"Oh, that," he says. "Could've been worse." And Declan limps out the door.

This morning, for Ben's birthday, I ran over to Shop 'n' Save and bought two double-chocolate cupcakes from the grocery store's surprisingly not-terrible bakery: a low-risk investment.

All week, since his note to Jane, things have been strange with Ben and me, forced and stilted and full of weird pauses and off-kilter emphases, as if we're performing a play David Mamet wrote for high school theater.

Willa, did you buy milk? I thought you said you would buy—

Yes, milk. Milk. Sorry, yes, milk. I forgot to buy it. I can go out now. I can—

No. No. No. I don't, I don't, it's okay. I don't need it.

So now I have cupcakes and milk and Ben's gift, a new issue of *The Overachievers* that I've been working on for a few weeks *(Life After College: The Underachievers)*, and a radical plan. I'm going to talk to him. I'm going to rescue our relationship: I'm going to pull us back from the ledge.

I'll start with *Happy birthday and I saw the e-mail.* I'll just cop to it, and then we'll be forced to discuss it all—how Jane figures into the equation of us; how even in her absence she's here, an indelible part of our relationship. Maybe it will be hard to admit how much we miss her and that we feel incomplete without her, but we'll work through it, because we love each other. And everything will be okay. I run my finger around the edge of one of the thickly frosted cupcakes and lick off the icing, and then, to even things out, I do the same to the other one.

I'm standing at the kitchen table laying out plates and whispering to myself when Ben comes home from work, only instead of slouching through the door and greeting me with the low-key, melancholy hello I've grown accustomed to over the past week, he's beaming. His face is flushed, his eyes bright. He peers around the living room as if he's seeing it for the first time, shrugs off his jacket, and peels off his blue sweater, stretches his arms above his head. He's even standing taller.

"Twenty-seven looks good on you," I say, forgetting, for the moment, everything I was rehearsing just seconds ago.

He bounds over to me and sweeps me up in a hug, murmuring, "Hi, Wilbur," into my shoulder. I'm so relieved that for a moment I am not myself; I'm this person Ben is holding, a bright receptacle for his love.

"Some pig," I say.

He pushes me away and looks at me intently and then kisses me, hard and passionate, like he means it and is also joking, both. His face is cold against mine. He snakes his hands up my shirt and rests them on my bare back. They're freezing, too, and I jump, I have the instinct to squirm away, but I don't; I relax into the feeling of Ben's icy hands.

"Mmm," he says, pressing his fingers into my skin and holding me. It's enough to be captured in this moment completely, enough to make me think that maybe it's not as hard as it looks, being happy.

"I have news," he says, still holding on to me. "Crazy good news."

"You *don't* have flesh-eating bacteria!"

"No! Turns out it's only leprosy!" He slips his hands from under my shirt and steps away, notices the cupcakes and smiles at me, a big hungry grin. I'm still breathing the scent of him, that pink soap they have at the library and the laundry detergent we're almost out of and the spicy, licorice smell that is Ben.

I pull out my chair and stand behind it. "Well?"

"Okay," he says. "You know I've been having . . . not exactly doubts about grad school, but hesitation. I mean, I want to go, and the applications are out there, but back when we were considering moving out east . . . I mean, Jane and I . . ." His gaze darts to the wall behind me, then back. "Ever since then I've been thinking maybe there's something else I should be doing, just for a little while, some kind of work, before I commit, before I get down to it. Something meaningful, something that doesn't involve the constant mental repetition of the alphabet and a nineteen-year-old pothead as my closest colleague. You know?"

I nod. Of course I know. I glance down at his present, wrapped in paper I made myself from a brown grocery bag. *The Underachievers* is a notebook full of cartoon sketches of Ben and me as we go about our regular lives, in superhero costumes. The Underachievers have breakfast. The Underachievers watch a movie. The Underachievers walk to the mailbox on the corner. Occasionally, in my book, one of us picks up a piece of trash from the sidewalk, or takes a spider from the bathroom wall and puts it outside. Lesser superheroes of greatly diminished expectations.

Ben sits down at the table and touches the edge of his store-bought cupcake. "For me?" he asks.

"Happy birthday," I say softly, smiling encouragement as the barometric pressure inside my body begins to plummet.

He takes a bite. A few crumbs dot his lower lip, and he licks them off. "I applied . . . a few weeks ago I applied to this program, not thinking I'd get in. I don't know. I did it on a lark."

I joined the marines! On a lark!

I sold my kidney! On a lark!

"I mean, I've never built anything before," he continues. "But I've been accepted. And they'll be paying me enough money to get by, maybe even to travel a little bit. . . ." He sits up straight all of a sudden and looks at me, and it's as if he's just been zapped by an electrical spark; he seems to realize with a physical jolt that this crazy good news of his—whatever it is—is going to affect me, too. "I'm going to Ecuador, Will. I mean, if I say yes. And if you think I should. It's a four-month program. I've wanted to go since high school. Well, you know that. I'm going to be helping to build an orphanage in Ecuador."

An orphanage! I see the word in my mind, and it pings around in there, ricocheting through my skull until it runs out of meaning. I'm still standing behind my chair. I grip the edge of it, hard. "I am so glad you don't have flesh-eating bacteria. What a relief."

Ben lifts his cupcake. "I thought you'd be happy for me. Four months isn't that long."

"I am happy," I say. Things you could do in four months: Train for a triathlon. Gestate practically half of a baby. Begin graduate school. Lose your boyfriend to an orphanage in Ecuador.

"I'll be back, you know," he says. He waves his free hand in a gesture of *pffft*. "Four months! I'm coming back."

Well, if you have to say it. "I know you are." We've been having this conversation in a dark apartment. It's only 4:45, but the sun has already set. "Duh! Of course you are!" I move to turn on the light, and the apartment is suffused with a homey, deceptive glow.

"I need to do something good," he says.

"It's just for four months." I pull out my chair and sit down across from him.

"Right." He seems pleased and relieved. He's probably already making a list of what to pack. *Soap, shampoo, condoms???*

"And the orphans!" I say. "They need you."

Ben's smile fades a little. "Come on." He reaches across the table for my hand, but I'm busy folding and refolding my napkin.

"Although," I say, "there are things you could do right here, of course. You know, local orphans just looking for a place to live. A nice bungalow by the lake."

"I guess," he says, furrowing his eyebrows, not sure if I'm serious; neither am I. "But, I mean, this is a once-in-a-lifetime opportunity."

"Homegrown orphans!" I say, shaking my head to dam the tears that are trying to escape. "With a much smaller carbon footprint than your Ecuadorian variety."

Ben's forehead wrinkles even more deeply, his affect morphing from puzzled to disturbed. "You're being kind of . . ." He would never actually say it.

"Locavorphans, is what they're called." I blink hard. "Pesticide-free and fresh to your table."

Ben scrapes his chair back and stands up. He moves to hug me. "I'm sorry. I'm sorry. I guess I kind of sprang this on you. It's just, I really wasn't expecting to get in. I kind of sprang it on myself. I haven't said yes yet, you know. It's not a done deal." He lets go of me, takes his plate to the kitchen and puts it in the sink with a rough clatter. "Maybe you need some time to process this, or whatever. Maybe I should just go out for a little walk. I'll go pick up some milk."

"I already got milk," I say quietly.

"Well, I'll go get some more." He stands behind me and lays his hand on my head. "Let's just . . . I'll be back in twenty minutes," he says. "Okay?" I'm silent, staring at the table—my plate, my origami napkin; Ben's still-wrapped present, untouched. "Okay?" When I don't answer, he grabs his jacket and answers for me: "Okay."

.   .   .

Alone in the apartment, I feel like I've just stepped off a roller coaster, my body thrumming, arms and legs shaky. I go into the kitchen and wash a pile of dishes. I'm placing them on the drying rack when the phone rings. For a sharp, quick second, I think that it will be Jane.

"Hey," Ben says. "I'm going to pick up a few things, as long as I'm here." I'm stopped cold. This voice. This man. My choice: Ben, not Jane. "Maybe I'll head to the co-op, too?" He sounds patient but uneasy, like he's trying to coax a cat out of a tree.

"Okay," I say, on cue this time. "Sure thing!" I force myself to sound carefree, to compensate for my previous clingy, tearful cynicism. "Take your time!" I say. "See you whenever!"

The balance of power between us has shifted. When did it happen? Just now, at the table, over birthday cupcakes? Or sometime over the past few months, after we became lovers? I was in control for all those years, even when he was with Jane. But now, suddenly, Ben holds the cards. And they're in Spanish.

Or maybe this is just what it's supposed to look like, the two of us bouncing back and forth on a seesaw, playing the game little kids play where they aim to balance in the middle, legs dangling: trying for equilibrium.

Four months really isn't that long—if he even goes. He didn't say he was definitely going, just that he'd been accepted.

I'm in the shower and feeling slightly better about things, just rinsing the shampoo out of my hair, when the door bangs open, and he pokes his head around the light blue shower curtain. "There you are," he says, as if I'd been hiding. "I bought oranges!" A peace offering: we both love oranges. Ben lets the curtain fall back and then, a minute later, the plastic crackles again, and he climbs into in the shower with me.

"Oh!" I say, smiling, surprised. "I'm sorry, were you on the shower schedule for six-fifteen?" There are lingering habits, remnants of a friendship imperfectly translated into love. More often than I would have imagined, sex begins with puppyish wrestling; our lust is sometimes tinged with a jokey kind of embarrassment. We are who we are—our bodies the willing participants in a game our brains play.

But not now. He steps toward me, braces himself with one arm on the tiled wall, and leans forward to kiss me, his head under the faucet, his face wet on mine, no joking to take the edge off, no paving the bridge with goofy laughter. "Because I was pretty sure I signed up for Tuesday," I say, and he shushes me. His body is urgent and his breath is fast and his hands are on me, on my face, my neck, my soap-slippery shoulders, hips, stomach; we're wet bodies and lips and tongues; he presses himself against me, his hands tangled now in my hair. He whispers something in my ear, but it's drowned out by the pounding water and my own loud, disoriented thoughts. The water goes lukewarm and then almost cold, but it doesn't matter, because the borders of my body have turned to liquid and I'm melting into him, every bit of me.

"Jeez," I say afterward, wrapped in a towel and lying next to Ben on the bed. "Shower sex. Such a cliché!" I've managed to forget everything that happened this afternoon and am basking in the foolish postorgasmic certainty that everything will be *just fine*.

"Oh, yeah, sorry about that," Ben says. He elbows me lightly. "I know you can't stand clichés."

"Pedestrian." I inch toward him. Little electrical tingles run up and down my skin.

He angles his leg over mine and crosses his arms above his head. "Hot, though." He turns his face to mine. "So, you're feeling okay about this, then?"

"Hot shower sex? Sure."

"No." He kisses my ear. "Four months in *Ecuador*." He pronounces the word with an exaggerated Spanish accent, as if to emphasize that we're just messing around here, just having a lighthearted little conversation.

A rush of warmth floods through me. "No, I'm . . . I thought we . . ." I adjust the towel that has fallen away from my chest. Humiliation is physical: a transformation of molecules, a shuddering rearrangement of the limbic system. What did I think? That fifteen minutes in the shower would be such a powerfully amazing experience that Ben would realize that he could not leave? That it would flip our imbalance and remind him of just how tremendously lucky he is to have me? "Well, I thought we were going to talk about it," I say finally.

"We are," Ben says. "We are talking about it."

"You said it wasn't a done deal. What if I tell you not to go?"

Ben sighs. "Willa, I don't know." Neither of us says anything for a long time, and then Ben finally does. "I don't want you to tell me not to go."

I reach up to touch my hair, which I can already feel is drying funny. Ben is staring at the ceiling, his eyes dark in the dim, shadowy room. There's a definition to his face that I've never seen before, never in twelve years of knowing him: a knife-sharp clarity in the set of his lips, the square of his jaw. Adult Ben, fully and completely. And as I'm taking in the new, decisive fix of his profile, I finally see exactly what is lurking here in the space between us— not just remorse over what we did to be together, not a stubborn obstacle or the pulse of missing her, but Jane herself; her long body; her thin arms; her pale skin; her curly hair; her clever, kind, accommodating self: Jane, human and warm and gone from us.

"Then I won't say it," I tell Ben. I curl toward him, rest my arm across his solid chest, squeeze myself closer to him, let the towel fall away, press my cool, bare skin against his. The radiator in the bedroom clanks on. Four months.

He half turns his body and edges up against me, his arms too tight around my rib cage, his face in my damp hair. We're thigh to thigh, ankle to ankle. I arch my back awkwardly so my stomach touches his. His elbow digs into the dip of my waist. I accidentally jab him with my knee; he grunts, but doesn't move away.

We can't get close enough.

chapter twenty-six

Seth tosses a small, poorly wrapped present onto my kitchen table. "So tell me more about this holiday of yours," he says, "this Hah-nu-*kah*."

"Well, it's a complicated story." I hold the tip of a lit match to the bottoms of the candles to melt them, so they'll stick into the holes better. "There was this band of rogue Jews. Bad-Ass Jews."

"Ah, yes, the Bad-Ass Jews. Of the Bad-Assian Mountain Range, near Assopotamia."

"Yes. And they were hanging out in the second temple, after they foreclosed on the first temple. And they found that, tragically, they did not have enough oil to make French fries, so they made potato pancakes instead."

"And that's how come we have eight nights of Jewish Christmas!"

"And why we give each other eight pairs of socks, one for each night!"

Seth picks up the lumpy little package he's brought and waves it in front of me. Back in the day, it was a running joke in my family that by the sixth night of Hanukkah, whether we needed them or not, we would be getting socks; while our Gentile friends were oohing and aahing over their new video games and the coolest technological accessories they'd gotten for Christmas, the Jacobs kids were unwrapping cotton footwear. *Kids,* our mother would say, dismissing our disappointed faces, *you can always use a nice pair of socks.*

"Oh, no!" I say. "But I cut off my feet and sold them so I could buy you a beautiful hat!"

"And I cut off my head and sold *it,* to buy you these socks."

"So tragic!"

Ben left two weeks ago. For three days I lay in my bed and I poked my fingers into the electric socket of my memory. Ben would not come back to me. Not come back. I cried and cried and cried and cried. My bed was covered in a damp blanket of crumpled white Kleenex and balled-up sheets of paper from my sketch pad, halfhearted attempts at drawings ripped out and discarded. By the end of the third day I didn't think I could cry anymore, but I was wrong, and that night I cried some more. My stomach was sore from it. My eye sockets ached.

On the fourth day, Seth came over with a box of Ho Hos and some Popsicles. "Willa," he said, "I swear to God, simple carbohydrates and refined sugars will make you feel better." He tapped his fingers on the Ho Hos, and he said it again. "They will Make You Feel Better." He sat me down at the kitchen table and unwrapped an orange Popsicle. "Here," he said, holding it out to me. "A little taste."

I didn't want to, but my tongue touched down on the syrupy ice-cold surface of it, and I took it from him, and the delicious shock of it! Seth was right; it made me feel a little better. Then I had a Ho Ho, and I felt sick, but also slightly more like myself.

Ben has written to me every day from Ecuador, just like he promised. His e-mails are full of the buzzy thrill of a new experience: his companions, the former priest from Detroit with the fabulously foul mouth, the middle-aged divorcée with a taste for tequila; the cloud forests, the hot springs; the roaming iguanas, the cockroaches as big as your head, the mosquitoes that can make you sterile. I think he made that last one up. His e-mails are vivid with delight and surprise, but not longing.

Sometimes, late at night, alone in my apartment, I yank the covers up to my chin and I stare at the dark walls of my bedroom and my heart pounds like a jailed psychopath in my chest and I think, *I have lost everything.* Once in a while I'll roll over and sniff Ben's pillow or wander into Jane's old room, and then I'm embarrassed, even at two o'clock in the morning in an apartment by myself. But it's in those dark, jangling, self-conscious moments that I know in my bones that he's not coming back. Not to me. "God," I say to Seth now, taking a deep, ragged breath. "It just really sucks."

Seth nods sympathetically, but I catch him suppressing a tiny smile. He can't help himself. He's been dating a woman he met recently at a city council meeting on water quality. Her name is Judy, and she works for the Department of Public Works. They talk about combined filtration systems and hundred-year floods and microbial contamination; Seth has been smiling, off and on, for two weeks now. He also looks like he's lost about five pounds.

He pulls on the novelty rainbow socks I got him with the separate compartment for each toe. "Can I tell you something?" He tugs his jeans—clean and hole-free—back over his ankles. "I always thought Kern was kind of a twerp."

"No kidding."

"No, I mean, I get that he was your best friend, or whatever, and I know he had a thing for you, so that excuses some of his twerpiness . . . but, I don't know. I always thought he had something up his sleeve. He had this smugness, this oozing smugness about him. Like he thought he was smarter than everyone else."

A flash of anger sparks in me, a match striking against flint.

Are we playing it again, Seth and I, this awful game of catch and release? Reverting to our age-old script, where I let myself grow vulnerable to him, and then he attacks? What does he know about Ben and me? What does he know about our history, our mistakes, the long road we've traveled to get to where we are. *Yeah, well, you're a jerk,* I think, hopelessly. *An ass.*

Seth, reading my mind, holds out his hand to stop me before I say anything. "Listen. I just mean . . ." He looks up at the ceiling as if it will drop the right words into his mouth. "I just mean, yeah, people change. So, fine, Kern's a great guy now." He's still holding out his hand, and I'm staring at it, stunned into silence. "But if it doesn't work out between you, just remember, he was a twerp once, okay? He really was."

And there it is for the very first time, the orange Popsicle sweetness of Seth, mine for the taking: *I will help you. You'll be okay.*

I light the Hanukkah candles and then try on the pink poly-blend socks he's gotten me, thin and cheap and available at convenience stores everywhere. I've been stupid and selfish and vain. Okay. But not about everything. I hold up my foot in a glamorous, foot-modeling pose, point it to the left, then to the right.

I want to say, *Thank you.* I want to say, *Louis, I think this is the beginning of a beautiful friendship.* Instead I stare at the four burning Hanukkah candles for a minute and then I look back down at my feet, and I wiggle my toes in their polyester home, and I say to my big brother, my friend, "You know, it's true. You really can't go wrong with socks."

epilogue

Back when we had no money, which was always, Jane and I used to go to the Art Museum on Free First Fridays. We could spend hours wandering around the permanent display; we both especially liked the collection of nineteenth-century daguerreotypes, the subjects anonymous, their faces pale and serious and ghostly, or preghostly, as if they were feeling an icy touch, in that peculiar long moment in front of the camera: the cold finger of death. And maybe they were! Or maybe they were feeling the cold finger of an empty stomach, or a full bladder. Who knew what was going on behind those impenetrable gazes? That's what transfixed us, Jane and me; that's what captured our attention.

In addition to poignant and haunting, we found those photographs to be strangely hilarious. We used to narrate them, moving from picture to picture, whispering to each other.

You know what bums me out? That I'll be dead before they invent tampons.

This guy next to me is not my husband, and he's pinching my ass. That's why I look so pissed!

I think now that those images spoke to us more deeply than we could admit back then, that they nudged uncomfortably at our own nascent fears, reminded us in the most visceral way that someday we, too, would be reduced to that fate, to a collection of moments that don't begin to tell who we are, that don't represent us at all.

Sometimes, on these excursions, I would bring my sketchbook and pick a painting to study and draw, while Jane would explore the exhibitions. Every so often she'd meander back to tell me what she'd seen and to check on my progress.

One Friday I sat down in front of a Degas and fixed my eyes on his lines, the angles of motion. I stared and stared, until, after a while, the colors blurred and the figures began to reveal their specific shapes, and then I sketched for a while, immersed.

I don't know how long Jane had been sitting next to me before I noticed her; I was that engulfed in my drawing, or Jane and I were so comfortable in each other's presence that her arrival was as unremarkable to me as my own left hand, my fingers manipulating the charcoal pencil, my skin.

I paused. My eyes were getting tired; I thought that maybe it was time to go.

"I love it," she said quietly.

"Oh, shut up." I was secretly delighted when Jane complimented my work. I hardly ever showed it to anyone back then.

"Keep drawing," she said.

"Nah, I think I'm done for today." I turned to her, so close beside me, her face pink from the warmth of the museum, arm bent to push back her hair, her right hand resting on her knee, and I felt in that moment that we were both overcome by an unexpected wave of sadness, a strange and heavy air current passing over us, through us. I wanted to press my cheek to her shoulder; I wanted to cry. My fingers closed around my pencil, its smooth, solid presence. What was this? Jane looked down, and then she looked back up at me and smiled, and the moment was over.

Later, after I packed up my book and my pencils and we put

on our coats and left the museum and headed outside into the
cool fall day, after we found our bus and made our way home and
stood together in the kitchen fixing sandwiches for our dinner;
later, much later, not that day or that night or even that year, I
realized that that melancholy moment between us at the museum
was nothing more than a permutation of love. I understood that
the ease of knowing you will love someone forever is always shad-
owed by the inkling that you might not: that even such a sweetness could end.

But by the time I understood, it was too late. It already had.

acknowledgments

For their wisdom, insight, patience, and friendship, my deepest appreciation to Jennifer Jackson, Julie Barer, Carolyn Crooke, Annie Rajurkar, Mitch Teich, Jon Olson, and Deb Rosen. My thanks to Sara Eagle and Andrea Robinson for their hard work on behalf of this book, and to Bridget Windau for her tireless and loving child care. I am grateful to and inspired by my parents, Ann and Jordan Fox. And finally, my love and profound gratitude to my husband, Andrew Kincaid, and to my daughters, Molly and Tess, who ensured that a book that ought to have taken two years to write took five. I love you.

A NOTE ABOUT THE AUTHOR

Lauren Fox is the author of *Still Life with Husband*. She earned her MFA from the University of Minnesota in 1998 and her work has appeared in the *New York Times, Marie Claire, Seventeen, Glamour,* and *Salon*. She lives in Milwaukee with her husband and two daughters.

A NOTE ON THE TYPE

This book was set in Legacy Serif. Ronald Arnholm (b. 1939) designed the Legacy family after being inspired by the 1470 edition of *Eusebius* set in the roman type of Nicolas Jenson. This revival type maintains much of the character of the original. Its serifs, stroke weights, and varying curves give Legacy Serif its distinct apperance. It was released by the International Typeface Corporation in 1992.

Typeset by Scribe,
Philadelphia, Pennsylvania

Printed and bound by RR Donnelley,
Harrisonburg, Virginia